Three Times a Murderer

BY PAUL HOWARD SURRIDGE

A chink in his psyche, a desire for women and hard drugs led him to kill three times.

FOREWORD

Dr. Dan Thomas was a highly intelligent research scientist but a chink in his psyche, a passion for women, and an addiction to hard drugs prove to be the perfect, lethal cocktail that led him to murder - not once, but three times.

CONTENTS

CHAPTER 1 – THE BREAKUP

Dr. Tanya Waters and Dr. Dan Thomas worked alongside one another for a global pharmaceutical company as research scientists in one of the company's vaccine development labs. Eventually, they became friends and a relationship evolved. Soon, they were working on a project to find a vaccine that would combat a rare virus that scientists believed could mutate and cause a worldwide pandemic.

Of course, developing a successful vaccine can take years and the costs were inevitably high, but so were the rewards for those companies successfully bringing their product to market before the competition.

Dan had always considered himself a fish out of water. Though undoubtedly a highly intelligent and brilliant scientist, he found lab work tedious and believed the rewards for people in his position were manifestly unjust.

He was not inspired by what he could do for humanity, but how his personality, skills and knowledge could be harnessed for his own financial benefit. The trappings of wealth appealed to him, and one way or another, he wanted the good life and would do almost anything to achieve it.

He held strong views on a wide range of issues, the more controversial the better. He took every opportunity to impress friends and colleagues with his knowledge seeing himself as a leader and an influencer, but he possessed an arrogant streak that many people disliked, often he would dismiss people rudely if they challenged him.

Dan liked to be seen with attractive women, and Tanya met the criterion. In recent years, he had dated a lot of partners; many more than he was prepared to admit to. It was not difficult for him to attract women and many of his conquests were immediately smitten with him but sustaining relationships had proved challenging. He was easily bored, and that boredom often led to arguments if for no other reason than to be provocative.

Tanya's personality, aspirations, and goals were vastly different from Dan's in almost every respect. She was not at all competitive and had no desire to be the centre of attention, preferring to use her skills for the betterment of mankind. Her few relationships had taught her little about men.

Dan swept her off her feet. He was so different from anyone she had met when growing up, or during her time in the lab, where her colleagues were, unsurprisingly, like her. Tanya quickly discovered Dan's negative traits, but despite her reservations, she continued with the relationship, believing over time she could change his ways. She, too, had fallen in love with him.

They were viewed by many people as an odd couple with few common interests. It was clear she was smitten with him, just as he was besotted with himself. Despite Dan's failings, he was popular, unpredictably interesting, and his charisma afforded him a wide range of acquaintances who were eager to spend time in his company.

Rarely did they socialize with Tanya's friends. Dan found them uninteresting and lacking in dynamism. Invariably, she was instead expected to join Dan's social circle. She tried her best to integrate but always felt the odd one out.

Within six months of first dating, they had moved into a basement flat in North London. Tanya had devoted herself entirely to her work before meeting Dan and rarely attended parties or social events. She was a novice. Dan was the reverse. He needed the kind of stimulation that came from such gatherings, including the use of drugs. For a while, Tanya knew nothing of his addiction and was horrified when she discovered him snorting cocaine. Despite her abhorrence for illegal drug use, though, she stayed with him. Reluctantly, she went to parties with him, knowing he would abandon her soon after arriving and she would have to fend for herself.

It was mid-June and Dan had been invited to a party in Highgate by a friend from his university days. They saw each other infrequently but Dan was nonetheless keen to go. It was at that party that he met Rupert Reece a wealthy businessman turned venture capitalist. Rupert was in his late forties and made his fortune in IT having sold his tech company a few years earlier.

Dan and Rupert hit it off immediately. They were both highly intelligent and able communicators and had much in common. At least, that was Dan's first impression.

He admired self-made millionaires like Rupert. As they became engrossed in conversation, Tanya was left on her own on the other side of the room. The party was teeming with people.

After almost half an hour of chatting together, Dan glanced across the room and saw Tanya sitting on her own. He knew he was guilty of abandoning her and wanted to bring her into the conversation to avoid a row later.

Rupert had also abandoned his wife, Fay, although she was used to his ways and was perfectly capable of looking after herself. She had become engrossed in conversation with a group of people she had met soon after arriving. Dan and Rupert decided they should find their partners and regroup as a foursome.

"Ah, there you are Tan. Why are you sitting on your own?" Tanya hated being called *Tan* but nothing she said persuaded him to stop using the abbreviation.

"You know I don't like parties. I only came because you insisted..."

"Oh, come on; make some effort, can't you? There are plenty of people to talk to!" She was irritated. "Dan, you know I'm here under sufferance, so why have you abandoned me... again?" He knew she was a reluctant party goer and given the choice, he would have left her at the flat to read a book or catch up with a scientific journal. Then again, he also knew that would lead to a lengthy discussion about his selfish ways.

"That's why I've come over, I've met this interesting guy, Rupert. He has made a fortune in IT and he's with his wife, Fay. I suggested we all get together...come over."

This was the last thing she wanted.

Her preference was to leave there and then and go back to the flat. After all, they had been there for over two hours. Wasn't that long enough?

"Do I have to?" Immediately after uttering the words, she knew it was a waste of time protesting and joined them.

"Rupert, this is Tan, my girlfriend."

"Hi Tan. I've never heard that name before...where does it originate?" Tanya looked at Dan disapprovingly. "Dan decided to shorten my name. I'm Tanya, and to be honest, I hate him calling me Tan...Good to meet you too."

Rupert paused awkwardly. "Oh. Okay. This is my wife, Fay. I don't think an abbreviation is necessary, although I could call you *F*, I suppose?" Rupert and Dan laughed.

Fay and Tanya looked at each and smiled mockingly. They were much less amused. Rupert was keen to find out more about Tanya. "So, what do you do, Tanya?"

"I work in the same lab as Dan, on final trial vaccine development. My PhD is in molecular biology.

"A clever girl..." Tanya was unimpressed with those three words. Yes, she was clever, but she was not a *girl* and did not like being referred to as one. Still, she forced a smile. Fay had her own questions.

"Gosh, I'm so impressed. It's people like you that play a part in protecting the world." Tanya smiled. "And you work with Tanya in the lab, Dan?" This was Dan's opportunity to impress Fay. "Yes, and strictly speaking, Tan is my superior. I'm not as devoted to my work, unlike her. I quite enjoy the science, but if I'm honest, I get bored in the lab and would prefer to be doing what Rupert's good at..."

Fay looked at Rupert. "And what is Rupert good at?" Dan was quick to respond.

"Making money!" His statement disappointed Fay and annoyed Tanya. Fay was keen to probe further. "Why do you think making money is preferable to saving the world, Dan?"

Dan knew his trite response was nothing short of pathetic and knew his answer to this second question needed more maturity if he were to retain any credibility.

"It's not. I think making money *and* saving the world has to be the goal, and I'd like to have a shot at both." Rupert liked that. "Good answer, Dan. But do you think you can do it?" "I'd like to think so..."

Tanya was unimpressed with Dan's response, knowing that he had no interest *in saving the world,* although she wished he had. If only he shared her thinking on life. The conversation between the four of them continued for twenty minutes before Tanya was ready to leave. She had got on reasonably well with Fay and accepted her card. Dan and Rupert also swapped details and agreed to meet up again soon.

"Dan, I like your thirst for making money. Perhaps there is something we can do together in the future...?"
"That would be great. I'll call you." Dan was pleased with himself. He was keen to stay at the party but knew Tanya wanted to go.

"Are you ready to go, Tan?" "About an hour ago!" She had wanted to leave the moment they had arrived. A small gathering of friends for dinner was much more her style. They said their goodbyes and left for the underground.

Dan was on a high after speaking to Rupert. He had also accepted a line of cocaine from him in the men's room. "I could tell you hated being there."

"Where?" She knew what he meant.

"The party!"

Tanya sighed. "We've been together over a year and we've attended at least four parties in that time, so you should know by now that I don't feel comfortable. I don't like parties. I don't see the point in them. All people do is drink too much and make small talk..."

Dan knew this to be the case on both counts. "I know, but for my sake, could you not try to enjoy yourself? You enjoyed talking to Fay, didn't you?"
"Dan, I don't want to row with you..." He stopped her mid-sentence. "Row? Who said anything about rowing? Did you or did you not enjoy chatting to Fay?"

"Not particularly..."

"Well, you seemed to get on together, you took her card."

"She gave me her card. I didn't ask for it. There's a difference." There was a stony silence on the underground. They emerged onto the street and walked back to the flat.

No sooner had they walked through the front door Dan went to the bathroom and snorted another line of cocaine. Tanya went to the bedroom and changed into her casual clothes. By now, Dan was buzzing.

Tanya had observed his mood swings after parties before and knew he had taken drugs. She found him difficult to deal with when he was high. She knew if she challenged him, he would become argumentative, and she hated conflict.

"I really don't know why you go to parties with me?"

"I'm happy not to, Dan. But if we are meant to be a couple, why would I stay here while you go out?"

"You could go out to a museum or a library or something?"

"In the evening, really?"

"Oh, come on Tan, lighten up."

Tanya had work to do before the morning. She was due back in the lab at 9.00 am. "Why don't you go back to the party? I've got work to do."

"Really? You're okay if I go back?"

"Yes, you go back. You clearly want to." In his drug induced state, he wanted stimulation, so he didn't hesitate. He was hopeful Rupert would still be there and they could talk more.

The fact that he had no hesitation in leaving her alone in the flat told her something. Her feelings for him had evaporated in recent weeks, so she made the decision there and then to end the relationship. However, having only recently taken the flat and jointly signed a lease, she knew when she moved out that he would insist she pay her rent for the period. It wouldn't be an unreasonable demand, but she knew she couldn't afford two rents in London.

After Dan headed off to the party, instead of preparing for work in the morning, she spent the remainder of the evening reflecting.

She was cross with herself for ever agreeing to get a flat with Dan. They only had one bedroom, so sleeping in another room wasn't an option. Dan would return early morning, likely drunk and like it or not, she would need to share a bed with him.

The following morning, she woke early. Dan had not returned. In some respects, she was relieved. If nothing else, it showed how contemptuous he was about their relationship. She got up, showered, dressed, and left for the lab. She had a couple of single girlfriends in the lab and decided to ask if one of them was prepared to accommodate her, at least temporarily.

Tanya was well-liked, both as a manager and for who she was. Most of her female colleagues knew what Dan was like and had feared from the outset that she would regret taking up with him.

Soon after arriving at the lab, she spoke to Emily, her closest colleague. Fortunately, she was looking for a roommate and agreed that Tanya could move in immediately. Tanya was relieved. Her challenge now was ending the relationship with Dan without any unnecessary drama.

Dan arrived in the lab late morning. He was visibly tired and ill-prepared for a days' work. They said little to each other until they found themselves in the rest room during a break.

"Why did you leave early Tan?"

"Why not? You weren't there, why does it matter?" Dan felt guilty.

"Look, I'm sorry. I know I should have stayed at the flat with you yesterday evening and not gone back to the party but..."

"It doesn't matter. I have decided I'm moving out. It's obvious we aren't compatible. I have agreed to share Emily's flat and will move my stuff out after work."

Dan was taken by surprise. "Really?! Moving out? What...ending the relationship? We only recently signed the lease."

"So, you're more concerned about the lease than me moving out? That says a lot about the relationship."

"I don't want you to go, of course I don't..." Dan seemed more concerned about his pride than losing her.

"We're over. I will move out later. I don't want an atmosphere between us and I'm sure you don't either?" Dan was annoyed. "You really don't expect me to pay your part of the rent, do you?"

"No. I will pay my share until you can find someone to replace me. I'm sure it won't take you long. Anyway, I must get back to work."

Tanya left Dan on his own in the rest room. Later that afternoon, she returned to the flat with a friend who had a van.

They packed up her things and drove to Emily's flat so she could settle in. She wasn't upset in the least. In fact, she felt relieved the relationship had come to an end.

Dan returned to the flat late. He had gone from the lab to a local pub and met up with friends. He expected Tanya to be at the flat when he returned, but she had already gone and taken all her belongings. He was shocked she had carried out what she said she was planning to do. His ego took a tumble.

He called her on her mobile. "So, you moved out then?"

"I think that's obvious. I said I would."

For the first time in a long time, he had found a girlfriend that he liked a lot, but also one who knew her own mind and would not be manipulated. That defiance and strong will appealed to him and he wanted to win her back. "Tan, I'm sorry for the way I have acted these past few days..."

"Few days? You have been like this since we first met, and I have been a fool to put up with it..."

"But look, we're good together, aren't we?"

"No, Dan. We aren't good together."

"If I promise to change, will you come back?"

"People don't change, it's who you are. No. I won't be coming back."

"So, what about the..." But before he had the opportunity to utter the word rent, she interrupted him.

"Rent. Yes, I will continue with the monthly direct debit in accordance with the lease, but if you move anyone else in, I expect you to inform me?"

"Sure. If that's what you want..." With that he ended the call.

Dan was furious that she had the audacity to leave him, but Tanya sighed with relief. She knew she had made the right decision but was concerned that there would be an atmosphere in the lab. They both had important jobs with high levels of responsibility. Their work demanded total concentration and she did not want either of them to be distracted; and, she was Dan's Manager and she didn't want him to abuse her position.

CHAPTER 2 – THE PLAN

Dan spent the evening drinking in the flat and decided to call Rupert. "Is it okay to call you at this time, Rupert? Dan here. We met at the party." Rupert was slightly surprised to receive a call at such an hour, especially from Dan. "Oh, right. Dan, good to hear from you. What's up?" "Just thought I'd make contact to see if we could meet up again to chat about business, ideas, that sort of thing?"

"Oh, right. Erm, yeah, sure. When did you have in mind?"

"Tomorrow evening if that's good for you?"

"Might be a bit tricky. Can you do daytime?" Dan had a work shift the following day, but decided he would call in sick and agreed to meet at Rupert's office in the city at 11.00 am.

He was pleased Rupert had agreed to meet. He believed there was synergy between them. More importantly, he wanted what Rupert had: money and power. The thought of continuing his work in the lab for much longer, especially with Tanya as his manager, did little to inspire him. He knew neither of them could brush their time together under the carpet. They had been close and ending relationships always created a certain amount of tension. He spent the remainder of the evening thinking about the meeting with Rupert and what he would say.

Dan woke early and unsurprisingly, discovered anew that Tanya was not lying next to him. For a few moments, he felt alone and vulnerable, but the feeling soon passed as he had breakfast and called the lab to report in sick.

He watched the news on TV before dressing in preparation for the meeting with Rupert.

It was 10.50 am when he arrived at Bank underground station and emerged onto the street. Rupert's office was a five-minute walk away, on Queen Victoria Street. It was a modern, glass fronted building that would impress any visitor, including Dan.

He introduced himself to the receptionist at the security desk and asked for Rupert. As he waited, he admired a large oil painting of horses and a magnificent bronze horse that hung from the ceiling like a chandelier. It was an extravagance he hadn't seen before in an office building.

Rupert's PA came down a spiral staircase to greet and accompany him to the board room.

"Good morning, Dr. Thomas. I'm Jane, Rupert's PA..."

"Oh, please call me Dan." Jane was impeccably dressed and, in Dan's eyes, a real beauty. Given half the chance, he would have asked her on a date, but he thought the better of it. It wasn't the first impression he wanted to give to Rupert.

"Have you travelled far, Dan?"

"No. A short ride on the underground." On his journey to the boardroom, he passed several executives all smartly dressed in suits and wondered if his jeans and corduroy jacket were inappropriate for the meeting. That said, he didn't own a suit. He wore a white lab coat at work and socially, jeans, a shirt, and the same jacket he was wearing did the job.

"Take a seat. Rupert will be with you shortly." The board room was opulent, comprising a large, beautifully carved rosewood board table surrounded by twelve leather chairs with matching rosewood inlays and drinks cabinet. Six TV screens were strategically placed around the room. To continue the theme from the reception area, original oil paintings of horses in rosewood frames adorned the walls and bronze sculptures were strategically placed.

The boardroom was on the top floor. One side of the room was entirely glazed and looked out over the city. At this height, it was possible to see the river Thames winding its way up to the Houses of Parliament and beyond.

For Dan, this would be the perfect working environment. He was lost in a daydream when he heard the voice, "Hi Dan, good to see you." Rupert was impeccably dressed in a royal blue suit with white cut-away collared shirt and waistcoat. Dan felt conspicuous in his casual clothes.

"Forgive my choice of clothing, I don't own a suit..."

"I wasn't expecting you to wear one. Most of our visitors, entrepreneurs in the main, look just like you..."

"Well, that's a relief!" Dan shook Rupert's hand.

Rupert sat opposite him and looked him squarely in the eye. "So, my friend, what can I do for you?"

Dan was a little nervous. It felt as though he was attending an interview and needed to say something memorable. "I wondered if there was a way we could work together for mutual benefit, but before I tell you what I have in mind, I wondered if you could explain a little more about what you do here?"

To Dan's relief, Rupert smiled. "Sounds interesting. Okay. As I told you at the party, I started an IT company some years ago and partnered with an old friend. Between us, we had several IT solutions developed for the banking sector and knew we could save them tens of millions. We pitched to the leading players expecting to be turned down, but incredibly, they all signed up. The contracts they signed were worth a considerable sum. Over the following three years, we enhanced those software solutions which guaranteed us enough income to expand the operation into other sectors where the technology had applications. Eventually, we were approached by a competitor to buy the business for a ridiculous amount of money and agreed to sell. My partner was keen to go on and develop other IT solutions, but that wasn't for me. I thought I knew enough about start-ups, so we dissolved our partnership and I decided I would invest my newly acquired wealth in other people's ideas as an *angel investor.* I was lucky. I found three people to invest in early on and they all went on to deliver great products to the market, giving me a substantial return on investment. Today, my investment company *Hedgerow* employs almost 60 people whose job it is to identify investable opportunities.

If I like them, I back them. Does that give you enough information?"

"Thanks, it certainly does." Dan was hugely impressed. Rupert smiled again.

"So, back to my earlier question – what can I do for you?"

"It must be obvious to you that I'm new to all this investment stuff, but I wondered if I should ask you to sign a confidentiality agreement or something like that?"

"No. I don't sign confidentiality agreements, Dan. Hundreds of ideas are presented to *Hedgerow* every year and in some cases with similar product ideas in similar markets, it would be impossible for us to do so. I think you'll find the same refusal exists with most venture capitalists.

So, I take it from your question that have a project plan you need financing? If so, I could get one of my analysts to look at what you've prepared and if they think it's worth me considering, they'll say so?"

Dan did not have a business plan to present to Rupert or any other potential investor. He squirmed in his seat for a moment, wondering how best to tell him what he had in mind. Finally, he spoke. "I don't have a plan, but I do know how you and I could make a great deal of money. I'll be the first to admit that it wouldn't be a conventional investment for you though..."

Rupert was intrigued. Like Dan, he was a chancer, a gambler. He had made millions from his legitimate business investments, but was not against taking the odd risk, especially if it justified the reward. Of course, though, he would never admit to any form of impropriety.

"Okay. Sounds interesting. And what do you have in mind?" Dan saw a glint in Rupert's eye. "I understand why you won't sign a confidentiality agreement and perhaps that would be the wrong thing for me to ask for, but can I ask for your personal guarantee that anything I tell you will be kept confidential between us?"

Rupert paused as Dan shuffled in his seat. "Would you like some coffee?" Dan was grateful for the opportunity to collect his thoughts.

"That would be great, thanks." Rupert got up and went to a 'phone situated next to the drinks cabinet. "Hi Jane. Can we have some coffee...Dan, what would you like?"

"Do you have a flat white?"

"Sure. Two flat whites, Jane. Thanks." He hung up, turned back round, and sat on the edge of the board table.

"I'm not sure I can offer you that guarantee either. Look. We met at a party, we got on, we shared a line of coke together, but that's about it...I have no idea what you're so keen to talk to me about and as you can see, I'm not exactly desperate for new investment opportunities, so if you want to tell me what you have in mind that's okay, but no guarantees."

Dan knew Rupert held all the cards. He was a shrewd businessman, and he was right - he knew nothing about him. In fact, as far as Rupert was concerned, Dan could be working for the police, fraud squad, or HMRC and was trying to catch him out. He knew his choice was to either to tell Rupert what was on his mind or walk away.

There was a knock on the door. Jane walked across to the table and put down a silver tray with the coffee and chocolate biscuits. "Can I do anything else for you, Rupert?"

No. That's fine. Thanks, Jane." She left.

Dan had had the time to consider his options. Of course, he would tell Rupert what he had in mind. Rupert handed him his coffee and sat back in his chair.

"Thanks, I understand, no guarantees." He took a deep breath.

"Okay. I won't bore you with the science, but suffice it to say, I have spent the past three years in the lab working on a top-secret project to develop a vaccine for a deadly virus that the scientific community around the world know will start to infect people globally in the next decade. It may well cause a pandemic. It isn't something that's discussed in the public domain and rarely within the scientific community because there is the legitimate fear that people would panic.

Believe me, if the virus got out, and inevitably it will, millions would die, and there would be nothing any healthcare system in the world could do to stop it. There are several global pharma companies working on a vaccine as we speak, but they are only at the early stages of development. I work in a small team of fifteen people that I supervise, reporting to Tanya. You remember we were at the party together?" Rupert nodded.

"This project isn't a priority for the company I work for, nor is it in their planning. They aren't expecting us to come up with a vaccine before anyone else, if at all, but I know that as a team, we are on the brink of a breakthrough. No one else working on the project knows how close we are to finding a formula that works. I have personally managed the early scale trials and all the evidence suggests we are on the verge of proving its efficacy. Of course, everything is subject to full scale trials and peer review and that takes time, but I know we are leading the race..."

Rupert listened intently but was itching to ask questions. "That's great. Well done. But I'm puzzled...why are you telling me this?" Dan paused.

"It's hard to explain, but the chance that my team might develop a vaccine ahead of anyone else is a remarkable feat. But what's even more remarkable, is that I'm the only person in our team, in the company...indeed in the world, who can put all the pieces of the jigsaw together.

Without me, we are just a small, insignificant team working on a project that's expected to go nowhere..." Rupert was still struggling to understand what Dan was telling him. "I can see you're excited, Dan, but I'm still trying to work out why you think telling me has any relevance?"

"Okay..." Dan knew he was arriving at that defining moment when he would have to tell Rupert what he had in mind, and he had no idea how he would react.

"You'll understand that any company coming to market with a vaccine to solve a deadly virus has the potential to make tens or even hundreds of millions over time?" Rupert nodded. "Sure. I understand."

"Well, a unique situation exists. I have already alluded to the fact that my company has invested in this as a 'B' project.

They don't expect us to find an effective vaccine. To them, it's just another, speculative project. As I said, my team don't know how close we are to finding a formula, and without my contribution, they never will.

I am the only person that has access to all the data, the formulas, the research, and the ability to present this to market. It would be extremely easy for me to walk away with everything relevant to this project without anyone knowing, resign, set up a lab with your investment, and bring a vaccine to market that would make us a fortune."

Rupert looked at him quizzically. "You know what you're suggesting is illegal if it's even possible? It would be fraud on a major scale - a conspiracy that could have you jailed for a significant time?"

Dan was pleased that Rupert had not asked him to leave at that point.

"I do. But believe me, I have thought this through in minute detail. The success or failure of this venture is in its timing. If I fail to act soon, it will become obvious to everyone in the team that we have made a breakthrough, it will be reported to the company's board, and the lab will be elevated to an 'A' project. Right now, I am the only one who knows how close we are, and even more importantly, the only one that can piece it all together. If I were to be run over by a bus today, the project would die on the vine. If we went ahead, together, there would be no chance of anyone finding out. I would cover my tracks. Plenty of people like me join Biotech companies every day and make great discoveries. I would just be another statistic."

Rupert was showing signs of interest.

"So, you're asking me to finance a lab for you?"

"Yes, but the cost wouldn't be that great..."

"And how much is *not that great?*"

"It would need to be a fully equipped to undertake this type of work, not a sham set up. It could possibly be used for new research once this project is completed. Initially, I would need to hire five lab technicians and a minimum of two scientists with my skillset.

Other key personnel would be recruited during the second year..."

"...And the cost?" Rupert was losing patience.

"My estimate would be in the region of £1 - £1.5m. We would also need to acquire suitable lab space..."

Rupert was not about to agree to fund the project, at least not yet, but he did have several questions. "What does Tanya think of the idea? Is she on board?"

Of course, Dan hadn't discussed the idea with her and if even if he had, he knew there was no way she would want to be involved. In fact, she would more than likely report him to her superiors. Tanya was as honest as the day was long and such an idea would surely be abhorrent to her. In an odd way, though, now that the relationship was over, it would make it easier for him to go it alone. He no longer had to worry about what she thought or whether she would find out. She was now just another member of the research team, albeit his superior.

"Tan? Yeah, she's on board." Rupert had only met Tanya for a short time at the party but even to him, Dan's assertion that she *was on board* seemed unlikely.

"Really, so you've discussed it with her, she's aware of the risks but she's still willing to be involved...she doesn't seem the type?"

In that moment, Dan knew that his off-the-cuff remark didn't sit comfortably with Rupert. "Yes, we discussed it. At first, she wasn't happy, but she's in love with me and I persuaded her it's what I want, so she agreed to be a *silent partner.*" Rupert continued the interrogation.

"And what happens if you fall out or split up? What risk is there of your *silent partner* becoming your nemesis?" Dan believed the only way of reassuring him that Tanya would not prove to be a liability was to be over-confident. "Really, we're a couple. We're good together. She loves me - there won't be a problem, believe me..."

"Okay let's put Tanya to one side for a moment, but for the record, you haven't convinced me that she won't be a problem. How do you plan to steal all the documents, materials, and data you need to bring this project live?"

This was the part that Dan had thought through in detail and he was more than happy to explain precisely how he would do it.

"It's really not that difficult. Security is lax in the lab. It should be much tighter. As I have access to the server and every workstation, I can download everything I need onto an external hard drive and literally walk out without anyone knowing.

I only need access to six computers. We all work shifts. I would make sure I got in early one morning or stayed late one evening, and when I was alone, it would take me no longer than an hour or so to save all the data I need."

"Sounds too easy. Okay, so let's assume you walk out with everything you need; how could you explain setting up a lab and copying everything your current employer is working on?"

Rupert knew he had not articulated his concerns that well but instead of rephrasing, he waited to hear what Dan had to say. "Research and development take a lot of time. To most people in other walks of life like yours, Rupert, we move at a snail's pace. I would need about two years to set everything up and to come forward with the formula for the vaccine. In that time, my current employer would be no further forward in finding the solution because they would head off in another direction. Look, it's hard to explain unless I go into the technical stuff, and with respect, I would lose you if I did. But trust me: my current employer will be busy wasting their time keeping this project going after I leave, and as far as I am aware, there is no other lab facility in the world that is anywhere near to finding a vaccine. What I would save onto that external hard drive and walk away with is worth a fortune." Rupert scratched his head. "Would Tanya resign too?"

Dan knew that Tanya was a stumbling block in Rupert's mind, but it was proving a challenge to quell his anxiety.

"No. It would make sense for her to stay where she was. She could ensure, not that there's much chance of the team finding the right formula, that the lab works on strategies that would take them in a different direction."

"To be clear, Dan, you're saying that within two years or so, you could launch the formula for a vaccine for this virus and the cash would then flow in?"

"It's not that straightforward. I believe within two years we would be able to undertake scaled trials, and once we were confident, we would need to conduct larger trials that would be subject to peer review. It all takes time..."

"So, not within two years, no?"

Dan knew how long it took to bring vaccines to market, but he didn't want to scare Rupert off. He tried to formulate an encouraging response, but Rupert stopped him. "Okay, so how long after the two years before we see a return on the investment, and does the initial investment cover everything, or do you envisage additional investment along the way?"

Dan held up his hands. "Look, I don't want to mislead you in any way. Yes, there will be additional investment, and overall, it could take four years from now to start seeing a financial return, but believe me, it would be worth it. Most of the investment has already been made by my current employer. You can tell I'm not a businessman, Rupert. I'm not an accountant either, but if I worked with you, I know my proposition would make financial sense."

"So, you have no idea what the final cost would look like?"

"I don't. And there's no point in me guessing. Perhaps we could work this up together if the project has any interest?"

Rupert shifted his weight from leg to leg. "I'd be lying if I said I wasn't interested, Dan, but I'm asking myself *Why I would want to get involved in an illegal venture despite the potential returns?* I run a successful business that has made me more money than I could ever spend. Why would I do it?"

"I can't answer that one for you, Rupert, but what I would say is that this project could be the most successful venture you've ever invested in - not just financially, but also in helping make the world a better place and solve a health crisis that *will* come about if a vaccine isn't found."

It was a compelling closing statement from Dan. "Okay. Give me a couple of weeks to think about it..." Dan didn't want to wait weeks. "I know you're holding the cards, Rupert, but could I ask that you get back to me in the next week?

As I said earlier, the longer we leave it, the harder it will be to acquire the data without the current team straying into territory where they understand what I've discovered?"

Rupert agreed to his request, they shook hands, and he then escorted Dan off the premises.

Dan was pleased with his performance. Under the circumstances, he couldn't have expected to achieve more.

He hadn't gone to Rupert with a water-tight business plan and had been unable to adequately answer most of Rupert's questions, but he remained interested, nonetheless. Time would tell if his overtures had worked. What immediately worried him, though, was his lie about Tanya going along with the idea. She was not on board; in fact, she knew nothing of his plan to commit a serious crime. She wasn't even his girlfriend anymore and the last person he would confide in was her. But how could he square that one with Rupert? That would have to wait for another day. He caught the underground and returned to the flat.

Dan didn't meet the stereotypical profile of a scientist. He was highly intelligent and extremely competent, if not brilliant at what he did, but he was a flawed human being. He was a risk taker, not content to work for the betterment of mankind as most of his colleagues were, instead longing to use his talents and intellect to better himself at almost any cost.

He spent the evening reviewing what had been said in the meeting with Rupert and considered what he would need to do if he were to back his project.

CHAPTER 3 – THE STUMBLING BLOCK

Two days passed and Dan reported for work as usual. As a test to check security at the lab, he took with him an external hard drive in his backpack, something that was prohibited in his contract. In theory, all lab employees should have been subjected to bag and possible body searches twice daily on arriving and leaving, but that rarely took place.

In fact, during the time Dan had worked for the company, he had only had a bag search twice.

As anticipated, he was able to breeze in and out of the lab with the hard drive in his backpack, without intervention. He thought about copying some random data from the server to the hard drive but thought better of it. If he were stopped and it was clean, it would result in a slap on the wrist, but to be caught with random data belonging to the company would result in instant dismissal and possible prosecution for breach of contract. It wasn't worth the risk for a dry run.

During his shift, he had two meetings with Tanya at her instigation. They were progress meetings - one on his own, the other as a team. It was clear to him that she had made her mind up the relationship was over and, consequentially, their exchanges were very business-like. There was no warmth, no flirting, as though they had never even had a relationship.

Dan had a considerable ego and her indifference toward him annoyed him. She had got the better of him. He had hoped she would be repentant, or at least show signs of regret, but it was not to be.

He had built a close relationship with her over the past year or so, but he wasn't in love with her and knew he would find someone else when the time was right.

That evening, Dan received a call from Rupert. "Dan, I've given thought to our conversation..." Dan drew breath.

"...I would be happy to do some preliminary work with you to draw up a business plan and, importantly, a financial and investment plan, but only if you agree to my terms."

Dan was full of nervous energy. "Okay, what terms do you have in mind?"

"I would rather not discuss the matter over the 'phone. Can we meet in an hour at the city bar opposite my office?"

Dan agreed and left immediately. As he arrived at the bar, Rupert was crossing the road having just left his office. They entered and sat at a quiet table. "Can I get you a beer, Rupert?"

"Great."

Dan went to the bar and returned with the drinks. He sat, took a log sip, then looked Rupert in the eye, keen to get straight to the point. "So, what are your terms?"

Rupert didn't hesitate either. "For me, this is a highly risky venture, Dan. Apart from anything else, what you have proposed is illegal, and if I were to fund this project, it would have to be on the basis that I couldn't be implicated in any way in your stealing company property, but before we even reach that point, I would need to be re-assured that the project is financially viable in the first place." He paused and looked at Dan for a response.

"Sure, I understand..."

"So, just to be clear, what I want you to do is complete a detailed pitch for funding. Before we leave, I will give you a memory stick where you'll find a template to complete. If you don't have the answers to any questions, just leave them blank or provide an estimate.

Once I have received and reviewed your responses, we will arrange to meet at my office, and together, we will build a business and financial plan that makes sense and hopefully justifies investment. Now, I'm stating the obvious here, but you shouldn't make any reference to your current employer, or how you plan to obtain the data. Is that okay?"

Dan nodded.

"Good. Now, I think we need to establish the ground rules before we go any further. If your pitch document and our planning session produce what appears to be a viable investment opportunity, I will set up a legal entity, a holding company, that will be used as a vehicle for the lab to operate through. The ownership, the allocated shares of that company, will be solely in my name and I will finance the business up to a maximum of £2 million. If the financial plan we draw up suggests the investment up to the point of launching the vaccine is likely to go beyond the £2 million, I would reserve the right to attract additional investment from other funders. People I know personally. The management of the business will be my responsibility. You will be hired as an employee...Lab Manager, or whatever title you think appropriate. You will run the lab, reporting to me, and if for any reason you are caught stealing your current employers' data or are subsequently accused of doing so, I will be shielded from the fallout. I will do nothing to help or support you. I will deny any knowledge of your transgressions. I will not risk my existing business activities for this project..." Dan had to interrupt.

"Forgive me, but it does sound a bit one sided? I take all the risk and you get all the reward?"

"Let me finish, Dan. The business must be structured this way to protect both yours and my best interests. I can't be seen to be complicit in a conspiracy to defraud your employer, and you shouldn't be seen to be doing so either. So, I hire a team of scientists who happen to develop a vaccine formula that works. At the point of selling the company, I reward you, my trusted Lab Manager, with a share of the net proceeds. I think 40% would be equitable..." Dan flinched.

"I can see the logic, but wouldn't it be more equitable if the split was 60% for me?"

"The balance isn't up for discussion, Dan. Those are my terms. Do you want to take it to the next stage and prepare the pitch document or would you rather abandon the idea now? I'm happy to do either."

Dan was left with little option but to agree. Rupert held out his hand. "Here is the memory stick with the questionnaire. Spend the next couple of days, or however long it takes you, to complete the form. Then, just give me a ring so we can make a date to meet."

They shook hands, finished their drinks, and parted company. Dan took the train back to the flat, stopping on the way for a stiffer drink.

Had he pulled off a potential deal that would make him a fortune or agreed to an arrangement that he would live to regret?

Time would tell.

When he got back to the flat, he looked at the questions in the pitch document to see the information he would need.

Most of the questions he could not answer, simply because the questionnaire was designed for people who had already prepared business plans and financial forecasts and could pluck relevant information from existing data. Then again, Rupert had already acknowledged that this wasn't a problem.

He spent an hour or so Googling information that would prove useful and filled out the form as best he could. The following day at the lab, he gathered the information he needed. Once back home, he completed the form that very evening and called Rupert to set up the next meeting.

Three days later, they met at Rupert's office. Between the two of them, albeit mainly Rupert's input, they produced a business plan and financial forecast that would take them to the point of agreeing with a manufacturer to make the vaccine, as well as an estimate of the worth of the business at that time.

It transpired from their analysis that the project would take almost four years to complete and would cost nearly £8m. However, the forecasted return on the investment at the point of sale was a staggering £84 million.

Dan was anything but surprised. He knew the reward would be tens of millions of pounds. In fact, he thought that £84 million was a cautious estimate. Either way, though, it was acceptable to both parties. Once again, Rupert needed to hear it from Dan that he was accepting of the business structure and conditions he had laid out at their first meeting. This time, Dan agreed without hesitation and they shook hands. There would be no formal written agreement between them; they would base their agreement on trust.

Dan had been keen to stress the urgency of getting on with the project to ensure that he could steal the data in a timely manner. Between the two of them, they sketched out a timeline of activities up to the point when the new lab would go live, including data acquisition, Dan's resignation, the lab set-up, recruitment, and the grand opening. For all of this, they forecasted almost ten months of the four-year plan.

It was agreed that Dan would spend the next couple of weeks in the lab making a list of the data he would need to steal, before copying it onto the hard drive. He would also draw up the specifications for the lab and its equipment together with job specifications for the team he would need to assemble. They agreed that Dan would only contact Rupert when he had completed these initial tasks.

Dan returned home. Throughout the journey, he went over the meeting with Rupert in his mind. He was pleased he had gained his agreement to fund the project, but at the same time, he was concerned that there would be no reference to his part ownership in the new business.

He was relying on the word of a man he hardly knew. Anything could happen within the lifetime of the project and where would that leave him? He knew if he wanted to make some serious money, he had no choice but to accept Rupert's terms, but he was also no fool. He knew there were risks involved in stealing the data and he also knew that setting up the new lab and transferring the intellectual rights of another firm's property was a serious criminal offence, and if caught, he would serve a lengthy prison sentence.

There was also the issue of employing a team that would be expected to work with another lab's research work without them finding out it had been stolen. He had not raised with Rupert the challenges he would face in migrating the data and making the transfer work, because he knew that it might well have dissuaded him from investing.

Dan faced serious challenges and had no idea how he would overcome them. Not least of all was the issue of Tanya. He also knew there would be a raft of other stumbling blocks that would emerge as time went on, each of which could scupper his plans, but he had no option but to accept that it would be tough if he wanted to reap the longer-term financial rewards.

He stopped for a beer before returning to the flat. Three hours later and feeling a little worse for wear, he slumped onto the sofa and fell asleep. It was nearly 4.00 am when he woke with a start, and a hangover.

The gravity of the deal he had struck with Rupert the previous day was beginning to dawn on him and the self-doubt was creeping in. Did he really think he could get away with it? Despite thinking through all the elements of the plan, so much could go wrong. He was desperate to tell someone, anyone, what he was planning, but he knew that was impossible. It would have to remain a secret, even from his closest friends.

His shift at the lab started at 11.00 am. He arrived a little late. Tanya had called an impromptu team meeting and he was last to arrive.

"Good morning, Dan." He nodded at Tanya and acknowledged the other people in the room but said nothing. "I have some good news, or at least I hope it translates into good news. I had a meeting with senior management yesterday, and after their review of our lab work over the past six months, they are planning to ramp up investment in our current vaccine project and have sanctioned an extension of lab facilities. They've also given me the green light to hire another 8 people for the project, which should speed up development..."

Everyone seemed pleased with Tanya's announcement apart from Dan. He knew these revelations meant that senior management now believed there was a serious prospect the lab would uncover a successful formula for the vaccine.

This would inevitably translate into greater security, increased monitoring, and added complexities that he had not factored into his thinking.

It was obvious that Tanya had drawn the same conclusions about the lab's progress as he had, and that it had put his plans at a major disadvantage.

He had no way of knowing what Tanya knew without asking her directly. Of course, prior to their break-up, it would have been an easy conversation to have, but in the current climate, it would prove more difficult to say the least.

As they all returned to their workstations, Tanya asked to talk to Dan on his own.

"Dan, I know our splitting up makes our relationship in the lab a little more difficult, but I would be grateful if we could separate that from the job we are paid to do." Dan was irritated that she would say such a thing.

"What the hell do you mean? Do you think I'm pining for us to get back together? Well, I'm not. We're over and, truth be known, we were never compatible anyway." Tanya was hurt by his comment. She was relieved they had spilt up, but she had been in love with him, at least earlier in the relationship, and emotions were still raw.

"Okay. If that's how you see it, that's fine by me. However, as your manager, I expect you to arrive on time for your shifts, and it would be helpful if you would show as much enthusiasm for the job as the rest of the team. Are you not pleased with the news?"

"What news?"

"The news about the additional investment?"

Dan was not pleased, but he wasn't about to say why. "Sure, of course I am. Anyway, I'll get back to work." He had wanted to avoid an atmosphere between them, but it was too late. As he walked back to his workstation, he knew that time was not on his side. If he were to execute his plans successfully, he would need to start sooner rather than later.

It was just after 3.00 pm when he completed the tests he was currently working on and decided to devote the rest of the afternoon into early evening assembling the long list of data requirements he planned to download onto his external hard drive.

For most of the lab technicians' work, it would be easy to access their computers using a common password to download relevant information, but not Tanya's. As lab manager, she had a unique password that only she and her immediate boss knew.

It was crucial that he accessed her computer if he were to acquire all the necessary information he needed. It was highly unlikely that she would have written the password down and put it in her desk draw, but it wasn't inconceivable. Dan knew he would need to gain access to her office when no one was around and rummage around in the hope he would strike lucky.

It was Tuesday. He knew that Tanya worked until 6.00 pm on Wednesdays. His shift would end at 7.00 pm and only two other people would be in the lab at the same time. He could stay beyond 7.00 pm and use the opportunity to search Tanya's desk when everyone had left.

The company's announcement about ramping up investment meant that from the following Monday, the lab would be operational twenty-four hours a day, making it impossible for him to download data from each of the key computers without being seen. He had to undertake the task when he was guaranteed to be alone, and Wednesday evening was the best chance he would ever get.

There was no guarantee he would be alone in the lab again in the days leading up to the new 24-hour working regime. The reality of what he was planning was beginning to sink in.

As he microwaved a meal, he checked through all the things he needed to do in the lab the following day and packed his rucksack with the external hard drive. It was unlikely security would be tighter in the morning, even after Tanya's investment announcement. It would likely take effect the following Monday when the new working arrangements started, but even that was only speculation. Taking the hard drive into the lab was riskier now than it had ever been, and he knew it.

He settled down to watch TV but found it difficult to concentrate. He slept badly during the night, waking up several times in a cold sweat. As dawn broke, he was already wide awake. Today was the day.

CHAPTER 4 - EXECUTION

He arrived at the lab on time with the rucksack containing the hard drive slung over his shoulder. To his relief, there were no security guards on duty.

He had at least overcome the first challenge. As he entered the lab, Tanya was coming out of her office and smiled at him. He smiled back and went to his workstation.

For most of the day, he suffered a level of anxiety he had rarely experienced before. He knew that within a few hours, he would be downloading data from six computers, a task that would take an hour and likely more. He had to do it without interruption, and he still had no idea if he would be able to gain access to Tanya's computer.

He took the first opportunity he had to snort a generous line in the men's room. The new security regime would also impact on his ability to smuggle in his daily consumption of drugs, but that was the least of his worries.

It was shortly before 6.00 pm when Tanya was due to finish her shift that Dan was called away to another part of the building. When he returned, it was only him and two other lab staff remaining, just as he had hoped. Within the hour they, too, would leave and he would be alone to execute his plan. The hour dragged by. Eventually, his colleagues did indeed leave the lab as scheduled, and he was alone.

He had meticulously planned out how he would spend his time and the order in which he would access each of the computers. He attached his hard drive to the first computer and while that was downloading, he went into Tanya's office to search for the password.

He had assumed the draw to her desk where he might find it would be locked, but it was open. He found nothing of interest. Ten minutes had already passed and only one of the six computers had been accessed. He withdrew the hard drive from the first computer and hooked it up to the second one before returning to Tanya's office.

He knew how organized and security conscious she was, however, he had to find the password, or his plans would be compromised. Under the circumstances he was extremely relaxed but not thinking rationally, partly due to the cocaine. He rummaged around her office in a random manner while trying not to disturb anything. He wasn't overly concerned, as he knew he had time to clear up now that she'd left for the day. At least, that's what he thought, but as it turned out, she had been in a management meeting in another part of the building and, to his surprise, walked right in at that very moment.

"What are you doing in my office?" She was shocked to see him.

"I...I thought I heard your 'phone ringing in your desk and came to see..."

Came to see what?" Dan was sweating. "I thought I could retrieve it for you..."

"My 'phone is in my bag. You couldn't have heard a 'phone ringing in my desk. Why are you really in here?" She was nervous but assertive in tone. Dan had always been the dominant partner in their relationship, and under normal circumstances, he would have exploded if she had used that tone with him, but these were far from normal circumstances.

He was in the middle of a serious crime, he was high, and he was vulnerable.

"I'm sorry. I really thought I heard a 'phone ringing..."

"I don't believe you. Why would you want to rummage around in my office? What are you looking for?"

Dan was backed into a corner. There was nothing he could say that would sound remotely plausible. The excuse of hearing the 'phone ring might just have worked with someone more gullible, but not Tanya. His heart was racing.

Ordinarily, after everyone had left the lab after a shift, individual computers would be switched off, but one was whirring in the background and its screen was illuminated.

Tanya turned to see which computer had been left on and moved toward it. Dan followed her. "Why is this computer on?" Now, he was panicking.

He knew that the moment she arrived at the computer, she would see the external hard drive on the desk next to it, downloading data. "I needed to access Jemima's summary report..."

But before he was able to complete the lie, Tanya saw the hard drive. "Dan, are you copying data off Jemima's computer?"

She turned to face him. She knew the seriousness of the offence he was committing, but why was he doing it? Dan stood perfectly still and silent. He could think of nothing to say. "Why are you using an external hard drive? What are you doing?"

Dan had to think quickly. "If I tell you what I'm doing, will you hear me out without interrupting?"

It was his only option. He had to tell her everything in the hope, albeit an outside hope, that she would either go along with him or allow him to abandon his plan without reporting him. She was frightened by what he might say but was prepared to listen. She unplugged the hard drive and switched the computer off, then turned to him. "Okay. Tell me."

The next few minutes would test Dan's oratory skills to the limit. What did he have to say to convince her that his plan was worth her involvement? Or, if he couldn't, how could he at least extricate himself from all this, put aside what he had agreed with Rupert, and get on with life as normal, as though nothing had happened?

"Look, I had no idea that you and I would split up..."

"Dan, I'm not interested in why we split up. That much is obvious, to me at least. I just want to know what you're doing rifling around in my office and copying data off a computer?"

Dan needed Tanya to listen to him without interruption.

"Tan, please let me say what I need to say and then question me by all means..." She sighed and nodded.

"You and I were together, and I thought we were an item long-term. I know we have different views on things...Yes, I want to make money more than you do, but I only wanted what was best for us as a couple - to be able to live comfortably, raise a family, have a nice house and a nice car...that kind of thing. There is nothing wrong with wanting to have a better life, is there?"

Tanya said nothing but concentrated on his facial expression. He looked worried and she knew by the glazed look in his eyes that he had been taking drugs.

Dan went on "Well, I have worked here in this lab longer than you, and I can see the great work that we have been doing as a team, but until your announcement about the new investment and employing more people, it seemed to me that this project was unimportant to the business. We were starved of proper funding and the impression I got was that we were not a priority project and management were just going along with existing funding in the hope that a miracle would happen. That frustrated me. You know, in my job, I co-ordinate everyone else's work in the lab and I knew we were getting closer to finding the vaccine formula. I suppose in my frustration, I thought if we were to make a breakthrough, the company didn't deserve to reap the rewards. You know I've been pivotal in bringing the various work strands together and that has led us to where we are, on the verge of a breakthrough. If it hadn't been for me, we would have gone off in the wrong direction..."

Tanya had to interrupt. "Where are you going with this, Dan?"

Dan was arriving at the crucial point where he had to tell her the truth. He knew she would be appalled by what she heard, but what choice did he have?

"Do you remember the party we attended, the one that effectively ended our relationship?"

"How could I forget it?"

"Well, you will remember Rupert then?" She nodded.

"You'll remember that he is a venture capitalist – he invests in startup businesses. Well, I got into a discussion with him after I returned to the party that evening about the work we did in the lab and he was really interested.

He asked me if I had ever thought of starting my own lab. I told him that I was frustrated that our current management were taking little interest in the work we were doing, and out of the blue, he said he would be keen to discuss ways in which he could invest in me in a new facility. One thing led to another and he asked me if it would be possible to acquire all the relevant details of the current vaccine project and transfer it to the new facility to give us a head start..." Tanya was shocked by what she heard.

"...You mean, steal the intellectual rights to our company's £8m investment so far? Just copy the data onto a hard drive and walk away, are you serious?!"

"It's easier than you think..."

"...But Dan, you're missing the point. What you're attempting to do is illegal. It's theft, an imprisonable offence. Did that not cross your mind? I cannot believe I'm hearing all this!"

"But listen, Tan. I know there are risks. I know it's wrong. But I am confident I can make the transfer of data to a new lab and we could bring the formula to market and make a lot of money!"

Tanya had heard enough. "I thought I knew you, Dan. Yes, you have odd ways of thinking, but I had no idea you were dishonest, certainly not capable or willing to be persuaded by someone else to undertake such a stupid fraud..."

Of course, he hadn't been persuaded by Rupert at all, but she wasn't to know.

"Tan..."

"Do not call me Tan!" It was rare that Tanya would lose her temper, but his revelation had pushed her over the edge. "Have you any idea how stupid you are? How warped is your mind? Did you really think I would go along with your plan, whether we were together or not? In a strange way, I feel sorry for you, but I can't ignore what I've caught you doing! I'm sorry Dan, but tomorrow first thing, I'm reporting you."

In a blind panic, Dan couldn't contain himself. Enraged, he grabbed her by the shoulders and pushed her back onto her desk and screamed at her, "Do you seriously think I would let you walk out of here knowing you would report me? Well?"

Tanya was shocked by his aggression and for the first time since they'd met, she felt genuinely afraid. "Dan, let me go! This is insane..."

But after taking a generous quantity of cocaine, Dan had lost control and with it, the ability to think rationally. He knew she would expose his attempted theft and now he had physically assaulted her. No apology would undo that. He only had one choice. He had to act. As Tanya screamed and struggled to get away from him, he grabbed her by the throat and squeezed.

As he stared vacantly into her bloodshot eyes, his grip on her neck tightened. It was too late to go back. He kept a firm hold until she stopped breathing and only then, did he let her go. Her lifeless body fell limply to the ground. Dan stood over her, breathing heavily, unable to compute what had just happened. He looked at her for some time but there was no movement. He grabbed and shook her in a feeble attempt to bring her back to life, but to no avail. It was as though he had been watching a violent movie on TV and was now waiting to see what happened next. He let her head drop limply to the floor and stood up, staring at her in disbelief.

He sat back onto a chair, facing her body, and started to weep uncontrollably. Several minutes passed before the reality of what he had done sank in.

He was in no fit state to think rationally, but he had to weigh up his options. He could call the police and an ambulance and hand himself in. He could try and clean up the scene of the crime as best he could and simply leave her lying there for the first shift in the morning to find her, or he could clean up and go through with his plan to finish transferring the data from the computers, then leave.

The shock of what he had done remained, but he mustered the composure and clarity of thought to take his time to do everything he believed necessary to cover up the murder. Painstakingly, he carried on with his task of collecting all the data he needed from the computers. His final task was downloading data from Tanya's computer but at the point at which she had discovered him in her office, he still hadn't found her password.

He went back and searched through her desk drawers but found nothing that remotely resembled a password.

As he got up from her chair, he saw a small *post-it note* on the side of the screen and peeled it off. The password! He successfully gained entry to her computer and downloaded all the material he needed, then hastily wiped the computers clean of fingerprints. Finally, within ninety minutes of murdering Tanya, he had packed his rucksack with the hard drive and left the building. There were no security guards on duty, nor were there any CCTV cameras to see him leave the lab.

For a man that had just murdered an ex-girlfriend and stolen valuable data from his employer, he was remarkably calm. He walked back to the underground and got a train back to the flat. Within ten minutes of arriving home, though, the reality of what he had done hit home. He broke out in a cold sweat and started shaking violently, sobbing hysterically. What had compelled him to throttle her? How could he have so cold-bloodedly left her on the floor and continued his mission to steal the data? What kind of man was he? Would he ever be able to recover from this nightmare? He opened a bottle of whisky and drank it down as though it were his last. A few gulps saw off a third of the bottle. In his state of mind, it would have been all too easy to finish it off and sleep away the nightmare, but he knew that would serve little purpose. The nightmare would never go away.

If he were to get through this ordeal, he had to think clearly, rationally. Otherwise, he may as well give himself up. He was desperate to tell someone what had happened, confess to a friend that would keep his secret, but he knew he could not. He had to live with what he had done and plan a strategy to move forward.

It was late when he went to bed and he was unable to sleep fearing that if he did, he would only recount the memory as a nightmare.

CHAPTER 5 - AFTERMATH

The morning came and he was desperately tired. He had been up most of the night trying to think of a way of getting through the next few days. He had to maintain his composure when he turned up for his shift in a few hours, knowing that Tanya's body would have been found by then? It was inevitable the police would want to interview all lab members, especially him. The other team members knew he and Tanya had been a couple until they'd split up the day before, so he would surely be a key person of interest.

With a couple of hours remaining before he needed to leave for the train, he took the opportunity to review the material he had downloaded from the lab computers. As far as he could gather, he had everything he needed. Just in case the police were to search his personal laptop, he decided not to transfer the contents of the hard drive just yet. Instead, he would hide it in the flat until the drama had died down.

After strong feelings of remorse endured the previous evening, he was remarkably level-headed.

He had convinced himself that he had not intended to murder Tanya. It was her outburst that had caused him to grab her by the throat. It was an instinctive reaction, so her death wasn't his fault and certainly wasn't premeditated in any way. He had to remain cool, calm, and focused. Despite her demise, as unfortunate as it was, he had the data that he had set out to obtain, and in time, he would learn how to put aside any thoughts of Tanya and achieve his objective.

When Dan arrived at the lab, security was noticeably tight. The police were there in numbers. Dan approached a policeman. "What's happened?"

"Who are you, sir?"

"I work in the lab."

"Okay, would you come with me please." Dan was led to a large room at the back of the lab where he met other members of the team, who were visibly upset. "What's the matter, what's happened?" Grace, one of the lab assistants told him that Tanya had been found dead on the premises and that the police were investigating. Dan feigned his shock at the news and wept more convincingly than he could have hoped. Grace tried to console him.

"So, what happens next, Grace?"

"The police are planning to speak to us all individually; we're waiting to be called." Just then, a policeman came over to Dan. "May I take your name, sir?"

"Dan Thomas."

"Okay. I can see your colleague has told you the news?"

"Yes...it's awful. Do you have any idea what happened?"

"Not yet, sir. We have forensics in the lab, but we plan to speak with all members of the lab team, if you don't mind?"

Dan could do nothing but consent. "No. Not at all." He sat down to wait with the others and the policeman left. When Dan's turn came to be interviewed, the detective inspector introduced himself and his colleague.

"Dr. Thomas. Thank you for speaking to us."

"No, I'm happy to assist..."

"...Just an informal chat if we may." Dan nodded awkwardly. "How long have you worked with the deceased?"

"A few years. We started dating a year ago but just last week, we broke up." Dan thought it wise to get out into the open his relationship with Tanya before being asked.

"Oh, I see. You were in a relationship with her? I am so sorry for your loss."

"Thank you, although we had split up..."

"Presumably, you still had feelings for her though?"

"Of course, I didn't want the relationship to end, but..." He knew he was revealing too much information that would only lead to further questions. "But what?"

"Well. Tanya ended the relationship because she thought we were incompatible, and if I am honest, I agreed with her. It was sad but we agreed to move on."

"That is unfortunate. Have you any idea why anyone would want to murder her?"

"Murder? Do you think she was murdered?" Dan knew he would need to show surprise at the question.

"It's not conclusive, but we have reason to believe she was strangled." He swallowed.

"Oh, my god that's awful. I have no idea who would want to kill her, she was so lovely to everyone."

"When was the last time you saw her?"

"I think it was around 6.00 pm yesterday when she finished her shift. My own shift finished an hour later at 7.00 pm"

"Was there anyone else in the lab at the time?"

"Yes, Grace and Peter, I think. They finish their shift at the same time as me."

"So, did you leave the lab at 7.00 pm at the end of your shift?"

"No. I stayed a little longer to finish up what I was doing, but it wasn't long after." "Had the others gone by then?"

"Yes, I believe I was last to leave."

"And you didn't see Dr. Waters – Tanya – again?"

"No. As I said, as far as I am aware, she left at 6.00 pm. I left and went home to my flat."

"Thank you, Dr. Thomas. The lab will be closed for the foreseeable future. Your personnel department have asked to see everyone in the Common Room, so I suggest you make your way there now. We may want to speak to you again."

"Of course." Dan got up and made his way to the Common Room, where a team from Personnel had gathered to offer support and advice.

They were all offered counselling and were informed that they would not be expected to return to the lab for the next week or so. They should wait to be informed when they should report back for duty.

With nothing else to do, Dan went to the local pub with his colleagues for a drink and to talk about Tanya's demise. For three hours, they recounted their memories of her and were particularly keen to comfort Dan for his loss. They knew their relationship had ended, but they were also aware of how close they had been leading up to her death. When they all left the pub, Dan he returned to his flat.

The day had taken its toll. He was not an accomplished actor and wondered if his performance during the police questioning had led them to think he was a suspect. He was tired and desperate to empty the bottle of whisky he had started the previous evening but thought the better of it. He needed to keep a clear head.

He called close friends and told them of the tragedy. He was in a desperate state. Stealing data was one thing but murdering someone was an act of barbarity and he knew he would never be able to erase what he had done from his memory. That evening, three friends came round to the flat for an impromptu supper. They were shocked by the news. They were convinced Dan and Tanya were a solid couple and were surprised to hear they had split up.

Dan played along, and the support he was given gave him the short-term comfort he needed. Little did they know.

With him not expected back at work for at least a week, he knew he had to occupy his mind. It would be all too easy to go into a downward spiral. But try as he might, as each hour passed the gravity of what he had done became apparent, he became increasingly stressed.

Over and over, he challenged his sanity. How could he bring himself to kill anyone, let alone Tanya, someone who he had been making love to only a few days earlier?

He decided he could not face the thought of serving a long prison sentence for murdering her, so confessing to the police was not an option. He had already told them informally that he had left the lab after 7.00 pm and as far as he was concerned, he had been the last to leave. Despite being a scientist, he knew little about the discipline of forensics other than a short module he studied at university. What he did know was that the tiniest piece of forensic evidence could prove his guilt. He recalled precisely what he had done to cover his tracks after he had strangled her. His fingerprints would understandably be all over the lab; after all, he worked there. He had made a point of cleaning thoroughly in Tanya's office, especially her computer, the desk, and the desk key.

He played the murder scene over in his head time and time again, and knew he had to distract himself.

For most people in his predicament, they would abandon the idea of using the data he had stolen to set up the lab, but not Dan. He convinced himself that Tanya's death should not derail his idea. In a perverse way, he even felt that making a success of the project would be the only fitting legacy for the loss of her life.

He had at least a week before he returned to work and set about working on the list of tasks he needed to complete before reporting back to Rupert.

Two days passed and he had barely taken a break and had enjoyed little sleep. It was mid-morning when his doorbell rang. It was the police inspector and a detective.

"Good morning, Dr. Thomas. You may remember me, I am Detective Inspector Ian Graham, and this is my colleague Detective David Finch. May we have a word with you?" Dan was slightly taken aback.

"Oh, yes. I remember. Would you like to come in?" The three of them went into the sitting room and sat down. "Can I make you a drink, inspector?"

"No, that's fine thanks."

"So, how can I help you?"

"It's just routine, sir. A terrible business..."

"Yes, I know. I can't stop thinking about Tanya...I can't sleep."

"I'm sure. When we last spoke, you told me that you had been dating the deceased for a year, is that so?"

"Yes, I can't remember exactly how long we had been seeing each other but we moved in here recently."

"And remind me, why did you split up the day before she was murdered?"

"Sorry, inspector. Are you saying that Tanya was definitely murdered?"

"No question, sir...what did you think happened to her?"

Dan knew he had to answer the inspector's questions confidently, but it wasn't in his interests to widen the conversation further than necessary.

"I don't know. I just can't get my head around why anyone would want to murder her."

"No, it's a tragedy...but if I may say so, you don't appear to be very emotional about her death?" He knew he had to react forcibly to that question.

"Not emotional? I have been beside myself these past few days. I can't think of anything else...what are you suggesting, inspector?"

"I'm not suggesting anything, sir, other than the fact that all your lab colleagues we have spoken to over the past couple of days have been extremely emotional, even tearful."

"I'm sure they have been, inspector. Can you not see that I'm putting on a brave face myself?"

"Of course, sir. I understand. So, you said you were the last person to leave the lab that evening.

Is it possible, now you have had time to reflect, that you may have seen the deceased in the lab before you left?"

"No, I didn't. I didn't see her leave the lab at 6.00 pm either as it goes. You will recall I told you that I had to go to another part of the building and when I returned, it was after 6.00 pm and there were only three of us left who were due to finish at 7.00 pm. The other two left at 7.00 pm prompt, but I stayed on to complete something I was working on." Dan was feeling a little uncomfortable with the line of questioning.

"Okay. We have been able to confirm that the deceased was strangled to death."

"Strangled? My god!" Dan acted shocked to hear what he already knew.

"We are asking everyone in the lab if they would be prepared to provide a set of fingerprints and take a DNA test. Is that okay with you, Dr. Thomas?" It wasn't what Dan wanted to hear, but he had no choice but to agree to report to the police station the following morning. After a few additional questions, the policemen left.

Dan was panicked. Why did he think it would be so easy to fob them off? It was obvious they would want fingerprints and a DNA test of all the lab staff. From his basic modules on forensics at university, he knew that fingerprints on another person's skin - in this instance, Tanya's throat -would not last long and the likelihood of him being detected this way was extremely unlikely. But what about the room?

He no longer had enough concentration to work on his list of priorities, so he instead chose to finish the bottle of whisky and sleep it off.

It was morning and Dan woke in a panic. He was due at the police station in two hours. He remembered it was his birthday. The postman arrived with several cards, one of which was from Tanya. She had obviously sent the card the day they split up. Her personal message read, *I hope you have a good day, Dan. I bought a couple of tickets for us to go to the cinema which are enclosed. Hope you can find someone else to go with. Despite everything, I miss you. Tanya.*

His emotions flooded out. Not only had he split up with a girlfriend he was serious about, but she was also dead, and he had killed her. His mobile rang. It was his mother.

He couldn't bring himself to take the call. He waited until it rang off, but it started ringing again almost straight away. This time, it was a close friend. Again, he let it ring off, then he sat back on the sofa and wept.

It was time to leave for the police station. As he arrived, two other lab employees were there in the waiting room. They were called forward one by one. Dan only had to wait a few minutes for his turn.

His DNA sample and fingerprints were taken by a technician, which only took a couple of minutes, but as he was leaving, the inspector caught sight of him.

"Thanks for coming in, Dr. Thomas. I hope you're managing okay? Dan nodded, then said, almost on autopilot, "My birthday today. I received a card from Tanya. She obviously sent it the day we split up. I was heartbroken."

"I'm sure you were, sir. Perhaps we could have sight of the card if that's not too much to ask?" He agreed to drop it off at the police station.

On the way back to the flat, he stopped at the pub for a few drinks. He 'phoned some friends who were unaware of Tanya's death. Then, he called his mother back. It was a much more difficult call to make. She liked Tanya and had hoped they would settle down together and raise a family. "Hi Mum."

"Hello, darling. Happy Birthday. What are you doing to celebrate?"

"I have some news for you..."

"Not bad news I hope?"

"I'm afraid it is. Tanya is dead." There was a silence. "Dead? What do you mean dead? How did it happen?" He could hear that she was tearful. "She was murdered in the lab..." His mother struggled to find the words to reply.

"In the lab, murdered?" Dan could not continue the conversation, at least not at this point. He was too emotional. "Look, I can't tell you right now, it's too difficult..."

"I understand darling, but please call me in the next few days when you're up to it?"

Dan agreed he would call again, then he switched his 'phone off and proceeded to get drunk. Somehow, he found his way back to the flat and slept until the morning.

CHAPTER 6 – A SUDDEN PROMOTION

The following few days were a complete haze. His 'phone remained off. When he eventually turned it back on, he had several voicemail messages and many more texts. Most were from friends and his mother to see how he was bearing up. There was also a voicemail from Rupert and another from the Inspector, both asking him to call them.

Mentally, Dan was at an all-time low. He was struggling to come to terms with what he had done.

The thought of setting up the new lab with Rupert now seemed pure fantasy. His prime concern wasn't being caught, and incarcerated for her murder, but how he could live with himself knowing what he had done. Only a psychopath can kill without remorse, and Dan was no psychopath. At least, he hoped that was the case.

He noted that the inspector's request for him to call back had been left two days ago. That had to be his priority. Before calling, though, he toyed with the idea of coming clean, confessing what he had done in the hope that a manslaughter charge would be levied upon him rather than murder. But did it matter which he received? Whatever the justice system dispensed, it would be inadequate. It would not bring her back, nor would it unshackle him from the guilt he would carry to his grave. It was the thought of his mother and her reaction to discovering that he had murdered her that convinced him not to confess. He called the inspector.

"Good morning. Dan Thomas for Inspector Graham...yes, he asked me to call him." Dan was not in the least anxious, more resigned to his fate, whatever that may be.

"Dr. Thomas. Thanks for calling me back. I wondered if you could come to the station for another informal chat. One or two things have come up in our inquiry and I thought we could cover them off with you."

"Sure, what time would you like me to call in?"

"Would 2.00 pm be okay with you?"

"Yes, that's fine. I'll see you later." Dan accepted that he had to be their prime suspect. After all, he had been in a relationship with Tanya until a few days before the murder. It was inevitable that his fingerprints and his DNA would be found at the scene and the police would have questions.

Next, he called Rupert. Tanya's murder had been reported on all the national and local news channels, so it was highly likely that Rupert would know.

"Rupert. It's Dan."

"Dan. Where are you?"

"At home."

"I saw the news about Tanya. I'm really sorry...do you know what happened?"

"No. No idea." He decided short answers would avoid him saying too much.

"You must be beside yourself with grief. Fay and I are so sorry for your loss. If there is anything we can do?"

"Thanks...I thought you might like to know that I have all the data from the lab I need on an external hard drive." Rupert was shocked that he would be thinking about such matters.

"Dan, I don't think we should be talking about this right now..."

"No. I'm fine. It takes my mind off everything else..."

"No, what I mean is that I don't think after what's happened this is a runner anymore."

Dan was angry with Rupert's dismissal of the project and wanted to tell him so but thought better of it. "Can we at least meet to talk about it? Now Tanya has gone, I need something to work on, something to look forward to..."

"Look... I'm unlikely to change my mind, but of course I will meet with you to have a chat. Can you make it this evening at 8.00 pm?"

"Where?"

"Come to my home. You have my address."

No sooner had Dan put the 'phone down than he received a call from the HR department of the Pharma company he worked for

"Dr. Thomas?"

"Yes."

"It's Kate Hollins from the HR department. As you know the lab is currently closed but the police have agreed we can resume work in 7 days. With the sad death of Dr. Tanya Waters, we would like to discuss the possibility of you replacing her as lab manager if you are willing to be interviewed for the appointment?"

With Rupert likely to step back from financing the new lab project, it made sense for him to agree to an interview. "Yes, thank you."

"Could you come to the HR department tomorrow morning at 11.00 am?"

"Yes, that's fine. I'll see you there, Kate."

Dan felt his mood change. For the first time in days, his spirits were lifted, but he knew it would be a roller coaster ride. For the time being at least, he would try to maintain a positive frame of mind. He got ready and made his way to the police station for the meeting with DI Graham.

Upon arrival, he was shown into an interview room. It was clear from the start that the cordiality he had been shown in the previous discussions had now taken on a more formal tone.

"Dr. Thomas. Thanks for coming in. You'll remember my colleague, Detective Finch?"

"Yes." Dan sat opposite the two policemen. "We've called you in to ask a few more questions following the investigations we've been making. You are not under arrest, so you are at liberty to leave the meeting at any point if you choose to do so..."

"That sounds quite formal, inspector...should I be asking to have a lawyer here to represent me?"

"A lawyer? Why do you think you would need a lawyer?"

"I don't know, but it feels like you're treating me under suspicion?" The DI paused and looked at Dan. "It's just routine, sir. You'll understand I'm sure that those working with the deceased and indeed, someone who was in a relationship with Dr. Waters would be the priorities to dismiss first from our enquiries?"

Dan knew he had over-reacted and wanted to reign back his concern. "I'm sorry, inspector. I have been under a great deal of strain this past week and I'm feeling pretty miserable."

"Yes, I can understand it has been a shock for you, Dr. Thomas. Of course, if you do feel you need a lawyer present, it is your right to request one."

"No. No. Please go on. How can I help you?"

"You told us the last time we met that you had ended the relationship with Dr. Waters a day before she was found murdered in the lab. Is that true?"

"Actually inspector, that's not quite what happened. Tanya ended the relationship with me."
"And remind me why she did that?"

"It's complicated inspector. It's personal." The inspector probed further. "I know this must be difficult for you, but it would help us if you answered the question as fully as you could."

Dan thought for a moment.

"It's not uncommon for people to spend time together, and in our case, move in together only to discover that we weren't compatible. I mean, I really liked Tan and we were close, but we had different views and opinions about things..."

"What sort of differences?"

"Does it really matter, inspector? I'm sure if you're married you will know what I mean?" The inspector persisted.

"No. I would be interested to know what you mean?"

"Okay. I enjoyed going to parties and being with friends, but Tan preferred to stay at the flat. That caused a few disagreements."

"But she went with you to the parties you refer to, didn't she?"

"Well, yes. Only a few days before she was murdered, we were at a party and she wanted to leave almost the moment we had arrived...it wasn't her scene."

"What didn't she like about the parties you took her to?" Dan wondered why the inspector was so keen to persist with the questioning.

"I've just explained she wasn't a party animal...that's all!"

"Was it the drug taking, Dr. Thomas?" Dan was surprised by the question. "Drug taking?"

"Yes, I understand that one of the reasons she wanted to end the relationship with you was because of your addiction to drugs." Dan was even more surprised by the question because it sounded as though someone had informed the inspector of his substance abuse.

"Who have you been speaking to, inspector? It sounds as though someone has suggested I take drugs and I certainly don't."

"Is that so, sir? So, if I asked you to take a hair follicle test, you would agree?" Dan felt distinctly uncomfortable.

As a scientist, he knew that such a test would prove conclusively that he had recently taken drugs, and he also knew that if he offered himself up for a test, the inspector would be keen to see the results.

"Inspector, I am no hardened drug taker. Occasionally for recreational purposes perhaps, but what has that got to do with Tanya and her murder?"

"I am just looking for the truth, Dr. Thomas, and I think you will agree that you have been less than truthful about your drug taking?"

"But what does it have to do with Tanya's death, and as matter of interest, who told you I take drugs anyway?" The inspector ignored the question and continued.

"Did you ever threaten violence against Dr. Waters during your relationship with her?" Dan looked at the inspector in shock. "Violence? No. Who on earth told you that?"

"Let me ask the questions, sir, please. You just answer them."

"I'm sorry, inspector. I'm not prepared to continue with this line of questioning, the substance of which is totally fabricated..."

"So, let me understand, you no longer wish to continue with this discussion?"

"No, inspector. I wish to leave. If you have anything to link me to Tanya's murder, then I suggest you arrest me, and I will then ask for a lawyer to represent me." Dan was fuming.

"Okay, sir. You are free to go.

You aren't planning to leave the area any time soon, are you?"

"No. I'm not planning to go anywhere." And with that, Dan got up and was shown the exit.

As he left the building and reflected, he knew he had reacted badly to the questioning. He should have gone along with the inspector's line of enquiry. He also knew that it must have been Emily, the lab technician that Tanya moved in with, who had told the police about their relationship.

In Dan's own mind, he convinced himself he had not murdered Tanya, which would serve him well when defending himself during police questioning. Then again, he appeared to be their main suspect and were unlikely to discount him based on his most recent performance. He wondered how long it would be before he was arrested.

He returned to the flat via the pub, it was becoming more than an innocent habit. He was worried, and his feeling of positivity and 'lifted spirits' from first thing that morning had waned. Now, he needed to *lift a different type of spirit* to get back on track. What he really wanted was a line of coke, but he had none, and was not about to seek out a supply. Perhaps Rupert would oblige later when they met at his home?

After drinking quite heavily, he decided to sleep before readying himself for his encounter with Rupert. He set his alarm.

It was 7.15 pm when the alarm woke him. He was hung over. He drank some water and got ready to leave for Rupert's home.

Rupert lived in a smart, quite large semi-detached house in Chelsea. As Dan arrived, he could not help but be impressed. He would often daydream, looking online at properties he aspired to own one day in smart parts of London, and Rupert's house certainly met the criteria. He rang the doorbell. Rupert had a butler who answered the door. "Good evening, Dr. Thomas, Mr. Reece is expecting you. Please follow me to the drawing room."

The entrance hall was a hexagonal shape with a marble floor. Statues and artworks were strategically placed not too dissimilar from in Rupert's office. Dan was awestruck. "Hi Dan, come in, take a seat."

"Mr. Reece, may I get you and Dr. Thomas a drink?"

Rupert looked at Dan. Of course, he still had a hangover from the pub. "Orange juice for me, please."

"Thank you, Roger. An orange juice for Dan, and a gin and tonic for me."

"Yes, sir." Roger left the room.

"Dan. Again, Fay and I are both so sorry for your loss. It must have come as a great shock." Dan smiled weakly and the two spoke for a few minutes about Tanya and how much Rupert and Fay had warmed to her.

Dan acknowledged the sympathy but was keen to change the subject. "I have to say, Rupert, I'm impressed with your house."

"You like it?"

"Of course, and a butler?" Rupert enjoyed adulation.

"Roger has been with us for three years."

"Wow. That's the kind of lifestyle I aspire to!" Rupert was keen to dispense with Dan's compliments and get on with the reason he had agreed to meet.

"Dan, I can see you are motivated to succeed in life and that is to be applauded. I am sure that one day you will achieve your objectives, but to be frank, I haven't changed my mind." Just then, Roger returned.

"Your drinks, Mr. Reece. Is there anything else, sir?"
"No, that's fine, thanks." Roger left the room.

"Why have you changed your mind?"

"It's a combination of factors. First and foremost, what we agreed to do is illegal, and as you can see, I have no need to commit a crime to make money. I should have used better judgement when I agreed to work with you on the project. If I need another reason, and I don't think I do, Tanya's murder and all the publicity surrounding the lab where you work means it would be foolish to contemplate executing the plans we discussed under the circumstances. I'm really sorry, Dan, I know it's not what you want to hear."

What Dan said next would be crucial if he had any chance of persuading Rupert to change his mind.

"Look. I understand why you are thinking the way you are, but I can absolutely assure you, there is no more risk now than when we originally shook hands on the deal. In fact, the risks are even lower."

"Why so?"

"Two things. Firstly, Tan's death. Though I am still trying to come to terms with what has happened, one thing that is certain is that it makes it harder for the lab to make any meaningful progress on the vaccine project. The second point is that I have a meeting with my employer's HR department in the morning to discuss my taking over Tanya's job as Lab Manager, which would give me total control over lab protocols. I can ensure we work on stuff that will be meaningless; that way, we have more time and more flexibility to ensure that when we get our lab up and running, we'll have even less competition."

Rupert listened to him intently, then replied, "But Dan, even if you do get the job, you haven't addressed my first concern. What you want to do is illegal." Dan didn't wait for Rupert to finish his sentence.

"I understand your concerns, but I now have in my possession all we need to make this happen. It wouldn't be the first time that intellectual rights in the scientific community have been breached. It happens all the time. Please, Rupert.

I know I can make this happen, and the fears you have will evaporate. Can I spend the next few minutes explaining the progress I have made so far?"

Reluctantly, Rupert agreed, and Dan spent twenty minutes presenting his case for investment in the new lab. It was a well-polished and detailed presentation and Rupert was impressed. Despite his overtures about the illegality of Dan's project, he had always enjoyed a challenge, including the drama of winning and executing deals. It wouldn't be the first time he had got involved in something *shady,* either. "I'm truly, impressed, Dan. You have certainly done your homework.

If one of my colleagues in my team presented me with such a slick presentation, I would have no hesitation in backing the project. However, I am still concerned about the risks, and as I said, I don't need to take risks to make money. I'm comfortable enough. That said, I would be prepared to re-think my decision..."

Dan couldn't wait to hear the terms on which Rupert would commit. He had won him over! Nevertheless, Rupert took his time. He got up and slowly paced the room as he spoke.

"We agreed a 60:40 split in my favor for my initial seed investment. If I agree to continue, it has to be on a 70:30 basis to compensate me for what I believe to be the added risks." Dan wasted no time in responding. He had persuaded Rupert to change his mind. The revised terms seemed to matter far less to him now; at least he had a deal. "You have a deal. That's fine by me." They shook hands.

"Okay Dan. Look. Go back and work for your employer for the next 4-6 months and keep in touch. When you believe the time is right, let me know and we'll put the wheels in motion."

Dan smiled and got up, leaving his orange juice undrunk. Now he was ready to celebrate his latest achievement. He returned to his local pub for a nightcap and went to bed. The following morning, he attended the meeting with Kate Hollins in the HR department. They were joined by the head of vaccine development for the company. The interview went well, and Dan was offered the manager's role. With it would come complete day-to-day control of the lab staff and their activities.

As he left the building, he knew he had a week before the team would return to work and he thought about Emily, Tanya's flat mate, and the stories he believed she had told the police. He wondered how he could make life difficult for her and possibly even finding a way of sacking her. She would be the last person to congratulate him on his new appointment.

The police had released Tanya's body to the family for the funeral and Dan was invited to attend. Tanya's parents liked Dan and wanted him there along with her other friends and colleagues from the lab. The funeral was scheduled on the Friday before the lab re-opened.

As was often the case, it was a wet and overcast day, a suitably austere day for a funeral.

Over a hundred people attended the church service and even more attended the crematorium. Dan felt huge remorse on the day for what he had done but he was happy to accept the condolences he received from the people who believed that he and Tanya had been in a relationship up to her murder. Few knew they had split up.

He was treated like a member of the immediate family as they nursed their grief. It was only Emily, Tanya's flat mate, who made no effort to speak to him. He was acutely aware that she had deliberately distanced herself. He caught sight of her looking at him, shaking her head as though she knew he was her killer.

Mentally, the solemnity of the funeral affected Dan. He left the crematorium alone and did what he always did under pressure: he went to the pub and got drunk.

The weekend was spent nursing another hangover. Monday morning arrived and he set off for the lab to assume his new role as *Manager.*

He brought the team together and thanked them for their attendance at the funeral, keeping an eye on Emily all the while. She remained unmoved by what he said and avoided all eye contact. He spoke about his plans for the months ahead and flagged up a change in direction for lab work, assigning new tasks roles and responsibilities.

It became quickly clear that he had under-estimated the team's awareness of how close they were to making a breakthrough on the vaccine formula. His attempt to steer them away from what they were currently working on attracted a lengthy interrogation of his assumptions, which he found difficult to defend.

He was sufficiently assertive to get his way, though, and despite clear reservations, they had no option but to agree to his new strategy. Of course, it was a strategy that he also knew would fail. He asked to meet with everyone individually after the *team meeting.* He was especially keen to spend time with Emily, knowing she would dread the encounter.

"So, Emily. Thanks again for attending Tanya's funeral."

"Why wouldn't I attend? She was a good friend, as you know."

"Let me get straight to the point. I was questioned by the police yesterday and it seems you have been giving them your opinion on my relationship with Tanya. Is that true?" "They questioned me, yes. So what?"

"What did you say to them?"

"Well, judging by your question, you know exactly what I said."

"That I was violent toward her, I bullied her, and I'm addicted to drugs?"

"Those weren't my words, Dan, but you know Tanya was unhappy in the relationship and concerned about your drug taking."

"Well, for the record, I am not addicted to drugs and I would prefer it if you kept your views and opinions about me to yourself in the future."

"Is there anything else, Dan?"

"Yes, there is...the experiments you've been working on... I am disappointed with the lack of detail in your reporting. I think your findings lack rigor and as a result, your conclusions are misguided. I will be looking more closely at your work in the future."

Emily knew her work was of an acceptable standard. More than that, it was excellent. Dan's comments indicated to her that he wanted rid of her, and her employment file would reflect the comments he had made, no matter how fictitious.

She also knew it was pointless raising the issue with his boss at this stage. After all, he had just been appointed and anything she said would be seen as reactionary against the improvements he wanted to instigate to improve the lab's performance. She would bide her time.

CHAPTER 7 – THE PAINTING

Just over a week later, Dan received a letter from a solicitor acting on behalf of Professor Tim Gerald, one of his university lecturers with whom he had got on especially well. He was a bachelor, partially disabled, and often suffered from depression. On numerous occasions, Dan had spent time with him, and he had been grateful for the company. They remained in touch. Dan was saddened to read that he had passed away and surprised to discover that he had been named in the will and invited to attend its reading.

Unbeknown to Dan, Tim was a wealthy man, having inherited a family fortune years earlier.

Despite his wealth, he had chosen to live life frugally, there was no evidence to show that he had ever invested his fortune or spent large sums of money on indulgences. It transpired that all his wealth sat in one solitary current account.

Without a family of his own, he had bequeathed most of his estate to the university to build a new library. He had also left generous bursaries for a sizeable number of students. Dan had been left £25,000, Tim's antique gold fountain pen, his personal collection of science books and journals, and a framed picture that Dan had admired on one occasion when he had visited him at his apartment.

Accumulations of dust and pipe smoke over the years had dulled the subject – *the image of a young woman looking into the distance*. A haunting image, perhaps depicting someone who had suffered the loss of a loved one? The irony was not lost on Dan.

Due to its poor condition, the image lacked definition and the effervescence of color had faded, something a good clean might fix. As far as Dan could detect the picture was not attributed to a particular artist.

The first thing he did as he arrived back at the flat was to put the picture on the wall. With £25,000 soon to be transferred to his account, he felt suddenly liberated.

Over the next couple of weeks, he settled into his new job. He was keen to work closely with the team, primarily because he wanted to ensure they adhered to his new strategy of experiments distracting them from discovering the vaccine formula.

He had to hold his nerve despite the team arguing that he was drawing the wrong conclusions from their experiments. The roles and responsibilities of his new job gave Dan the power he needed. He believed putting pressure on people and bullying them was a part of a manager's job. Of course, the reverse was true. Dan alienated several members of his team very quickly, including Emily, who asked for a team meeting to clear the air.

It was obvious they had meticulously planned what they wanted to say to him across a range of subjects. Emily was charged with leading the assault. At first, she reiterated what most of them had said after Tanya's death, that they *were sorry for his loss and hoped he would be able to cope without her.* Of course, the inference was that his recent irrational decision making might be down to grief rather than incompetence, although it still left the possibility of incompetence as a firm possibility. The truth was, neither were true. Emily's attempt to send Dan a subtle message was not lost on him. She loathed him and had never offered him her personal condolences because she knew he had bullied Tanya, he was a drug taker, and he could conceivably be her murderer. As she spoke, Dan looked at her with distain.

Drug taking within the scientific community was thought to be rare, but Dan was no ordinary scientist. He was brilliant without trying, but he was conflicted by his drug addiction, his ego, and his aspirations for the kind of wealth and lifestyle that Rupert enjoyed. His work in the lab, whilst paying a reasonably good salary, was far short of his expectations even in his new role.

Emily relished the prospect of delivering the team's concerns and gave a confident and polished performance, outlining the areas of unease they had about his strategy. Dan listened attentively, taking the opportunity to look at each member of the team for their reactions as she spoke. None of them wanted to catch his eye, preferring instead to concentrate on what Emily was saying.

Everything she said, every argument she put forward, every challenge she made was right, and Dan knew it. He knew he was taking them on a merry-go-round because it was his precise plan. His arrogance had led him to underestimate their capacity to know that they were close to discovering the vaccine formula.

Throughout Emily's speech, Dan chose not to interrupt. He would wait until she had concluded. He had various options open to him. He could agree with everything she said, which would make him look foolish and incapable of undertaking the manager's job. He could wholeheartedly disagree with her, painstakingly going through her points and justifying why she was wrong, but even he would have difficulty arguing cogently against the truth. He could agree with some of her assertions, but challenge others, but what would that achieve? Or he could resist commenting at that time on the basis that he would need time to review Emily's presentation before responding. He chose the latter.

The meeting concluded.

Dan knew he couldn't get away with fobbing them off for long. It wasn't as though they were clutching at straws with their critique; they knew precisely what he knew, they were close to discovering the formula. The more he thought about Emily, the more he despised her. She was a thorn in his side. Without her, the team may not have moved against him. They were all aware of the facts, but it had taken someone like Emily to be the shop steward, the mouthpiece, pushing and shoving for what she wanted.

Dan decided to take the next day off, so he 'phoned in sick. After breakfast, he glanced at the picture on the wall that Tim had left him. The frame was 20cm square – it was the frame that had first drawn his attention when he saw it in Tim's flat.

Dan knew little about art. He had no idea whether it was a print, a copy, or an original but he believed the subject matter was late 19thcentury.

He removed the picture from the wall and placed it on the sofa. The frame certainly looked original. He looked closer at the painting lying beneath decades of dusk and nicotine. He went to the kitchen and fetched a tea-towel and washing up liquid and attempted to clean a corner of the painting. As he gently rubbed the canvass removing the dirt, a faint name appeared: *Paul Gauguin,* a name of course he was familiar with.

As he looked more closely, he convinced himself it was more likely a print of the original work, at best a good copy. He Googled 'Gauguin works of art' but saw nothing that resembled the picture he was looking at.

He had a friend, Timothy, who worked as a restorer at Sotheby's in London, so he decided to take a photo of the portrait on his mobile 'phone. He made sure it clearly showed the signature and emailed it to him seeking confirmation in his own mind that the work had no value. Within the hour, Timothy responded. *Hi Dan. Thanks for photo. Unable to determine anything without seeing it. If you plan to be near our Mayfair auction room, drop in for a coffee and bring the picture with you I'll take a closer look. Cheers, Tim.*

It had been some time since the two of them had seen each other, so Dan immediately called him back and arranged to meet at the auction rooms that same afternoon.

Dan arrived early and sat in a waiting room clutching a plastic supermarket bag containing the picture. He browsed through recent sale catalogues when Tim arrived and took him upstairs to his office for a coffee. They chatted idly for a couple of minutes before Tim took a cursory look at the picture. His instinct was that the picture was indeed an oil painting and not a print. He suggested asking his colleague, Dr. Peter Braithwaite to confirm his opinion. Dr. Braithwaite was a world-renowned 19th century art expert who rarely appraised pictures at the drop of a hat, but as Dan was a friend of Tim's, he agreed to look at the picture.

Dan was chuffed but expected a swift prognosis that the picture was worthless.

Peter examined the frame closely, then turned to the painting itself.

Using a magnifier, he spent many minutes silently looking at the signature. Then, he turned his attention to the brushwork before shuffling off with the picture into another room. Dan and Timothy looked at each other. "Dan, I think you may have something of interest. The fact that Peter is consulting a colleague suggests to me that the painting could well be an original, although the provenance may be difficult to link to Paul Gauguin himself. There were many copies of his works at the time." Dan was excited but before he could say anything, Dr. Braithwaite returned.

"May I call you Dan?"

"Of course."

"Dan, I can confirm that this is an original 19th century artwork and may well be attributed to Paul Gauguin. However, to prove or disprove its provenance, we would need more time. Can you leave the painting with us?" Dan agreed and was given a receipt for the artwork. They would be in touch.

CHAPTER 8 - CHANGES

He returned to the flat excited. It was early Friday evening and he had arranged to attend a friend's housewarming party in Southwark, South London. His hosts were Max and Tulip Steele. Max and Dan had been at boarding school together and had stayed in touch. Max was an investment banker and Tulip a psychologist. They were a successful, well-healed couple and another example of a lifestyle that Dan aspired to.

Dan and Max were the same age, had similar views on most subjects, and always enjoyed each other's company on the occasions they got together. Dan had had a growing feeling of envy, though, as Max had seemingly done more with his life than he had. More importantly, he had made a substantial amount of money in his chosen career.

When Dan arrived at the party, Max showed him around their new home, Dan was silently envious. As the evening wore on, the house became quite crowded. Dan knew several people and mingled quite happily. He was desperate for a line of coke. As he headed for the kitchen to refill his champagne glass, he bumped into Rupert and Fay, and was surprised to discover that they knew Max. "Rupert! Didn't expect to see you here...small world."

"Oh, hi Dan. So, you know Max and Tulip?"

Max and I were at boarding school together..."

"Right..."

"And you. What's your connection?"

"Max joined my firm a few months ago." Dan was surprised. "Oh, really? Wow! It *is* a small world."

Fortunately for Dan, Rupert offered him a line of coke which they consumed in the bathroom before rejoining the party. He was keen not to take up too much of Rupert's time and mingled some more. A while later, he got chatting to Max and discovered more about his move to Rupert's firm.

Rupert was paying Max a flat £400k a year plus anticipated bonuses worth another half million pounds. These were eye-watering sums of money and Dan was even more envious.

He had drunk far too much champagne and, mixed with the drugs had become noisy and over-confident, which was not lost on Rupert.

Dan approached Rupert and insisted they talk about the lab project. This was the last thing Rupert wanted to do and especially at a party. "Dan, I think you've had too much to drink. We can talk about this another time. May I suggest I get you a taxi?"

Ordinarily, when anyone suggested Dan left a party because he was drunk or high, it would result in a scene. He would often become aggressive and argumentative, but on this occasion, he kept his wits about him and knew it was time for him to leave before he wrecked his relationship with Rupert and Max. "Sure, that's fine. As you said, we can talk about this another time." Rupert arranged for a taxi and Dan said his embarrassed goodbyes before returning to the flat.

As the alcohol and drugs wore off, he felt angry with himself. He knew it had been a mistake to try and talk to Rupert about the lab and wondered what people had said about him after he left.

He also knew this experience had to serve as a wake-up call. He had to change his ways.

He could no longer indulge in excessive drinking and drug taking if he expected to be taken seriously. Relying on his intellect, charm, and oratory skills to get by was no longer enough. He saw his friends settling down into long-term relationships and building careers and, in the case of Max and Rupert, earning a substantial living. He was being left behind.

He desperately wanted what they had.

Up until Max's party and the encounter with Rupert, he had had a positive self-image, at least most of the time. He was someone that people wanted to be associated with. He was good at commanding people's attention and they listened to him, but the people he impressed were mainly his friends and those of his own generation. In a wider social and business context, he was a novice and had a great deal to learn.

It was late. He went to bed but slept badly. He kept replaying in his mind the encounter with Rupert and being *sent home* in a taxi. He would 'phone him later in the morning to offer an apology. He got up late in a reflective mood. He had kept turning over in his mind everything that was wrong with him and his life. Dominant in his thoughts the fact that he was a murderer, and there was still the very real possibility that he would be arrested. For the rest of the day, he suffered feelings of anxiety and depression he had never experienced before.

In the early afternoon, his 'phone rang. It was Rupert.

"How are you feeling today?" He seemed genuinely concerned.

"If you want the truth, I'm feeling terrible. I was going to call you to say sorry for my behavior at the party."

"It's not necessary, Dan. I know you've been through a lot, especially with Tanya's death."

Dan admitted he had recently been drinking and taking drugs to excess but had decided to stop doing both and focus his attention on their project.

He hoped his confession would win Rupert over, but the reverse was the case. "Look, Dan. What are you doing later this afternoon? Can we meet and talk? My home at 5.00 pm?" Dan agreed. He was pleased he would have the opportunity to clear the air and would attempt to persuade Rupert that it made sense to press on with the project now, rather than wait several months. After all, what was there to be gained by waiting?

When he arrived at Rupert's home, he felt more positive in himself, having had the chance to think through his strategy. Rupert's butler greeted him and took him into the drawing room, where he offered him a drink. He settled for an orange juice as he had done before. Rupert would join him shortly.

Looking around the beautifully furnished room with its fine artworks and sculptures was confirmation that this was the lifestyle he aspired to. His commitment to stop drinking and taking drugs was the starting point. He felt like a reformed character and could not wait to start his new journey towards power and riches.

Rupert entered the room and greeted Dan. "How are you feeling, Dan?"

"Great. Really good...I've done a lot of soul searching today, and I know I need to change my ways... I'm not planning to drink or take drugs again..."

Rupert sensed that he was in a fragile and vulnerable state and wanted to let him down gently without causing a scene. "...You don't have to promise anything to me, Dan."

"No. I understand. But my performance at the party and our chat this morning was a wake-up call. I now have a clear understanding of what I need to do about our project and believe..." But before he had a chance to explain what he had in mind Rupert intervened.

"Okay, I understand how you feel, Dan. You are under a lot of strain right now, and I'm not judging you - really, I'm not - but I have to tell you that despite my reassurance the last time we met that I was committed to the project, I have decided to withdraw. I'm sorry but I know it would be the wrong thing to do."

Dan was stunned. It was not what he was expecting. He looked at Rupert in dismay. "But I thought we agreed...?"

"I'm sorry Dan. It's my fault for agreeing in the first place and indeed for changing my mind on two occasions."

The conversation continued for almost an hour. During that time, Dan tried his hardest to persuade Rupert to change his mind, but he remained steadfast. He tried to reassure Dan that his conduct at the party had nothing to do with his decision.

In fact, he said if Dan ever had any other *legitimate* projects that needed funding, he would consider them without hesitation. Nevertheless, it was far from the result Dan wanted to hear. Still, he had no option but to accept Rupert's decision. They agreed to stay in touch, and he returned to the flat.

Oddly, he did not feel in any way angry with the outcome of the meeting with Rupert. He had done his best to convince him to change his mind but deep down, he knew his plan was flawed in so many ways. He had convinced himself over time it would work, but the reality was that almost everything was against him, not least of all the legality of what he intended. Of course, Tanya's murder was a consequence of his actions, and her death would never be a price worth paying for a plan that was destined to fail. He knew it was unlikely he would ever come to terms with murdering her. How could anyone be accepting of ending another person's life? It would haunt him for as long as he lived.

Dan's next shift at the lab started at 11.00 am the following morning and he would have to respond to the points Emily raised in the team meeting. As Rupert was no longer backing his project it made sense to abandon any idea of setting up his own facility and get the lab back on track. He decided he would tell Emily and the team that his assumptions had been wrong, and they should go back to what they had previously been working on with immediate effect.

He hoped they would accept his aberration was down to the stress of losing Tanya. He knew it would sound implausible to Emily, but he was unconcerned about her views and opinions.

He arrived at the lab early and called a meeting. The team displayed a degree of apprehension as he started to talk...He had spent time reviewing all the data and concluded that he had been wrong in his assumptions. He thanked them for their diligence and hard work. He especially thanked Emily for her eloquent presentation at their last meeting and asked to speak to her privately. Everyone was relieved and returned to work. It was obvious Emily had been taken by surprise and wanted to hear what he had to say to her in private. "I've treated you badly, and I'm sorry Emily. You were right in all you said at the last meeting, hence my announcement to the team today. I hope we can move on in a positive way from here."

Emily was not about to forgive him or backtrack on her assertions about his relationship with Tanya, but she at least offered him a smile.

"Now I have been appointed lab manager, I wondered if you would consider taking on my previous job as supervisor?" She was even more surprised by this suggestion, considering their history. She immediately wondered if he had a hidden agenda.

"I must admit I'm surprised by your offer," she responded, "but I'm afraid not. I've found another job and was about to hand in my notice."

Her announcement came as a shock to him. It was clear they didn't get on and his appointment as lab manager had been the last straw. She couldn't work in an environment where she loathed her boss, a man she suspected had something to do with her friend's murder. "Oh...right...so when are you planning to leave?"

"It's in a letter of resignation I have for the HR department. I'll hand it in later this morning."
"So, you're not going to tell me?"

"It's in my letter, Dan. I'm sure HR will inform you." With that she returned to her workstation.

As Dan returned to his office, he was seething. Of course, he had a motive for offering her the supervisor's role - *keep your friends close and your enemies closer* - but he was incensed she had got the better of him. He had not anticipated she would resign, but the fact she had meant she would no longer be there to undermine him. The company's policy, because of the secrecy of the work they undertook in the lab, was to pay people for their notice period but to ask them to leave with immediate effect.

Emily would be gone by the end of her shift.

The following morning Dan met up with his boss, the lab director, whose role was to persuade the board to invest in what he considered worthy and profitable research projects, taking responsibility for their set up and operational performance.

Dr. Phil Cameron was one of the company's most successful scientists. He had been with the company for almost 30 years, working his way up from a lab assistant.

Over that time, he been responsible for the successful development of several vaccines and cancer drugs that had generated global sales worth tens of millions in revenue. He was in his mid-fifties and had devoted his life to his career. He liked Dan, but he was disappointed with what Emily had said about him in her resignation letter and was eager to hear his side of the story.

"Morning Dan. How have things been going since you took on the manager's role?"

Dan smiled. "Good. Yes, good, I think we're settling into..." Phil interrupted him straight away. "...I was disappointed to hear that Emily resigned."

"Yes, a shame. I spoke to her about the supervisor's role before she told me she was leaving."
"Do you know why she chose to leave?"

"To be honest, Phil, we didn't get on. I'm sure you're aware I was dating Tanya before..."

"Yes, I was aware. Her murder on our premises has been a huge shock for everyone. In all the years I have worked in pharma companies, I have never come across such an incident. I just hope the police find the culprit, and soon, for everyone's sake."

Dan lowered his head and paused for a moment. "It's been tough..."

"I can imagine.

So, you and Emily didn't get on...why?"

"I'd rather not go into too much detail. I'm still...feeling a bit low about it all. But Emily was a friend of Tanya's and to be honest, I think she was jealous of the relationship."

"And what about drug taking, Dan?" Dan was taken aback. He could not believe that Emily would mention his drug taking in her resignation letter.

"Drug taking? Is that what she alleged?"

"What you do in your private life is none of my business, Dan. If you're denying Emily's allegation, we will leave it there.

However, I do need to remind you that anyone found taking recreational drugs or are under the influence of alcohol on company premises is liable for immediate dismissal." Dan was irritated that he was being given a lecture.

"Phil, with respect, you really don't need to read me company policy. I emphatically deny taking drugs, either on or off the premises."

This was not the kind of conversation he had wanted to have with his boss, and it tainted the rest of the discussion. That said, he gave a compelling presentation, outlining his plans for revamping the lab and upgrading work practices, as well as setting out his ideas for integrating the new team as they joined the facility. Phil approved Dan's proposals, shook his hand, and left.

CHAPTER 9 – THE HOLIDAY

Having arrived back at the flat after his shift, he picked up the mail. One letter was addressed to Tanya and was from a travel company. He opened the envelope.

It was a reminder that the final installment for a two-week safari holiday they had booked at the Queen Elizabeth National Park in Uganda was now due. They were scheduled to leave in a fortnight. With recent events, he had completely forgotten about the booking. At first, he thought of cancelling the holiday until he saw that Tanya had paid a non-refundable deposit of £3000. The balance was an equivalent sum.

Rather than go alone, he toyed with the idea of finding a replacement for her. It was short notice, but he was confident he could do it. He made a few 'phone calls and sure enough, Susannah, a friend, was delighted to accept.

They had dated in the past, but she had been unwilling to enter a serious relationship with him, knowing he had been unfaithful with one of her close friends. They agreed to meet the following evening to discuss their plans.

Susannah had read about Tanya's murder, and had seen TV reports, but had no idea she was Dan's girlfriend until he told her. She was different from Tanya in so many ways. Tanya was academic, logical, and rational, whereas she was wired for fun and excitement and relished challenges out of the ordinary. She worked for a marketing agency managing cosmetic brands and, like Dan, she loved partying. She was an attractive woman who lived life to the full and had a wide circle of friends.

She was attracted to Dan and was prepared to give him a second chance if the holiday brought them closer together.

Dan was attracted to her too, physically at least, and enjoyed her fun-loving attitude to life but had never seen himself with her long term.

They met again over the next two weeks before the start of the holiday. After working long hours in the lab in preparation for the trip, Dan was ready for a break and thought he could put on hold memories of the past couple of months and enjoy himself. Little did he know what awaited him.

They would fly from London Heathrow to Kampala, a nine-hour flight, then an onward bus ride to Kasese that would take another five hours with a short hop by jeep to their camp. On arrival at Heathrow, they discovered their flight was running four hours late. Eventually, they boarded the plane and had an uneventful journey. When they got to Kampala, they were tired. They collected their luggage and a half hour later, in sweltering heat and humidity, they transferred to a rickety old bus that had seen better days. There was no air conditioning, and the journey took almost six hours to complete. The bus was full, mainly tourists and locals heading for work in the safari villages in the national park. It was a rough ride, and they were desperate for a rest. Dan and Susannah were shown to an open top Land Rover that took them to their final stop - The Darafiki Camp Lodge.

The camp comprised 14 individually thatched clay lodges that were superbly appointed in a style that appealed to well-healed westerners. Internally, each property comprised two sumptuous bedrooms, a sitting room, a bathroom, and a small utility room.

The outside housed a private plunge pool with decking for a BBQ. The camp blended in perfectly with the surrounding bush.

Every evening, after a long day on safari, guests would meet to share a meal prepared by local chefs and enjoy being entertained by local musicians. Dan and Susannah settled into their lodge at 5.00 pm local time and immediately fell into a deep sleep.

They woke suddenly to the sound of a ringing bell, a call to join fellow guests for supper. Wearily, they dressed and joined the other guests around the campfire. Most of the other guests were from the USA, UK, and Germany.

Dan and Susannah soon made friends with an American married couple of a similar age – Chuck and Ashley - who had arrived before them. They had supper and enjoyed a few hours together before returning to bed. Everyone had been given their itinerary and instructed to meet at 6.30 am sharp the following morning for their first day's safari.

Neither of them slept well. The sound of wild animals at night in the bush took time to adjust to. It had also been a long and arduous journey.

After breakfast, the guests were split into groups of six who would travel together for the duration of the holiday in canvass topped jeeps. Each group would go in different directions each day within the national park.

They were briefed on what they could expect to see on their excursions, together with a list of safety instructions. They were also warned that jeep travel could be uncomfortable and were encouraged to hire cushions – an idea all the camps used to generate much-needed additional revenue. Dan and Susannah declined the offer, only to regret their decision almost immediately.

Chuck and Ashley were keen to accompany them, so they climbed aboard behind them. The jeeps each had a driver and an experienced tour guide who knew where animals were more likely to be seen. They headed off straight away, the early morning mist still covering the plain around them. There was a chill in the air. Visibility was limited at first but as the sun gained strength, the mist disappeared, and the temperature soared. The driver stopped after the first hour to remove the canvas top.

They were under strict instructions not to leave the jeep unless they were told to do so. There had been incidents in the past when animals had got close to vehicles and people had panicked. Instead of remaining perfectly still, they had got out of the jeep and ran into the bush. On rare occasions, this had resulted in dire consequences.

It was their first day, and they were suffering from heat exposure and the inevitable soreness of travelling on rock hard mud tracks in a vehicle that appeared to have no suspension. They wished again that they had hired the cushions. As they got deeper into the bush, though, animal sightings became commonplace, and discomfort turned to excitement.

They stopped for a sandwich lunch in a designated safe zone, where they were able to stretch their legs and recuperate before returning to camp. They got back just after 4.00 pm, giving them time to shower, change their dusty clothing, and relax before supper. The following morning, they would head in a different direction. They went to bed early knowing they would leave at 6.30 am. This time, their destination was Lake Edward, which ran adjacent to the Democratic Republic of Congo. It was hot first thing. The driver removed the canvas top and they headed out. It would take them four hours to arrive, with occasional stops. The dirt tracks they followed were rock hard and everyone was suffering despite the use of cushions. After several complaints, the driver slowed down and detoured from the main route onto softer ground.

They were three hours into the journey when they stopped in a quiet area the tour guide thought safe, enabling them to stretch their legs once more. Soon after getting out of the jeep, they heard rounds of gunfire in the near distance. The guide reassured them it was park wardens sending out warning shots to poachers, but he was wrong.

From nowhere, six men in combat clothing carrying semi-automatic rifles appeared in front of them, forcing them to the ground. The driver and the tour guide were beaten with canes in front of the tourists before being marched into the bush. The group were terrified.

Moments later, several shots were fired. The assailants returned their clothing spattered with blood. They had killed them in cold blood.

They all remained perfectly still and said nothing. As they were taunted and provoked by the gang, several women, including Susannah and Ashley, screamed in fear. One of the assailants struck an elderly woman several times and she fell to the ground.

There had been incidents of kidnapping and loss of life in the region in the past at the hands of the ADF – a rebel group from Uganda who were based across the border in Congo. The ADF had begun life as a force attempting to overthrow Uganda's President Yoweri Museveni but had morphed into a criminal group who focused on looting and killing people at random. They saw the value, when they could, of taking Western hostages for ransom.

They had also been accused of attacks on the Ebola treatment centres that were trying to suppress an outbreak in Congo. Worryingly, they had also been linked to ISIS and al-Shabaab.

Dan and the others had their hands tied behind their backs and were told to stay silent before being marched into the bush. The kidnappers took everyone's possessions from the jeep, then two men drove it away. The temperature had soared to 30c and everyone was suffering and desperate for water.

Dan, Susannah, Chuck, and Ashley were marched one behind the other. They were followed by an elderly American woman who was panic-stricken and finding the pace and the heat too much for her. She pleaded with one of the men to release her.

He struck her several times with his cane and she fell to the ground, where she was unable to get up. By now, Dan and the others had stopped walking and turned to witness her captor untie her hands. She slowly got to her feet crying uncontrollably. Again, she pleaded with the man to free her. He waved his rifle, giving her permission to run into the bush. She looked at the man with fear etched on her face and started to run, screaming as she went. The men laughed as they watched her, allowing her to get about sixty feet away from them before shooting her in the back and leaving her for dead. Dan had seen enough, and in a moment of madness, he ran toward the woman as the gang fired shots over his head. He stopped dead in his tracks and turned to face the group. A gang member ran toward him as Suzannah screamed out, begging them not to kill him. One of the men hit him with his rifle butt and he fell to the ground.

Several minutes later, he was forced to get up and join the group, blood running down his cheeks from a head wound. They were ordered to continue walking. After an hour in the blazing sun, they stopped and were told to get down on their knees and face their captors.

With terror in their eyes, they turned briefly to each other expecting to be shot, but of course they were assets too valuable to be disposed of, at least not yet. The men laughed seeing the fear etched into their faces. They were untied and given water, then positioned under a tree where they were shaded from the burning sun.

Their kidnappers smoked as they chatted and laughed together, clearly in the mood to celebrate.

They had five wealthy westerners as captives, which could potentially amount to a considerable ransom.

After fifteen minutes, the hostages were tied up again and forced back into direct sunlight and the blazing heat. They walked for another hour as the blood-red sun started to disappear on the horizon. It would soon be dark. As they came into a clearing, an old army truck awaited them, likely stolen during a recent conflict. Exhausted, and badly sunburnt, they were bundled into the back of the truck and driven off. Two men and a driver were in the front of the vehicle engaged in a heated argument. The group now comprised five – Dan, Susannah, Chuck, Ashley, and Stefan, a German who spoke perfect English. Quietly, Dan took the opportunity to discuss their predicament. It was agreed it was pointless jumping off the back of the truck with their hands tied. Even if they were successful in escaping, what were their chances of finding refuge? They knew by now they had been kidnapped for ransom and were likely being taken to a hiding place. They were valuable assets and hopefully, for this reason alone they would be kept alive.

The truck suddenly pulled up. It was an uncomfortable journey that had taken twenty minutes. By now it was dark. They were dragged from the back of the vehicle and lined up before being taken into a shack. Dan took the opportunity to glance around the site. The area was lit up, revealing several relatively small buildings in the encampment with a sizeable number of rebels milling around in combat jackets.

It had been a grueling day in the bush, where they had witnessed the shooting of the American woman, their tour guide, and the driver. They were exhausted, stressed, and fearful of what may happen next. One of the guards came in and to their surprise, he spoke a little English. He turned on the light and untied them. The room was about 30 feet square. He read a list of instructions and told them there was a toilet at the back of the room. They could move freely around the shack, but he warned them not to try and escape. First thing in the morning, they would be interviewed.

Their abduction was probably one of many. Escaping seemed impossible as there were no windows and they had been told the only door would be locked. It was hot and the room was airless. An overbearing smell lingered. Of course, there was no air conditioning. It would be a long, hot night attempting to sleep on soiled mattresses that had been left on the floor. As the man left, another arrived with food and much needed water. Then, he left and locked the door. Throughout the night it was possible to hear the rebels talking in the distance. Trucks came and went.

At 6.00 am, the door was unlocked, and their breakfast arrived, comprising a jug of water, an assortment of cooked yams, beans, ground nuts, cabbage, and papaya. There was just about enough for them all. At 7.00 am, the interviews would get underway with *Boss Man,* as he was referred to. The stress and exhaustion of the previous day was imprinted into their faces, but they had recovered sufficiently to discuss how they would get through their ordeal.

They speculated about the interviews and felt sure the key objective was for the rebels to work out how valuable a ransom they could demand for their release.

7.00 am came and went. They were on edge. Eventually, the door was unlocked. Nearest to the door was Ashley, who was told to follow the guard. She was overwhelmed with fear and wanted to scream but thought the better of it. Chuck helped her up and held her tightly before letting her go. She walked to the door before turning and attempting a smile for her fellow captives. The door was locked behind her.

Chuck was emotional, wondering if he would ever see her again. Susannah and Dan comforted him. Stefan, who was next in line, sat quietly, pondering his fate.

Ashley was escorted to a building approximately 30 yards away. As she passed other huts, she heard American voices and assumed other hostages were being held. Her guard prodded her in the back with his cane as an indication to gain pace.

She entered the building and a man in a heavily braided uniform and beret was sitting behind an oblong table. She believed he was 'Boss Man' – he was in his early fifties.

He had a weathered look about him, thick set with deep scars on his left cheek and a loud deep voice. "Get your belongings." He pointed to the table where all the possessions that were taken from the Jeep the previous day were spread out.

Instinctively, she went to pick up Chuck's rucksack. They were a married couple, and she would naturally pick up his items too, but she quickly put it down again, knowing he would be going through the same process in due course.

She collected up her hat, her rucksack, and a lightweight jacket, then took them across to him. He told her to empty the contents of the rucksack onto the table. She obliged. He reached over for her passport, mobile 'phone, and purse containing cash, traveler cheques, and credit cards. He took the cash from her purse and put it in his pocket together with the credit cards and cheques. Then, he opened her passport. "You're American...Ashley Craig...yes?" She nodded.

"On your own...?"

"No. I'm with my husband, Chuck."

"Do you know why you are here?" She paused before answering, wanting to avoid saying anything provocative that she might regret.

"I think you have taken us hostage and want a ransom."

He smiled. "You are right, Mrs. Ashley Craig. How much do you think you are worth to us?" He smiled again, then yelled at the guard standing at the back of the room to get her a chair. He did as he was told.

"Sit, please sit." She sat opposite him and waited a while before answering his question.

"I don't know. We aren't rich people..." He laughed, then shouted at her. "

How much?" She was shocked by his change of mood.

"Ten thousand dollars?" He laughed again.

"We ask $500,000 dollars for you. You get the money, or we kill you!" She was stunned. He continued to laugh.

"But how can I get the money...?" He barked at her.

"You will be told what to do. You will get the money, or we will kill you, you understand?"

The interrogation continued for a while before she was returned to the shack. One by one, the other four went through the same process. In each case, $500,000 was the asking price for their release.

They had a maximum of 30 days to raise their individual ransoms. If they failed, they would be executed and fed to the animals. So far, they hadn't been split up but there was no guarantee that would remain the case. The clock was ticking.

There was no doubting the sincerity of the threat. The fragility of their situation was plain to see. Food and water arrived late afternoon. They were desperate for both. It mattered little what was being served up: there would be no complaints. After eating, Stefan told Dan and Chuck that he was planning to escape. On his journey to be interviewed, he had noticed that there was a pathway not far from their shack that led into the bush.

Of course, he had no idea where it led or his chances of escaping but he had to try. He was convinced that whether they raised the ransom money or not, their captors would execute them anyway, and he wasn't prepared to sit around waiting for the inevitable.

Dan admired Stefan's courage. He didn't come across as someone that would take undue risks; the last person in their group he thought would try an escape. Dan and Chuck questioned him.

Firstly, how would he escape the shack they were in? The door was always locked after their guard had brought them food and water. But Stefan had noticed something the others had not. Above the door, there was a ledge. On it, he had seen something protruding and discovered a key. He had waited until everyone was asleep the previous night to see if it fitted the door, and it did. Dan and Chuck were excited by his discovery, but even with a key to get out, how could he escape the camp undetected? It turned out Stefan had an answer for that question, too. When he had tried the key in the door and discovered it worked, he had gently opened the door and peered out. There was no one in sight.

He had assumed, as the others had, that someone would be guarding them twenty-four hours a day but then, logically speaking, why would they? The door was locked and there was no way out.

Stefan went on to explain that he planned to wait until about 2.00 am and if the coast were clear, he would slip out and make his way to the path on a reconnaissance mission. He would spend the next hour or so trying to determine whether an escape had a good probability of success or not, then return by 3.00 am. If he believed it was worth a try, he would either go alone the following night or better still they could all go together.

Dan and Chuck listened attentively. Finally, they shook his hand and agreed it was worth an exploratory mission. Neither believed their respective partners would take the risk of an escape but agreed to have the conversation.

The five of them huddled together and Stefan explained his plan before waiting for Ashley and Susannah's response. To Chuck's surprise, Ashley agreed it made sense to try and get away. She, too, had concluded that their chances of staying alive irrespective of whether they raised the ransom or not were slim, but had kept quiet, not wanting to panic anyone. Chuck hugged her. He was proud of her bravery. Unsurprisingly, Susannah had an opposing view, believing they would almost certainly be caught and executed without a second thought. She was adamant she would take her chances and stay behind. This placed Dan in an invidious position. His inclination was to risk an escape, but he had to remain with Susannah. It was unthinkable that he would leave without her. He knew it was pointless attempting to persuade her as she was clearly fragile, and even if she agreed to the plan, she might prove to be a liability if they ran into trouble. No. He had to decline the offer. The other three, with Dan's encouragement, agreed that Stefan would go out at 2.00 am for the reconnaissance trip as planned. Based on his assessment, they would either escape there and then or abandon the idea completely. There was no point enduring another day of captivity.

Susannah was relieved that Dan had not tried to change her mind. It was early evening and they decided to get some sleep. Chuck's watch alarm was set for 1.50 am, giving Stefan enough time to prepare for his departure.

They were all wide awake before the alarm went off. Stefan was ready to leave. They wished him well as he went to the door and slowly turned the key to avoid making a noise.

The door creaked as he gently pulled it toward him just enough for him to survey the scene. The coast was clear. He turned to the others and smiled nervously as Dan and Chuck patted him on the back and wished him luck. He edged his way out of the hut and dashed toward the path. They immediately closed the door behind him, leaving it unlocked for his return. They listened closely for any signs of commotion or, worse still, gunshots. Several minutes passed and it remained silent outside. Chuck and Ashley were apprehensive, but they were ready to leave and waited anxiously for Stefan to return. Dan had considered in his own mind the likely consequences for him and Susannah once the escape was discovered by the guard in the morning. He feared they might be tortured for information or even killed. He resisted sharing his thoughts with her, knowing she would freak out. Once again, Ashley spoke to Susannah and tried to persuade her to go with them, but she had made up her mind.

Forty minutes later, the door creaked, and Stefan crept in. He was out of breath and had both good and bad news. The good news was that getting outside the encampment without being detected was easy. The bad news was that it was pitch dark and he could see little as the path quickly turned into a dirt track. He had been unable to figure out if it led anywhere other than deeper into the bush.

Travelling in the bush on foot at night had its own challenges, not least of all, encountering predators looking for their next meal.

There was no way of working out if the track would eventually lead them to safety or not. It was also the case that if they left now, they would only have an hour or so before sunrise and could easily be spotted.

Their experience so far suggested the guard first came into the shack late morning, which would give them a fair amount of time to be miles away. Then again, they were expected to start making ransom calls in the morning and that process would likely start early.

Ashley and Chuck listened closely, weighing up what Stefan had to say. Their minds were unchanged. They were ready to go.

Within a few minutes, the three of them had made their decision. They hugged Dan and Susannah for the last time, then the two watched as the others sprinted toward the path and out of sight. Dan locked the door and returned the key to the ledge. Then, he changed his mind. If they had to return in a hurry, they would want immediate access. He decided to unlock the door again. He would lock it later.

It was impossible for either of them to sleep. The hours past and they heard nothing, so they assumed the escape had been successful. Dan was worried what would happen to them next. There was no way of knowing what time it was as they had previously relied on Chuck's watch. He went to the door and opened it slightly. The sun was up, and he estimated it was about 7.00 am. A few rebels were milling about. He left the door unlocked again and returned the key to the ledge.

His theory was simple. The guard would think he had mistakenly left the door unlocked when he had brought them supper the previous evening. Dan and Susannah would argue that they had been asleep and unaware of the escape. He doubted such a tale would in any way protect them, but it was worth a try.

By now, Susannah was visibly stressed and unable to stop shaking. The guard was due at any time and their fate would be known. Dan did all he could to reassure her.

Just then, there was a noise outside. The guard attempted to put the key in the lock; it opened freely. He was surprised but no more than that. He was carrying a wicker basket with their breakfast, which he placed on the floor. At first, he failed to notice anyone was missing, but as he raised his eyes, he looked around the room in disbelief. He shouted at Dan. "Where they...where they gone?" He was clearly panicked, knowing how serious this was for him.

He pointed his pistol at Dan's head. "Where they gone?" Rather than wait for an answer, he checked the toilet and the reality hit home that they had escaped. He ran out of the shack shouting.

Within a couple of minutes, several guards came over and dragged them both outside, pointing rifles at their heads. Boss Man arrived at the scene. He looked at them and ordered them onto the ground. "Where are your friends? You will tell me, or I will shoot you."

He pulled out his pistol and pointed the barrel at Dan's head.

Dan looked up pleadingly, denying any knowledge of their whereabouts in the hope that they might get off the hook "They must have left in the night when we were asleep..." Boss Man struck him over the head with the pistol and grabbed Susannah by the hair, dragging her away screaming. Semi-conscious, Dan was shoved back into the shack and dumped on the floor, where he passed out.

When he came to, he had no idea how long he had been unconscious. His head was bleeding, and he was in a good deal of pain. He vaguely remembered Susannah being dragged away but no more than that. He had to find out what they had done with her. Fearlessly, he banged on the door continuously until a guard came and forced his way into the shack. He demanded to know where Susannah was, but he was pushed to the floor. "Where is she...where is she?*!*" The guard kicked him repeatedly as he coiled up to protect himself. It was stifling hot, and he could barely breathe. His clothes were soaked in sweat and blood.

After a couple of minutes, the guard left the shack, and the door was locked. A few minutes later, he returned with two other men to take Dan to Boss Man for an interrogation. As he entered the room, he was ordered to sit down. Again, he demanded to know what had happened to Susannah. There was no answer. He asked again but was struck on the head for the trouble. For over an hour, he was interrogated about the escape, but he stuck to his story despite believing that Susannah had likely told them everything.

He was given an ultimatum; tell them what time they had escaped and how they got out or be tortured.

He remained silent. They stripped him naked and forced him to stand facing a wall. One of the men used his cane to lash his back at least 30 times before he fell to the ground. He was in agony but maintained his composure. Again, he said nothing. Next, his knees and shins were beaten with a metal rod.

The pain was too much for him; he passed out and was dragged back to the shack unconscious and dumped on the floor. Later, he came round in a cold sweat and a great deal of pain. He was drifting in and out of consciousness. He could barely move and had no idea that two days had passed. Food had been left on the floor next to his blood-soaked body and both had attracted a swarm of flies.

Several days passed, he had little contact with his guards. He was unwinding mentally and talked to himself continually. He had lost the will to live. A guard came in and forced him outside. It was the first daylight he had seen in days and the sun blinded him. As he lay on the ground, a truck drew up next to him, showering him in dust. Two of the rebels jumped out of the front and removed the tarpaulin. Wiping his eyes, he looked up in horror to see the remains of Chuck, Ashley, and Stefan dumped on the ground next to him. It was a grotesque sight. They were riddled with bullets and had been beaten badly.

Their torsos were covered in blood and Ashley had been stripped naked. Dan wanted to scream out, but he had no voice. He was too dehydrated to shed any tears. By any standards, the rebels had committed a barbaric act. It would forever be engraved in Dan's memory.

The ordeal wasn't over, though. He now had to witness their final act of cruelty as they dragged Susannah's naked body before him and dumped it on top of the other three corpses. She, too, had been brutally murdered and likely raped.

He was dragged back into the shack, begging his guards to shoot him too; to end his life, he wanted to die. For him, life was now a living hell and he wanted it all to end. The guards laughed. They smashed the only light bulb in the shack and locked the door behind them. It was now pitch black, save a shaft of light that penetrated a small hole in the door.

CHAPTER 10 - RESCUE

It had been almost two weeks since the group had been discovered in the bush and taken to the camp. The authorities had been informed that the jeep had gone missing on safari and those on board had not returned. It was rare for kidnappings to take place in the region, but there were more incidents than the international community were aware of. The government was keen to play down the risks of holidaying in the country, fearing the tourist trade and much needed foreign exchange would dry up.

A task force of soldiers had been sent to the area where it was thought they had gone missing. When the remains of the tour guide and driver were discovered in the bush, the hunt for the tourists and their abductors intensified. It was thought likely from previous abductions that the rebels responsible for kidnappings invariably crossed the border into Congo, where they were less likely to be caught.

There were many remote sites deep in the bush where camps had been set up for hostage taking. The gangs had refined their operations over the years and had been successful in extorting millions of dollars from governments, major corporations, and wealthy individuals, so much so that new and larger camps had been discovered abandoned after short periods of time. It made no sense for rebel groups to stay long in any one location knowing they would eventually be found. It was big business, and it was highly lucrative.

News of the gruesome discovery leaked to the American, German, and British media, who picked up on the story that five western holidaymakers had been abducted.

As Dan's captors had disposed of four of them, he was now the only one left who could be used as a bargaining chip. The BBC and other main channels covered the story extensively and as a result, Dan and Susannah's families, work colleagues and friends were hounded by the press, who were eager to find out anything they could that was newsworthy about the couple. It had also not escaped the notice of the police either, as they wanted to question Dan further about Tanya's murder at the lab.

Dan remained captive in the shack in a depressed state as his mental and physical health deteriorated. It was stifling. What little air entered the building hung unpleasantly. His squalid conditions attracted vermin, and flies were ever present. Boss Man waited for him to recover sufficiently that he could make a ransom video pleading for his life. The room had been set up for one purpose: to interview and video record captives for broadcast on Western news channels.

He was instructed to say everyone was alive and he had been selected to be the spokesperson for the group. The ransom was $2.5m for their safe release. The deadline was 14 days for a payment to be transferred to a nominated account, or they would all be executed. Dan knew the chances of him being released alive were slim, even if his plea for help was successful. The gang had already demonstrated what they were capable of. The threat of torture if he failed to make the video was enough for him to agree to their demands. They seated him in front of the camera. His physical and mental state would shock those that knew him. He was a changed man, a shadow of his former self. He knew what to say and what not to say. The video camera was switched on.

"My name is Dan Thomas. I am a British citizen. I am being held with Susannah Mortimer, also from Britain, Chuck and Ashley Craig from the USA, and Stefan Schmidt from Germany. We are all alive and being treated well, but we need your help if we are to be released. Please, please..."

He broke down in tears and paused for a moment as the video continued to record. The emotional drama was precisely what his captives wanted to see.

"....please help us. Our captors are demanding $2.5 million dollars for our safe release. Payment must be made within the next 14 days. If the ransom is not paid, we will be executed. Please help...please!" The recording ended.

Dan had done what was expected of him. He had pleaded for his and the others lives.

When the video was released on all the main international networks, there was an outcry. Various groups lobbied individual governments to step in and pay the ransom to secure their safe release, but the response was unambiguous. *We do not pay ransoms for hostages.* Governments around the world would often make such statements, but then use diplomatic channels behind the scenes to negotiate with kidnappers. At least, that was Dan's understanding. He had to believe that the ransom would be paid, and he would have a chance of being released alive. He was unaware that within a few days of the video's release, his captors had engaged in discussions with at least one government who were prepared to negotiate for everyone's release, but like many negotiations, it had started off badly and further communications had ceased for a period. The 14-day deadline came and went but negotiations continued and were making progress, so no further harm came to him.

Imprisoned and not knowing whether it was night or day, let alone how many days had passed since he made the video, his will to live was ebbing away even further.

Food came and went each day, but he had no appetite. He was surviving on the little water he received. One morning, shortly after receiving his daily rations, he heard a disturbance outside. Something was up. It was unusual to hear the rebels talking, let alone shouting. There was never a sense of urgency or drama. Today was different. Soon, he heard gunfire and that panicked him. Were they shooting the hostages? Would he be next?

While the behind-the-scenes negotiations between the kidnappers and representatives of the three governments were in progress, the pace was too slow for the kidnappers and they had given a final deadline of 72 hours to be paid the $2.5 million or the hostages would die. Their tone and the finality of their statement spooked the government negotiators, who feared lives would be lost and the resulting political backlash would be significant. What the kidnappers were unaware of, though, was that their location had been pinpointed by the British military, who had been instructed to draw up plans for a rescue mission.

The rebel strongholds were anything but. The fact that Ashley, Chuck, and Stefan were able to walk out of the camp unnoticed was testament to that fact.

There was little time to debate the merits of the rescue plan. With special forces on standby, the decision was made to go in with ground forces, who would be helicoptered to a location not far from the encampment, but far enough away not to be seen or heard.

The commotion Dan heard was a reaction to intelligence Boss Man had received, informing him that special forces had been spotted only a few miles away.

It was not uncommon for rebel groups to be spooked. Their encampments were designed for a speedy exit into the bush, where they would hide out until the coast was clear. Depending on the number of hostages they were holding, and the progress of ransom negotiations, they would often kill less able hostages, taking the more able and valuable with them. This was precisely what was happening.

As the rebels assembled and prepared to leave, Dan heard repeated gun shots. They had gone into several shacks and shot those they believed would be an incumbrance. Dan's door swung open. He knew nothing of their plans but found himself joining seven other escapees and within 15 minutes, they had been bundled onto the back of a truck. From there, they were driven at speed into the bush. Several of those on board had been held hostage for almost a year in the camp and their physical and mental well-being eclipsed Dan's. He was certainly the youngest on board. Most were middle aged Americans – both men and women - and a Spanish woman whose husband had been shot dead before they set off. They were all traumatized by their lengthy incarceration and now, they had had to deal with witnessing the slaughter of their fellow hostages.

The trucks sped through the bush, a route they were familiar with. Twenty minutes passed and special forces covertly approached the camp.

The troop commander heard truck engines in the distance but had no idea the camp had already been evacuated. He sent his men in and they reported the rebels had indeed gone.

They searched shack by shack and came across the freshly shot corpses, nine in all. One elderly man was still alive but died soon after, unable to provide any intelligence.

The commander of the attack force rightly assumed that the rebels had been tipped off that they were closing in on them and made their escape. He had hoped he could take the camp by stealth and in doing so, rescue the hostages unharmed. He had no idea if all the hostages had been shot and left for dead, or if they had taken their most valuable assets with them. He had to assume the latter. This had not been the outcome he and his political bosses were seeking. To mount a covert strike against rebel groups and fail in such a marked way with the loss of so many lives would not go down well with the public back home.

As the rebels had only recently left the camp, the commander ordered his troops back to their land vehicles to mount a search.

The rebels knew the terrain well. They had cleverly planned emergency hideouts in case they were attacked, and today was an opportunity to put them to the test. Fifteen miles west of the encampment, and well into Congo, they arrived in a hilly area where drive-in caves had been prepared to conceal the trucks and their human cargo. The convoy stopped and the hostages were ordered to get out.

One American woman had not survived the journey and lay dead in the back of the truck, where she was left. They were led deep into the caves. Armed with semi-automatic rifles, the rebels camouflaged the trucks in a hurry and took up strategic hiding places at the top of the cave in anticipation that special forces may well find their location. Boss Man knew whoever was after them would be highly trained and not easily won over.

The land was parched, and the dirt roads made it difficult for the force's commander and his men to identify the direction the rebels were headed. They stopped to look at their maps. As far as it was possible to work out, there were two likely directions they would take. One would take them deeper into the bush and the other, toward a hilly region. The commander was an experienced combat soldier, and he instinctively knew they would head for the hills.

It made sense to take up positions on high ground or find caves to conceal their whereabouts and he was right. What concerned him most was that the rebels knew they would be followed and if there were hostages among them, they might be in an extremely vulnerable state. The priority for the commander was the safe return of the hostages and his men, not capturing the rebels at any cost. It was a tricky balance. The time for negotiating the ransom had passed. It was now a combat mission and time would tell how successful it would be.

The rebels were now settled in and had concealed the trucks extremely well and taken up defensive positions above and around the caves.

Boss Man knew it would be difficult for anyone to penetrate their position as the dirt road leading up to the caves was the only way in and they would be spotted with ease, or so he thought.

As the special forces approached the hills out of earshot of the rebels, they stopped again to think through their strategy. If their enemy were in the hills hiding, waiting for them to arrive, they were at a disadvantage and could be ambushed. It was decided that they would abandon their land vehicles and go on foot. Stealth was the only way of surprising them.

Unbeknownst to both the commander and Boss Man, the rebels had almost twice the number of men. This made it appear that they had an advantage, but of course, that was not always the case. The rebels were largely untrained thugs, murderers who had either been forcibly conscripted as children or joined voluntarily to be guaranteed being fed when starvation in the villages was endemic.

The special forces, of course, were the opposite. They were specially trained, disciplined troops that had mastered the art of warfare.

The sun was high above them and the temperature had risen to 32c as they slowly made their way toward the hills. The dirt track being the only way to the caves was not lost on the commander. He ordered his men to split up and take a detour, some going left and the others right.

They were instructed to approach the hills from the north, knowing it would add over an hour to their journey time. They would stay in touch by radio.

It was 2.40 pm when the troops reached the northern flank of the hills and reported back to the commander. Using binoculars, they observed seven rebels on top of the hill ahead of them, approximately two hundred yards away. The terrain leading up to the foot of the hills was challenging to navigate. They estimated it would take a further thirty minutes to get into a position undetected, where they could make a surprise attack. The commander gave them the go-ahead and asked them to report back when they were in place.

Successfully attacking the rebels on the hill was only a part of the task ahead of them. The commander suspected they would also be entrenched in the caves, and if they were, the hostages would also be hunkered down, making it extremely difficult to rescue them without casualties. There were so many unknowns. A call came over the radio. The troops were in place and ready to attack.

Working on the assumption that the caves were in use, it made no sense to storm the rebels on the hills with gunfire, which would only alert those in the caves and risk the lives of the hostages in turn. They had to kill their targets one by one using knives, only opening fire if that strategy failed. The commander gave his order to attack.

Fortunately, the rebels had spread out and were relatively easy to pick off.

They were highly experienced in torture techniques and cold-blooded murder, but naive when it came to man-to-man combat and lacking the discipline and basics of warfare. They called out to each other instead of remaining silent, alerting the troops to their individual positions. The rebels had wrongly assumed the attack would come from the dirt track leading to the caves. They had no idea the insurgency would come from behind. One by one, the troops picked off their prey, silently cutting their throats until they were all dead. They then reported back to the commander that their mission had been accomplished.

Phase two, the most delicate part of the mission, lay ahead: how to safely free any hostages being held in the caves, while capturing the remaining rebels with a minimum of bloodshed so they could be brought to justice.

The commander and the troops that remained with him on the south side were able to see the mouth of the cave through their binoculars and were confident that the area was unguarded. Of course, what lay beyond the entrance was unknown. He gave the order for the troops on the hill to work their way down to ground level and report back when they were in position to storm the tunnel. The commander and his men gradually moved toward the cave entrance, where they would all meet up.

Everyone knew the success or failure of the next phase had little to do with competency, logistics, planning, or discipline.

It would be determined by pure luck, as they had no way of knowing how many rebels were left, where they were in the cave, their fire power, or how they could overcome them without having to open fire themselves.

From experience they knew that ill-trained and ill-disciplined rebel fighters often tried to flee rather than fight when they knew the odds were against them. The big question was whether they would attempt to kill their hostages in the process, assuming there were any left.

Having assembled close to the unguarded cave entrance, the commander issued his latest orders. Three men would go in first, quickly followed by another three. Their job was to survey the scene, slitting the throats of any rebels they came across. Gunfire was only to be used as a last resort. The remaining six troops and the commander would follow shortly after. Having come across the camouflaged trucks, the first wave of troops checked to see if anyone was guarding them. They were in luck - no one was in sight. As they slowly and deliberately moved forward, they heard voices in the distance. The further they entered the cave, the darker it became. As their eyes adjusted, they were able to work out the configuration of the space and where people were situated. At that very moment, a rebel walked toward them. It was impossible for the troops to hide. The soldier leading the movement leaped forward, grabbed the man tightly around the throat, and plunged his knife several times into his chest.

When he was satisfied the man was dead, he set him down to one side, giving the others enough room to maneuver around the corpse. They moved forward.

The remaining rebels were sitting in a circle on the ground, talking. They moved closer. It was the perfect scenario for an attack. To the right of the men appeared to be a small group of people huddled together, the assumption being they were the hostages. They needed to be protected at all costs.

So far, the mission had gone according to plan. The commander was now at the front of the group and would decide their next moves. His objective was to protect the hostages and detain the rebels without a shot being fired, but that, even to him, seemed a remote possibility.

Rifles ready, they were instructed to move quickly and noisily toward the rebels, taking them by surprise and frightening them into surrender. Their plan worked, save Boss Man, who was standing separate from the group holding a semi-automatic rifle. He saw them approaching and fired several rounds at the troops. Two were hit and fell to the ground. Then, he opened fire on the hostages. The soldiers didn't hesitate, shooting him dead where he stood. Then, the commander rushed over to the hostages. Three of them had received fatal wounds but one was still alive. The rebels were rounded up and eventually transported by helicopter to Kampala where they would at some point stand trial. Many of them were young boys.

One of the soldiers had died in the attack and another was seriously injured. He, too, was transported back to hospital in Kampala alongside the only remaining hostage, Dr. Dan Thomas.

The mission was considered a failure, despite the bravery of the commander and his troops on the ground. An Inquest would determine they had executed their mission to the best of their abilities, but they had failed to secure the safe release of the hostages except Dan. The failure of the mission was attributed to a tip off Boss Man had received that troops had been spotted not far from the camp, which gave them time to flee, murdering most of the hostages in the camp before they did. The second failure was assuming all the rebels had been sitting on the ground prior to the attack, leaving Boss Man free to shoot at will.

Dan, the only surviving hostage, remained heavily guarded in a Kampala hospital where he recuperated for two weeks before being flown back to the UK amidst a media frenzy.

Millions of people worldwide had been following the story and wanted to hear what he had to say.

His ordeal had left him mentally and physically scarred. He had endured torture and near starvation and had witnessed the grotesque sight of his three friends and Susannah’s mutilated corpse unceremoniously dumped on the ground in front of him. They were memories that would haunt him for the rest of his life.

CHAPTER 11 - ESCAPE

Back in the UK, Dan shunned publicity and demands for interviews. He was too fragile and needed time to mend. Several months passed and he barely saw anyone he knew other than family and a few close friends. He hid away from everyday life and ignored social media and emails. Gradually, he regained his mental and physical strength enough to agree to an exclusive TV interview to talk about his ordeal.

Dan had always been a good communicator and he had not lost that skill, but the experience he had endured had changed him as a human being. He could no longer be accused of being self-obsessed and arrogant. Instead, he was introspective and humble. He spoke eloquently and emotionally about the courage of his fellow captives, especially Susannah, and of the special forces who had saved his life. He acknowledged how lucky he had been to escape the rebels alive. He wanted nothing more than to get back to a normal life, or as normal a life as possible under the circumstances. One morning, he decided to wade through a mountain of mail. One letter was from Dr. Peter Braithwaite – the art expert he had met at Sotheby's who had been reviewing his painting. He had also left several voicemail and text messages for Dan, unaware at that time of his ordeal. He opened the letter, read it, then re-read it. It had been quite some time since he had something to smile about. Peter was eager to inform him that the painting he had left with them to appraise was indeed an original Paul Gauguin oil painting. In his view, should the painting be presented for auction, it would command a recommended reserve price of £600,000. Dan looked at the figure several times. He couldn't believe his eyes. The letter was dated three weeks earlier, so he decided to call Peter.

"Peter. It's Dan Thomas..." Before he had an opportunity to say why he was calling, Peter offered an apology for harassing him. Of course, he didn't know that Dan had been *indisposed* at the time. They spoke for ten minutes with Peter confirming Dan's picture was a valuable treasure and wondered if he had the intention to keep it or sell it at auction. Dan agreed it should be auctioned and gave instructions for it to be listed in the next available catalogue. Peter confirmed the next relevant auction at the sale room was in six weeks.

During his rehabilitation, his employer offered to help him in any way they could and held his job open for him. Despite the likelihood that his painting would return him a sizeable sum of money from the auction, meaning there would be no need for him to work for a while, he was nonetheless keen to return to the lab to take up his old job. He decided he would keep his good fortune about the painting to himself until it was sold.

From the moment he arrived back in the UK, the police, especially Detective Inspector Ian Graham, had been keen to interview him about Tanya's murder, but they knew they had to find the right time to do so.

He had been through a horrendous ordeal. He was fragile and the focus of considerable media attention, so they chose to back off until the time was right. After Dan had left the country on safari, they had tried to contact him to interview him again. They were unaware he was away on holiday and had subsequently been kidnapped.

They had visited the flat several times during the following month and grown suspicious, wondering if he had absconded fearing they were closing in on him. A warrant was obtained to search his flat in his absence and two things came to their attention. Firstly, a receipt for a safety deposit box at *Stasher* where he had stored the hard drive, and secondly, a hard copy of the business plan he had prepared and discussed with Rupert to set up the new lab. Both were of significant interest to their enquiries. DI Graham had obtained a court order that allowed him to access the safety deposit box, where he discovered the hard drive. Having accessed its content, it became clear the data had been stolen from his employer and was related to the business plan they had already found. It was easy for them to discover Rupert's business details and an appointment was made to interview him under caution.

Rupert was horrified to learn that he was to be interviewed. He called Dan several times to find out what he knew but got no answer. He'd 'phoned him at work, too, only to be told by a new staff member in HR that he'd left. What she meant to say was that *he had left for a holiday*. Like the police, Rupert also feared that Dan had fled, perhaps abroad, knowing the police were on to him.

With that knowledge, Rupert had no choice but to tell the police the truth, at least in part. He told them he had met Dan at a party. In conversation, he had told him of the business plan and was looking for an investor.

Rupert had agreed to review the plan and believed the idea of setting up a new lab seemed compelling enough sufficient for him to *consider* getting involved, but he denied ever agreeing terms. What he absolutely and emphatically denied was that he knew Dan's plan involved stealing data from his current employer. Rupert was, after all, a venture capitalist. He looked at propositions on a regular basis and this was no different. Of course, the police had in their possession email exchanges between the two men proving that terms had been agreed as well as how much Rupert was prepared to put into the business.

In exchange for giving evidence for the prosecution at some point in the future, Rupert was guaranteed that no action would be brought against him personally. If he were to be implicated in any way in what was an illegal plan, his reputation and his business would be on the line and he was not prepared to take that risk. He had no option but to agree to their terms. Dan would be hung out to dry.

Dan had been back at the lab for two weeks. Having returned to the flat after work one evening, the doorbell rang. He assumed it was a reporter but when he got to the door, it was in fact DI Graham and Detective Finch.

"Oh, hello inspector. I wasn't expecting you." DI Graham put aside the pleasantries. "Dr. Thomas, I am arresting you on suspicion of murdering Dr. Tanya Waters."

He read Dan his rights and insisted he accompany him to the police station for further questioning. This time, it would be under caution and Dan would be offered legal representation.

Fifteen minutes after arriving at the police station, the questioning had begun. "Dr. Thomas. Just to confirm formally what you have previously told us in our enquiries about your relationship with Dr. Tanya Waters. Is it true that you were in a relationship with the deceased up until the day prior to her murder?"

"Yes, inspector."

"Is it also the case that the deceased ended the relationship with you because of your drug taking and alleged violent conduct?"

"I admitted taking occasional recreational drugs, yes, but I did not say that I was physically abusive toward her."

"Is it also the case that on the evening of the murder, you claimed to be the last person in the building, leaving the lab sometime after 7.00 pm?"

"Yes, that is true."

"And that you have no recollection of seeing Dr. Tanya Waters at any time after 6.00 pm?"
"Yes. Inspector."

"And you can also confirm that when you left the lab that evening, you saw no one else on the premises?"

"As far as I can recollect, I saw no one else. I have been through a difficult ordeal recently, inspector, and my memory is not what it used to be. But yes, I'm sure I saw no one else. Security is not what it should be at the lab; there are no CCTV cameras anywhere, although I believe they are currently being installed."

The inspector wanted to know more. "I see. So, this is something that occupies your mind, is it? You have checked, have you, how easy it is to enter and exit the building unseen?"

"I am not sure what you're suggesting, inspector, but yes, I am aware of the security issues."

"Did you ever report your concerns to management?"

"No, inspector. I didn't think it was my job to do so."

"Not your job? If I worked in a lab that was trying to develop an important vaccine, Dr. Thomas, I would want to ensure my work was being protected. I am surprised you *didn't think it was your job*?"

"And your point, inspector?" Dan was rattled by the questioning but held his nerve.

"I put it to you, Dr. Thomas, that on the evening in question, when Dr. Tanya Waters was brutally strangled, you knew there would be no security on duty. This gave you the opportunity to steal data from your colleagues' computers, which you planned to use to set up your own lab. You were surprised to discover Dr Waters was indeed still on the premises and that she caught you in the act of downloading data on to an external hard drive. Is that not the case?"

Dan was shocked rigid that the inspector was perfectly describing what had happened that evening, but how the hell did he know about the hard drive? "No, inspector, none of this is true." The inspector persisted.

"And I put it to you, Dr. Thomas, that after the deceased caught you in the act, you got into an argument with her and in a moment of rage, you strangled her."

"No, inspector!" The inspector was confident he had his man and pushed harder.

"So, you deny copying data from your colleagues' computers and murdering the deceased?"

"Yes, I deny both, inspector."

The inspector went on to explain to Dan that after trying to track him down, not knowing he had been kidnapped, they had sought a court order allowing them to search his flat and in doing so, had discovered the receipt for the storage locker and the business plan he had discussed with Rupert. "I further put it to you, Dr. Thomas, that you cleaned up as best you could and casually left the building, knowing you wouldn't be seen by anyone and that the body of the deceased would be found the following morning." Dan was completely thrown off balance by the inspector's claim.

"None of this is true, inspector. I left the building after 7.00 pm and I was alone when I did."

"Let me ask you the question again, Dr. Thomas. Before you say you left the lab on your own, had you in any way tampered with any of your colleagues' computers in the lab?"

"Tampered with their computers?

I don't understand what you mean by *tampered?*"

"Had you opened any of your colleague's computers that evening, either to view or download data?"

"Clearly, you know that I downloaded data on to an external hard drive but not on the evening in question. I did that the previous evening as I was planning to work from home. It was part of my job to extract data and provide a technical analysis for management."

"Did you normally do that in the presence of your colleagues or after work?"
"Sorry inspector, what has this got to do with Tanya's murder?"

The inspector pressed on with his questioning. "Answer the question, sir."

"No, it's not often the case that I would access colleagues' computers after office hours, but I was running late on a report and stayed late to finish it. I wasn't committing a crime in doing this, inspector." Of course, he *had* committed a crime. The inspector had also checked it was against his contract of employment to copy any data and remove it from the company's premises.

"Dr. Thomas, I believe you are lying to me. You copied data onto a hard drive and were caught in the act by the deceased and you murdered her. You took the hard drive off company premises and stored it in a locker until you thought it safe to access it. Prior to this, you had prepared a business plan to establish a new lab to use the stolen data and sought an investor. Further, you had meetings with at least one potential investor who is prepared to testify to this fact. But let me turn to the strangulation of Dr. Waters. We have reason to believe that on the evening in question, you did indeed strangle the deceased. A forensic examination of her neck suggests that the imprint left on her skin matches your own fingerprints. How could that be?"

Dan knew he was sweating. What he was unable to determine was whether his brow was sweating also. He resisted the opportunity to mop his forehead, knowing that it would only draw attention to his now nervous state. "Inspector, the only explanation I can offer is that earlier in the day, when Tanya and I were alone in the lab, I tried to embrace her, but she pulled away from me. We had split up the previous evening and I was trying to make amends. I did put my hands on her shoulders, and I may have even put my hands around her neck to bring her closer to me."

"So, you admit you put your hands around her neck?"

"I may well have done, but that was earlier in the day, not in the evening."

"May well have done, Dr. Thomas? Either you did or you didn't?"

"Okay, I did, but it was harmless and over in a second. But as I said, that was earlier in the day."

The interrogation went on, lasting for almost two hours. Dan's performance was less than convincing, but so far, the inspector had been unable to extract a confession.

He hesitated to charge Dan as he believed he did not have quite enough evidence and needed certainty. If for no other reason, he knew that because Dan was currently viewed by the public and media as a hero, the last thing he wanted to do was charge him with a murder he was unable to prove without a shadow of doubt.

It was then that the inspector made the biggest mistake of his career. He allowed Dan to leave custody rather than hold him for further questioning. When Dan left, he promptly 'phoned his boss and said he wouldn't be in the following day.

As he left the police station, his experiences as a hostage in the camp locked up in the shack flooded back to him. In no way could he contemplate spending the rest of his life behind bars. He went over and over what he had told the inspector and knew his performance was less than convincing. They seemed to have all the evidence they needed to charge him, so why let him go?

He returned home in a paranoid state. He worried that the police would place a surveillance team on him, and he would be followed wherever he went. He was unable to sleep that night and the stress of not knowing when the police would charge him took its toll. He drank heavily, something he vowed he would never do again. Despite his celebrity status and constant requests from the media for interviews and friends calling, he felt isolated. Prior to his suffering at the hands of the rebel gang, he would have relished the attention he was getting, but that was then. Now, he feared everything was unravelling around him and he would be exposed for what he really was – a murderer.

As much as he wanted to unburden his mind onto another living soul, he knew that was impossible. He was like a caged animal, unable to escape and unable to express himself in a way that people would understand and take pity on him. He was a pariah, and sooner rather than later, everyone would know what he had done, and he would be a social outcast.

The life he had enjoyed prior to murdering Tanya, and his time at the hands of the rebels had damaged him mentally. He was now in a state of constant anxiety. He knew he had to get away, to escape the inevitable, but how?

Overnight, he slept little as he tried to hatch a plan that would give him his freedom. He knew Rupert had been interviewed by the police and from what the inspector had said, he would be a witness for the prosecution if he were charged and brought before a jury. It was early morning. Dan was desperate to know what Rupert had said, so he called him. He had a new mobile phone and a new number after his old handset had been taken from him while he was being held hostage. Rupert answered the 'phone. "It's Dan..." Rupert was astonished to hear from him as he had assumed he had been charged and was in custody. "Dan...Why are you calling me...where are you?" Dan knew Rupert had betrayed him, believing he could save his own skin irrespective of what may happen to Dan. Rupert had agreed to invest in his business idea, knowing it was illegal. Even though he had changed his mind later, it was enough in Dan's mind to make him a co-conspirator.

If he were to serve time in prison, then Rupert should not get off *scot-free.* "I won't beat about the bush, Rupert. I know you betrayed me to the police. I don't know precisely what you've told them, but they see you as a prosecution witness if they charge me."

Rupert was shocked that Dan had not been detained after the police had told him categorically, he was their prime suspect in Tanya's murder. "Look, Dan, I think it's best we don't communicate again."

"I'm sorry you feel that way, Rupert, but you really didn't think you could act against me and get away with it?" Rupert was fearful. He knew Dan had been through the hostage ordeal and was likely to be in a distressed state.

"I'm not sure I know what you mean, Dan?" Dan told him in no uncertain terms that he possessed enough evidence to show unequivocally that Rupert had agreed to invest in his business plan in the full knowledge that the lab would be using data from his previous employer. In other words, they had both conspired to commit fraud. Once Rupert heard this, the two men agreed to meet discreetly within the hour. Dan knew he had little time to escape the clutches of the law. It was more a case of when, not if he would be charged with Tanya's murder. He had to get away.

There was an immediate atmosphere between the men from the outset. Rupert was desperate to protect his liberty and assets almost at any cost, and Dan knew that would be the case. His pitch was a simple one. He knew that Rupert owned several properties in the UK and a few in exotic locations overseas.

As things stood, Dan would find it impossible to leave the country without the police being alerted, so he had no option but to remain in the UK.

In exchange for his silence about Rupert's planned involvement in the illicit business, he demanded that Rupert find him a property to disappear to, somewhere remote where he could hunker down until things died down. He would also arrange for Dan to have a fake passport, so that when he received the money from the sale of his painting at Sotheby's, he could discreetly slip away abroad and start life over.

Dan knew his demands were not beyond Rupert's capability. He had bragged about some of the things he had done in his past when they were high on cocaine, which had shocked Dan at the time. At first, Rupert was adamant he wanted nothing to do with his demands, but Dan's oratory skills convinced him that his bests interests would be served by assisting him. It was agreed that Rupert would obtain a new passport for him and would arrange for a discreet place for him to stay.

Within 48 hours, Dan was on his way to a remote cottage in the Cotswolds and within a fortnight, he had a new passport.

Before leaving for the cottage, he returned to his flat, hoping, praying he would not be followed. As quickly as he could, he got together everything important to him that he could carry in a large rucksack, and he was off. The cottage was beautiful and sat on almost three acres of woodland. It was fully furnished in Rupert's decorative style. In a barn, Dan found an old motorbike that he would use during his time there.

The nearest property to the cottage was over a mile away. It was the perfect hideout. Before making the journey, he had withdrawn almost twenty thousand pounds from his account - the inheritance money he had received from his university professor – which would enable him to fund his existence.

Few people had his new pay-as-you-go mobile number. If he were to escape the country and start a new life, he knew he could not risk contacting anyone, even his closest friends. However, he had to speak to his mother first. She would be worried about him, but what would he say? Several days passed before he plucked up the courage to call her. He explained that after returning from his ordeal as a hostage, he had received a visit from the police, who were convinced that he murdered Tanya. He feared they would charge him despite his innocence and in his fragile state, he could not contemplate spending time in prison. He knew he would have a mental breakdown or, worse still, commit suicide. He was planning to leave the country to start a new life and would let her know when he was safe.

She begged him not to go. If he were innocent and she knew he was, he should stay and argue his case. She believed in the justice system and it would not fail him. Of course, she was unaware of his guilt. Eventually, after almost twenty minutes on the 'phone, she had no option but to accept his plan. He promised he would stay in touch. After the call, he destroyed his 'phone. He had several others he could use.

Despite feeling all alone and stressed, he tried his hardest to think about his future, where he would go, and what he would do with his new life. Changing his appearance was essential. Within hours of arriving at the cottage, he had cut his hair short and shaved off his beard.

Then, he went into Chipping Campden on the motorbike to take passport photos to send to Rupert. He had agreed with him that his new name on the passport would be Roderic Charles. The inspiration came from a label in one of his shirts. He knew the auction of his Paul Gaugin painting was due in a fortnight. He wanted to attend the sale in person but that was now impossible, so he would join online anonymously. He could not risk being seen again in such a public place. What worried him was how he would get his hands on the sale proceeds, assuming the painting was sold on the day. He still had his bank account, but the withdrawal of the twenty thousand pounds had to be the last transaction on the account if he were to disappear and assume a new identity.

It was mid-afternoon when he decided to call Dr. Braithwaite at Sotheby's to discuss the auction and tactfully discuss how the funds could be transferred. Peter was eager to tell Dan that there had been a great deal of interest in his painting from both UK and international buyers, and from previous experience, he anticipated the reserve of £600,000 would quite likely be exceeded. He told Peter he wanted to be an anonymous seller. This was common practice, especially with the rich and famous, who were often eager to shun publicity.

In Dan's predicament, the last thing he wanted was to attract unwanted attention. Of course, Peter agreed to his request. The more delicate question was whether he could nominate an account that the sale proceeds could be transferred to, other than in his own name. This caused Peter some consternation as the auction house was legally bound to transfer funds to the declared owner and to report the sale to Her Majesty Revenue and Customs if it were a UK resident, which of course he was. If funds were transferred to a third-party name designated by Dan, proof of identity would be required in several formats – passport, bank details, council tax bill, etc. It would not be easy. The only person that was fully aware of Dan's circumstances was Rupert. He could provide the proof of identity that Sotheby's demanded, but would he be willing to get embroiled in the plan? Dan had already coerced him into providing the cottage and the new passport, so he hoped he would accept one last request.

Rupert reluctantly agreed to drive to the cottage with Dan's passport the following day. This would give him the opportunity he needed to secure one last favor. Even if Rupert agreed to *launder his money,* he knew it would come at a price. Dan would need to cover the tax that Rupert would have to pay, as well as a *fee for his trouble*. What choice did he have?

Rupert arrived with the passport. Dan had threatened to expose his part in the lab project, and he did not like being threatened or coerced, especially by someone like Dan – a person over whom he had hitherto had control.

Again, there was an atmosphere between the two men. Dan explained about the auction and the challenge he faced transferring funds if the painting sold. Rupert wanted him out of his life, so he no longer posed a threat to him or his business interests, and the sooner he went abroad, hopefully never to be seen again, the better. He chose to request rather than demand Rupert's help with the money transfer. Rupert had little choice but to agree. He would put Peter and Rupert in contact so that all the formalities and proof of identity could be completed.

Over the next few days, bored with the cottage and its remoteness, Dan used Rupert's motorbike to explore the region while he had the opportunity to do so. As soon as the auction was over and the money was transferred, he would make his move abroad. He had decided to settle in Cyprus. There was a vibrant ex-pat community and English was spoken widely. He would not tell a soul where he was planning to settle, other than his mother. Once the publicity machine announced that Dan was Tanya's alleged murderer and he had absconded, everyone would be on the lookout for him. He would have to sacrifice his wide circle of friends forever; he couldn't risk his whereabouts leaking out. It would be a completely new start. A new life.

He received a text message from Rupert, confirming that he had passed on his details to Peter at Sotheby's, and Peter was content that proceeds could be transferred to Rupert's account soon after the sale. It usually took 3-5 days for funds to clear.

On the strength of that news, Dan bought a one-way ticket to Nicosia, a day after the auction under his new name of Roderic Charles. He booked a hotel room for a fortnight to give him time to decide where on the island he wanted to set up home.

He was constantly on edge, fearing he would be apprehended before he had a chance to leave the country or indeed at the airport before his departure.

The day of the auction came around quickly. The sale catalogue had been distributed widely and contained over 200 lots. Dan's painting was lot 24. Most of the items for sale were 19th century artwork and some furniture. The auction room was full of prospective buyers and the number of people logged on for the auction exceeded 100, including Dan. Dealers and wealthy private individuals from across the globe were represented. There were two specific lots that had aroused people's attention. A JMW Turner oil on canvas that had not been seen at auction in sixty years and Dan's Gauguin. The fact that Dan's painting had never come to market before, made it especially rare.

The auctioneer breezed through the first fifteen lots. Most of the items barely sold for little over their reserves. Dan knew little about art, but Peter had told him that the first half an hour of an auction gave an indication of how bullish, or not, buyers were on the day.

When it was his turn, the auctioneer announced, "I come to lot 24. An oil on cavass attributed to Paul Gauguin: *Girl looking into the distance*. The catalogue entry describes this item in detail.

"This artwork was an unknown piece until it was recently discovered. It has since been authenticated by the Gauguin Trust. A great deal of interest has been expressed in this fine work. Who will start me off at £300,000? Thank you, sir. £400,000 in the middle of the room. £500,000. £600,000. £700,000. £800,000. Who will bid £900,000? Thank you. One million pounds?"

Dan watched the auction on his laptop with a disbelieving smile on his face. Several minutes later and the auctioneer said, "At five million, five hundred thousand, are we all done? Six million, thank you, sir. We have an online bid for seven million. Are we all done at seven million? At seven million, going once, going, twice...seven two. Am I offered seven five? Seven five. I'm selling at seven million, five hundred thousand. Going once, going twice, *sold* for seven million, five hundred thousand pounds."

The attendees clapped as the auctioneer's hammer came down, sealing the deal. The reserve of £600,000 had grossly underestimated its market value. This was not the first time that an unknown work of a famous artist had attracted such interest.

Dan was speechless. He did a quick calculation and after paying the auction fees and VAT, he would likely net around five million pounds. He 'phoned Rupert to tell him the news, but he already knew, as he had also been online watching the sale. The cash would be transferred to Rupert's account within days. Dan would open a bank account upon arrival in Cyprus, enabling Rupert to transfer the funds across to him.

Having worked out the tax implications, Rupert had calculated this would reduce Dan's net proceeds still further, to a figure of around £4,000,000.

It would set him up for life.

He was desperate to share his good news with someone, anyone, but that was impossible. Instead, he opened a bottle of Rupert's champagne from his cellar and consumed it alone.

He woke the following morning with a familiar hangover. He packed the few possessions he had and called a taxi to take him to London Heathrow to catch the flight to Nicosia.

Having checked in, he made his way to passport control. This would be the first big test. Could he, Roderic Charles, get through using his new passport? Luck was on his side as he breezed through both passport control and security. His flight was due to take off in an hour.

He had learnt to drive a car as a teenager but had never owned one. Generally, he liked the look of sports cars, especially Bentleys and Aston Martins. As he waited in the lounge, he saw a stand promoting a *spot the ball competition* to win a Bentley Continental. He wandered over and sat in the car. Now he was a millionaire, he could afford to buy one, but he never would. He bought a ticket and recorded his name, his mother's address, and his mobile 'phone number on the form. Then, he returned to his seat.

CHAPTER 12 - NICOSIA

When the flight was called, he boarded and within 20 minutes, the plane had taken off. Dan was a free man. It was a 4-hour 40-minute journey. He sat next to an attractive English woman about his own age, who was travelling to Nicosia on business. They flirted throughout the journey. As they exchanged names, he accidentally blurted out *Dan Thomas,* then quickly corrected himself and used his new name - Roderic [Rod] Charles. The woman, whose name was Charlotte, was slightly taken aback. After all, who forgets their own name? She had heard the name Dan Thomas only recently but failed to bridge the connection. Of course, she, like most people, had been following the hostage crisis and seen him arrive back in the UK on TV. Fortunately, his face wasn't familiar to her now, which was no surprise because he had cut his hair and shaved off his beard soon after arriving at the cottage.

Dan knew his slip could be his downfall. If he were to start a new life under an alias, he had to remember who he was, or at least who he was pretending to be.

By coincidence, Dan and Charlotte were staying in the same hotel in Nicosia, so they agreed to share a taxi at the airport. It was a hot, sunny day and the air conditioning in the taxi failed to work. Even with the windows open, they were sweltering. Dan's mind was taken back to the shack he had occupied as a hostage in the bush and went quiet, which Charlotte was quick to pick up on. He wanted to tell her what he was thinking. In fact, he wanted to tell her everything about him and his life, but he knew that from there on, he had to live a lie, daily, constantly.

He would have to fabricate a life story that he could recount in an instant to all those with whom he came into contact. It wasn't how he wanted to live, but he had little choice if he were to avoid a lengthy prison sentence. He had chosen Cyrus as his new home knowing there was no extradition treaty between the UK and the island. If his real identity were discovered, he hoped he could successfully fight a case against being sent back to the UK. That gave him some comfort.

They eventually arrived at the hotel – The Cleopatra. It was centrally situated, just a few minutes' walk from the old part of the city and its shops, bars, cafes, and nightlife. They checked in.

He suggested they had dinner together that evening and Charlotte agreed. She needed to do some preparation later in the evening for a meeting in the morning, but it could wait. They went to their respective rooms to relax and agreed to meet at 8.00 pm in the bar. For a new life, Dan had packed only a few clothes when he left the UK. He would be staying at the hotel for at least the next few weeks until he found somewhere more permanent to live and that would give him time to buy a few more things. His main challenge would be inventing a life story for himself. That would not be easy. He had an hour before he would sit down to dinner with Charlotte, and inevitably, the conversation would focus on their lives, where they lived, what they did for a living, who they knew, and their views and opinions on a wide variety of subjects.

For a one-off date, or a cursory conversation, he could virtually say what he liked and get away with it, but with people who would in some way, or another become a part of the fabric of his life, he would need to invent, rehearse, and commit to memory a life story that was plausible that he could recall at the drop of a hat.

He had to believe his own lies.

On the plane, he had carefully avoided answering too many personal questions, preferring instead to focus the conversation on Charlotte and her work. So far, he had only told her that he was taking a long break from the UK and would initially base himself in Cyprus. He was a scientist, so from a job perspective, it made sense not to lie about his occupation when they talked over dinner.

They had only just met but he really liked her. In fact, he liked her a great deal and wanted the encounter to go well. He wandered down to the bar. She was already there and looked stunning. He was not unaccustomed to dating attractive women - Susannah and Tanya had been good examples.

After a few drinks in the bar, they left the hotel in search of a restaurant. The evening was a great success, and it was plain they enjoyed each other's company. He had told her a pack of lies, some of which he liked and thought he could build into his imaginary past life, and others he was less comfortable with.

On balance, though, he felt he had done a good job in convincing her that Rod was a *nice guy* and someone with whom she would be prepared to start a relationship with.

It was almost 11.00 pm and she was mindful she still had some prep work to do for her business meeting in the morning. They agreed she would spend an hour in her room and then make her way to Rod's room for a nightcap.

They woke at 8.00 am after a physically demanding night. Charlotte panicked; she only had forty-five minutes to get showered and dressed, and travel to her planned engagement. Fortunately, the venue was only a few streets away. After the meeting with a prospective client, which was scheduled to last about two hours, she planned to wander the streets of Nicosia and shop before making her way back to the airport for the return journey to London. Dan insisted that he accompany her on the shopping trip, and they agreed a rendezvous point at 11.00 am.

His chance meeting with her was a distraction he could well have done without. For the next few months at least, he needed to keep a low profile, blending into his surroundings, and finding a more permanent place to live. But he had fallen for her. He was keen the encounter didn't end as she got into the taxi back to the airport. She had feelings for him too, but neither of them had talked about seeing each other again.

She came out of her meeting and saw him across the street. She ran over to him with a big smile on her face.

Her meeting had gone well, better than expected, which meant she would need to spend more time in Nicosia in the year ahead.

Over coffee, they both agreed they wanted to start a relationship. She had finished with her boyfriend some months earlier and as Dan was a free man it dovetailed nicely. As they wandered around the shops, they discussed how and when they would meet again. She had unused holiday to take from work, so they agreed she would travel back to Nicosia to stay with him for a fortnight. She would return within a month. They had lunch before she set off in a taxi for the airport. He was in a good mood. She had been just the tonic he needed on his first day in Cyprus, so much so that he had almost forgotten he was in Nicosia to start a new life avoiding arrest for murdering his girlfriend! During the following week, mindful that he would soon receive the £4m from Rupert, the net proceeds from the sale of the painting at Sotheby's, he started to look at available homes to rent or buy.

Nicosia was expensive, and after reviewing a few properties, he concluded that it would be best to rent for a period to make sure he wanted to live there. For an ex-pat to buy property was a lengthy process and would involve being subjected to a barrage of questions about his identity. He found a sizeable three-bed furnished apartment in a smart part of town and agreed to take it for an initial twelve-month term. He could move in within a fortnight, which perfectly dovetailed with Charlotte's return. Life was good.

He 'phoned his mother that evening. He had already told her prior to escaping the UK that he feared if he stayed any longer the police would eventually charge him with Tanya's murder. Despite his innocence, if a jury found him guilty, he would receive a long prison sentence. She knew he was mentally fragile, and she believed him when he said that he feared he would end up taking his own life.

She answered the 'phone. Before he had a chance to tell her that he had arrived safely in Nicosia and found an apartment to rent, she had news for him. He had won the *spot the ball competition* that he entered at Heathrow airport and Dr. Dan Thomas was now the owner of a £188,000 Bentley Continental GT, which was sitting on her driveway.

He was immediately thrilled with the news, but he had been a fool because he entered the competition in his real name, and his mother, in his absence, had provided the lottery company with photos for the company's publicity. His mugshot and name and the fact that he bought the ticket at the airport would be seen widely on social media and in the press.

To add to his woes, his mother had also told the company that he now lived abroad, although she had had said where. Of course, his fear was that his win would become known to the police, who would make their own enquiries. Their first port of call would surely be his mother. He knew she would be unable to lie convincingly, or even at all. She would be pressed to provide his whereabouts and would oblige.

He was now the proud owner of a brand-new Bentley Continental GT that he could not access or had a need for. He asked his mother to get a friend to drive the car into her garage and leave it there until he gave her further instructions. He could only hope his win would not attract any undue attention.

He decided to 'phone Rupert's mobile to find out when he could expect the paintings sale proceeds to be transferred to his bank account. The call failed. *Unknown number.* He attempted the call several times but received the same message. He 'phoned Rupert's office, but he was told he was away on business. He also 'phoned Rupert's home, but again there was no answer. Over the next few days, he called Rupert's home and office many times but failed to speak to him. He was beginning to feel anxious.

He told his mother that he would call her regularly. He had had the sense not to give her or Rupert his mobile number; only Charlotte had that. Perhaps that was a mistake, but how could he have avoided giving it to her?

A week passed. He had become familiar with downtown Nicosia and had met several interesting people, both locals and Brits that had moved to the city. He was beginning to establish a network of contacts that would give him the company he craved. He had started to drink, albeit not heavily, but he was desperate for a line of cocaine. He lacked the confidence to ask any of his new acquaintances where to get a stash not knowing how well his request would be viewed.

Most days, he spoke to Charlotte on his mobile and the relationship was blossoming. She was desperate to see him again. Dan had also met an attractive local Cypriot woman of his age - Dr. Savvina Constatina - a science lecturer at the University with whom he had started an affair. She was unhappily married and escaped home as often as she could to be with him in his hotel room.

Charlotte was due in two days and there had been a delay in him moving into his new apartment. It was likely he would get the keys during her visit. The conundrum he now faced was how best to manage the two women. During Charlotte's holiday fortnight, he had to devote all his time to her, which meant putting Savvina on hold. She was becoming increasingly attached to him and was hoping he would ask her to leave her husband and move into the new apartment. He was attracted to her, too, but the thought had not crossed his mind.

He decided he would tell her on the 'phone that he needed to return to the UK for a fortnight and would contact her the moment he returned. She was disappointed to hear the news but volunteered to drive him to the airport. For obvious reasons, he declined her offer.

Charlotte's flight was due in at 2.00 pm. He had agreed to pick her up and arranged for a taxi to do the return trip. The flight was on time. As she came through customs, she beamed at him. She was excited at the prospect of cementing their relationship, especially as she had already fallen in love.

He was pleased to see her too, but like so many things in his life, it was complicated. He wanted Charlotte, but he also wanted Savvina, despite the emotional baggage she came with, but in his current circumstances, the last thing he really wanted was to get embroiled in her marital issues. It was too complicated. What was *not complicated* was that he enjoyed sex with both women.

Entering the hotel with Charlotte, he headed straight for the elevator. FLOOR THREE. As a long-term guest, he had been given a suite for the cost of a double room, comprising a large bedroom, bathroom, sitting room with easy chairs, a sofa, a desk. He also had a balcony overlooking the street. It was more than comfortable. Just as he turned the key in the door, he remembered that Savvina had left some of her clothes in his wardrobe. He had planned to ask the concierge to store them during Charlotte's visit but had forgotten. He fumbled with the key, pretending that the door wouldn't open. They would have to go back down to the lobby to sort it out. Fortunately for him, Charlotte had mentioned in the taxi that she was looking forward to a glass of champagne upon arrival, so he took her to the bar and ordered a bottle of their best.

He went across to reception to get another key and in doing so, took the opportunity to speak to the concierge and ask him if he would immediately go up to his room, empty the wardrobe of Savvina's clothes, and store them for him. The concierge liked him and appreciated his dilemma. He returned to Charlotte in the bar, quite relieved.

This episode was a sanguine lesson for him. It was beginning to dawn on him that he had to be less complacent if he were to avoid being caught out on several fronts. He was beginning to settle into life in Nicosia as a local, but not as a murderer, a wanted man, a fugitive. Unless he paid attention to detail, he would slip up and only have himself to blame. This time, he had been lucky. The concierge would bail him out.

Twenty minutes later, with most of the champagne consumed, they made their way back to his room. On the way, he had an opportunity to exchange a smile with the concierge, who confirmed the clothes had been removed.

Charlotte flopped down on the bed. She was tired, but not too tired for Dan's overtures. After a few hours of intimacy, they showered and dressed ready for dinner. He had been in Nicosia long enough to have found all the best restaurants used by the locals rather than the tourists. Apart from the food and drink being more authentic, it was half the price. They had a wonderful meal and walked hand in hand for some time.

Dan had devoted time since first arriving in the city to discover its past and enjoyed telling anyone who would listen what he knew. He told Charlotte about the long history of Nicosia, from its first habitation during the Bronze Age all the way up to the civil war in the 60s and 70s. Charlotte was impressed. When they returned to the hotel room, they were both tired and slightly drunk. Within minutes, they were fast asleep.

It was just after 3.00 am when Dan stirred. He heard a key in the lock.

Since he had started to date Savvina, aware of the challenges she had in her marriage, he had encouraged her to use his hotel room as an escape, a refuge if she needed it. As the relationship had intensified, she visited more frequently, and he was pleased when she did. The hotel staff knew her well. She had her own key to his room. Of course, having announced he was returning to the UK for a fortnight, he had not thought that she would attempt to use his room in his absence. He was wrong.

The concierge who removed her clothes from his room was off duty, and none of the other staff were aware of his infidelity. Why would they be? He got out of bed naked as the door opened fully and the lights came on. He stood and faced Savvina as she walked into the room. They were both in shock. Why was he here? Hadn't he returned to the UK? And bearing that in mind, why was she here? If that had been their only dilemma, it could have been resolved in an instant and they could have been cuddling up in bed in no time, but the problem with that was Charlotte, who was occupying the bed.

Once again, he had not thought things through. It did not occur to him that Savvina would use his room whilst he was away. His investment in the relationship was not as deep as hers, partly because he had another woman in his life. Like Charlotte, though, Savvina had fallen in love with him, and in her mind, it was only a matter of time before she could divorce her husband and set up home with him. So, why wouldn't she use his room?

By now Charlotte had come to and was beginning to take in what was going on. She got out of bed. Savvina was highly strung, an emotional woman who was in marital turmoil, and the only person she felt she could trust was Dan. She demanded to know the obvious – what was this woman doing in his bed? Dan was used to getting out of scrapes. He had a certain charm, eloquence, and emotional intelligence that often smoothed his way through life, but even he was unable to magic up an explanation that was believable. Even if he had, he then faced the same challenge in reassuring Charlotte that what she was witnessing was only a figment of her imagination.

It was now nearly 3.10 am, when most guests would be asleep, but not now. For a few minutes that seemed unending, Savvina shouted and screamed telling him precisely what she thought of him. He chose to stay silent, as did Charlotte, who was eager to hear what she had to say. Dan thought it appropriate to put his dressing gown on.

"Well, are you going to say anything?" Savvina was in tears and not about to storm out and end the awkwardness. No, she wanted answers.

"I'm sorry..."

"Is that all you can say?" Having heard him dribble out an apology, Charlotte was also eager to know what he planned to say to her?

"And me, where does that leave me?"

It was obvious to everyone that he was having his cake and eating it, but just knowing the truth was only part of the equation: he had to pay for his deception and in full measure.

Surprisingly, at least to him, the two women sat down on the bed together, demanding answers to a series of questions as if they were jointly prosecuting the case against him. As he stood there, watching their lips move in slow motion and the pained expressions on their faces, his mind wandered back to Tanya and Susannah, another two beautiful women who had occupied space in his life. He had also let them down. In fact, now he thought about it, he had let so many women down over the years in his quest to provide sustenance for a growing ego. He had paid little if any genuine interest to the wants and need of others. He was selfish, self-obsessed, and lacking any meaningful social intelligence. As he returned to the present moment, he was able to distinguish the words that were coming from their lips, at least enough to understand that both were angry and unforgiving. Finally, each woman took comfort in the other's dilemma and jointly demanded that he got dressed and left the room. He obliged and went down to the lobby and sat silently, berating himself for his stupidity.

Why had he not seen the possibility that Savvina would use his room while he was supposedly back in the UK? What escaped him were the flaws in his character. He did not see what the women saw. To them, he was a man who used women for sex and to bolster a demanding ego. He had all the charm and good looks and was prepared to do and say anything to win them over. He was prepared to let them fall in love with him, knowing he would eventually let them down. They were, of course, exactly right.

Twenty minutes later the women came out of the elevator. It was almost 3.45 am. Charlotte had packed her suitcase and Savvina was demanding to know where her clothes were. He now had the humiliation of admitting they were in the concierges' lock up. He went to fetch them and both women left the hotel without saying another word to him.

He went back to his room to discover they had shredded all his clothes while he waited in the lobby. It was inconvenient, but a small price to pay for the anguish and hurt he had caused them. He slept soundly and woke just after 8.00 am. As he sat up, he looked around the room, seeking confirmation that it wasn't a dream. His torn garments provided the confirmation he was seeking.

CHAPTER 13 - DOM

Dan remained in his room for the rest of the day.

The feelings he experienced were nothing new to him. It was as though he were coming down from a *high* after taking a generous amount of cocaine. He felt miserable, depressed, reflective, and worried about his future. His 'phoned pinged. He expected it was a message from one of the women, but he was disappointed. It was the estate agent, confirming that his new apartment was ready for him and he could pick up the keys at his convenience.

Other than the clothes he had put on when the women asked him to leave the room, he had nothing to wear.

It was early evening, he was hungry, and the shops were still open, so he decided he would shop first and have a meal afterwards. His spirits were raised: at least he had something to occupy his mind.

He bought all the clothes he would need for the foreseeable future and dined in one of his preferred restaurants where he had taken both Savvina and Charlotte. The restaurant was busy and predictably noisy as people enjoyed the atmosphere. A woman he had met and chatted to in the street a few weeks earlier entered the restaurant and came over to him, so he invited her to join him.

His mood changed instantly. He was pleased with his purchases and was now enjoying dinner with another attractive women who was showing an interest in him.

Dominique Church was about five years older than Dan, an American originally from Illinois who now lived part time in Nicosia. She was an independent film maker specializing in documentaries and had travelled widely over the years. He was hugely impressed with her and demanded to know her life story. Not only was she interesting and different in so many ways from the other women he had dated she had a talent for storytelling which had him spellbound throughout the evening.

Then, it was his turn. First, she wanted to know why he had so many bags of clothes at that hour of the evening. Where did he live? How long had he been in Nicosia? What did he do for a living? Was he single? There was no stopping her. Her journalistic talents came to the fore.

Dan was able to repeat most of the story he had fabricated for Charlotte and he got away with it, but he also made the mistake of telling her about his time as a hostage. Of course, as a documentary filmmaker, she was fascinated. She wanted to know everything. He, too, was also a good storyteller, so they got on extremely well. It was obvious the international news about his encounter with the rebels had passed her by. Until recently, she had been filming in New Zealand, which was good news for him as she only had his story about the experience; but her inquisitive mind was not going to leave it there.

It was after midnight and they were last to leave the restaurant. He asked if she would like to join him for a nightcap back at his hotel room, having told her that he was about to move into his new apartment. She agreed to his invitation.

It was odd for him, but he felt strangely nervous asking her back. It had nothing to do with the fact that only hours earlier, he had said goodbye to two other women he was dating, but because she was a powerful, no-nonsense, tell-it-like-it-is type woman who he believed was his intellectual superior. She was knowledgeable about a wide range of subjects, possessing an in-depth knowledge in all the areas where he thought he excelled. He had met his match...and more.

The concierge was back on duty and astounded to see that he was accompanied by yet another beautiful woman: how on earth did he do it?

Dominique [Dom as she preferred to be called] was happily there for sex, there was no beating about the bush. Two hours later, and exhausted, she offered him a line of coke and his eyes lit up. At last, he had found a source of supply for his habit. As they took a second line, she was eager to return to his story about being held hostage. She wanted to know what had happened minute by minute; everything from the moment he booked the trip to his return to the UK and the media interest. In some respects, it was a cathartic experience for him because she allowed him to pour out the horror as it unfolded, and as a documentary maker, she lapped it up. Most people wanted the story's veneer; she wanted *the goriest details.*

What he omitted from his storytelling was Tanya's involvement; it was she who had originally arranged the safari and paid the deposit before he had murdered her and invited Susannah instead.

Dom was gripped by his story but would certainly have been even more so if he had told her the truth, the whole truth, and nothing but the truth. That would wait.

It was almost morning, and they were dog-tired. They had sex for a third time before she left, agreeing to meet later in the day at his new apartment. He slept for a few hours and had a late breakfast before picking up the apartment keys from the estate agent. The apartment was larger than he remembered. It was beautifully furnished and perfect for his new life.

A taxi transferred his worldly possessions to his new home, including the clothes he had bought the previous day. He later sat on the verandah with a beer overlooking the street below. The sun was dipping and there was a cool breeze.

He wondered if he would ever hear from Charlotte or Savvina again. It was more likely he would see Savvina on occasions as she lived only ten minutes away and frequented the places he went to. Despite what had happened less than twenty-four hours earlier, and aside from his arrogance and insensitivity, he had strong feelings for both women and would welcome the opportunity to date either of them again, although on balance, as Savvina was embroiled in a complicated and messy divorce, it was probably better he made no attempt to rekindle the relationship.

His 'phone rang. It was Dom. She would be 15 minutes. He was excited at the prospect of seeing her again. To him, she wasn't as physically attractive as the other two women, but she was attractive in so many other ways; a powerful woman who had carved out a demanding but hugely exciting life for herself. She was a straight talker who knew what she wanted and invariably found a way of getting it.

The doorbell sounded and he let her in.

After hearing his hostage story, she had spent the morning conducting her own research about him and knew he had not told her the whole story – in fact, in her estimation, he had lied to her. She had discovered the media footage of him being rescued from the bush, as well as his hospitalization in Kampala and his return to the UK.

She had also unearthed media stories about Susannah and her death at the hands of the rebels, as well as Tanya's death in the lab. She knew that he was about to be charged for her murder by the UK police but had absconded under an alias before they could apprehend him. She also knew about his Gauguin painting and even about him winning the Bentley. She pretty much had the full story, but not quite. What she wanted to know was whether he was guilty or innocent of Tanya's murder, and that could only come from him. Dan was shocked that she had uncovered so much about him in only a few hours. He emphatically denied murdering Tanya - whether she believed him or not was irrelevant, though. She was a filmmaker and had stumbled across what could potentially be the most dramatic story she had ever unearthed.

Her challenge was persuading him to allow her to make a documentary about his life. Confronted with the findings of her research, it was clear that back in the UK, all the dots had been joined up. The police had somehow discovered that the painting sold at Sotheby's was his. That could only have come from either Dr. Peter Braithwaite or Rupert. Of course, he had tried on several occasions to contact Rupert to find out when he could expect to receive the £4m from the proceeds of the sale and was now wondering if he had deliberately avoided him and told the police everything.

He was mindful that he had threatened to expose Rupert's part in the lab fraud if he failed to arrange interim accommodation in the Cotswolds and, of course, obtain his fake passport, so they weren't on the best of terms.

Would he ever see his money? He very much hoped so but had his doubts. With only half of the cash left from the £25,000 he had received from his inheritance he knew he could not expect to sustain himself financially for more than a few months at best. Then what?

The fact that Dom knew about the Bentley had to have come from his mother. Perhaps she had been interviewed by the police under caution and had let slip a good deal more about him than he would have liked. CCTV at Heathrow would have identified him despite having shaved off his beard and cut his hair. In that case, they would also know he had boarded a flight to Nicosia on a one-way ticket. He had naively thought he had found freedom in Cyprus; that he had escaped his past and could start a new life with a stack of cash cocooned from reality. The truth was that at any moment, the media or the Cypriot police could knock on his door and that freedom would crumble in an instant.

Dom wasted no time in telling him what he already knew. He had to get out of Nicosia; he was as vulnerable there as he would be if he were renting an apartment in central London. There was even the risk that Charlotte would be confronted on her return to the UK with the news that the man she had fallen in love with and travelled to Nicosia to spend a fortnight with on holiday, was in fact the infamous Dr. Dan Thomas – murderer. It was highly probable that she would then immediately report his alias and whereabouts to the police. It appeared everything was closing in on him.

In addition to her apartment in central Nicosia, Dom owned a run-down villa that she was refurbishing in Alona, in the Greek Cypriot area of the island about 45 km from Nicosia. She suggested he could stay there for as long as he liked until the drama blew over. However, she wanted something in return: his agreement that she could make an exclusive documentary about him.

Only a few hours earlier, he had been drinking beer on the verandah of his new apartment watching the sun go down and thinking that life was good.

He was daydreaming of putting the past behind him and building a new and exciting life with the millions he was due to receive. Now, with Dom's revelations, he was a wanted man on tenterhooks again, constantly looking over his shoulder and wondering how many days he had before he was apprehended, charged, and imprisoned for a considerable time, if not for life. He had no option but to accept her offer. Having only taken the apartment that day and paid six months' rent in advance, he was leaving. The few possessions he had brought into the apartment earlier were re-packed and put into the trunk of Dom's Land Rover and they were on their way. They spoke little during the hour-long journey. He had too much on his mind. He was weighed down with the plight he found himself in. How could it all have gone so wrong? He needed to 'phone his mother soon after he arrived.

Alona was a small enclave in the hills and Dom's villa was a distance from any other property, in a remote spot. The perfect hideout.

As they approached from the west, it looked derelict but as they pulled up alongside the property, it became evident how much work Dom had undertaken. She had an eye for design and possessed the practical skills to do almost all the work herself. Despite his malaise, he was impressed. He had already concluded from their first encounter that she was a dynamic woman with wide-ranging talents and an abundance of life experience. He now saw himself as a schoolboy and her, his boarding school matron. He would do as he was told. Having toured the villa and shown him his room, she offered him a line of coke to raise his spirits, which he readily accepted. Then another, and another. She wanted him relaxed and free thinking - there was no time to waste. As a professional filmmaker, she had mastered the art of extracting real life stories and knew it could be a lengthy process. Unlike most of her research subjects, she had slept with him and there was a level of affection, but unlike most of his conquests, she was not in love with him. At least, not yet. He was a project to work on and if she also had sex with him, that was fine too.

They had supper and drank vodka until they were both in a mental haze, chatting idly about their early lives. She was born in Illinois, the only daughter of a wealthy businessman who was shot dead in a bank raid. He had been there for a meeting, a random killing - she was nine at the time. Her mother remarried a few years later and within a year had divorced.

She subsequently died from breast cancer and Dom, at the age of nineteen, had inherited the family business, property, and various overseas assets. She was at college studying film making and drama at the time and was advised to sell the business and some of the other assets, freeing her up to live life. She had received almost ten million dollars.

Despite only recently having met her, Dan knew that there was no sense in holding back on his own life story – she already knew almost all there was to know about him. He wanted to tell his story, but in a way that was sympathetic to his cause, using his incarceration at the hands of the rebels as a valid reason for his actions and his fleeing the country, not a sensationalist piece that would grab headlines and vilify him. They agreed in their mental haze they would be totally honest and open with each other, and that she would aim to tell his story faithfully. Of course, he would need to bend the truth in an exaggerated way if he had any chance of winning over his detractors, including the police.

The rest of the evening and night flashed by and neither had much recollection of what happened. It was mid-morning when they woke in the same bed. The sun had been up for some time and it was already hot. As Dom prepared food, he called his mother. The signal was poor in the hills and the broadband was almost non-existent.

The moment she answered the 'phone and knew it was him, she broke down in tears.

He had told her before he left Rupert's Cotswold cottage that he was leaving the country, fearful that he would be charged with Tanya's murder but claiming his innocence. Of course, she believed her son. If he said he was innocent, then he must be innocent! Then, after he had left the country, all hell broke loose, and she was inundated with the police and media demanding to know where he was and what she knew. She found out about the sale of the painting at Sotheby's, which he had omitted to tell her. Upon his instruction she had asked a friend to park his Bentley Continental in her garage and not tell anyone that it was there. She had done as she was asked, but it was one of the first things the police had found when they searched her house.

The last thing he wanted was his mother to bear the brunt of his transgressions, but he could do little about it. She tried to persuade him to give himself up and return to the UK, and if he was innocent of Tanya's murder as he claimed, he should have nothing to worry about. She was right - that was precisely what he should do if he were innocent, but he wasn't and was convinced that the police now had enough evidence to prosecute him. He ended the call promising to stay in touch.

They finished breakfast. Dom needed to return to Nicosia to carry on her work editing the New Zealand documentary she was making. Unlike Tanya, Susannah, Charlotte, and Savvina, her thinking and decision making were not clouded by love or infatuation.

No, she was level-headed, and her foremost ambition was to make his documentary, which would be the highlight of her career to date, with the objective of making her an award-winning film maker. She liked him. She enjoyed sex with him. She found him quite interesting but would be prepared to sacrifice him on the altar of ambition at the drop of a hat.

Before she left, she gave him a generous supply of cocaine. She was a regular user, so this was a natural thing for her to do. She wanted to ensure her prize asset wouldn't be discovered so gave him strict instructions on where to go and where not to go locally if he felt he needed to escape the villa to maintain his sanity. She had a moped he could use. There were also plenty of jobs to do around the property and he relished the idea of lending a hand to occupy his time. She had made it clear that she would carry on her life as normal and would not be staying at the villa with him. She would only visit occasionally until she had finished her current project. He was not to call her mobile unless there were an emergency; she would not contact him either. The freezer was full and would last him months if necessary.

He watched her drive away, then went inside to make coffee.

For the rest of the day, he did a lot of soul searching; he was worried about his mother and the stresses and strains to which she was being subjected.

He wondered if she would cope. He also wondered if Charlotte had stayed in Nicosia to complete her fortnight's holiday or returned to the UK to discover who he really was. He also thought about Savvina, and whether he would ever see her again.

More worryingly, he speculated about how close the police were to discovering his whereabouts and what chance he had of avoiding a long custodial sentence.

The only thing he could justifiably claim was that he was the legitimate owner of the proceeds from the sale of the Paul Gauguin painting, but the chances of getting his hands on that cash were remote. He pondered whether Rupert still had the money or whether it had been handed over to the police.

A week had passed, there was no word from Dom. Time passed slowly. He undertook some basic remedial work on the property but little else. As he had a generous supply of cocaine, it was a daily ritual that he would get high. One line of coke a day became three and occasionally four as he drifted in and out of an abnormal state of awareness. His addiction was taking root, so much so that he was unable to tell what time of day it was and how he had spent his time.

Another week passed without seeing anyone at all. He was on the verge of a breakdown and he knew it. He had no choice but to try and ween himself off his daily fixes if he were to survive. He had been on the edge after murdering Tanya but had proven then that he had the will power to *get clean,* at least for a period. It wouldn't be easy though.

Fortunately, his salvation arrived. Dom drew up in the courtyard. He rushed out and held her tightly as though she were a long-lost lover; she was slightly taken aback by his emotion. He cried non-stop for ten minutes. Dom was a much stronger character than he was, and she knew his mental state was due to an over-indulgence of cocaine and that it had been a mistake to leave it for him. They went inside. The villa was extremely untidy, and it was obvious he had been high most days. She was unsympathetic as she could control her use of the drug. He was clearly an addict. It wasn't an easy conversation to have with him, but she made it clear that she was removing all the cocaine from the villa and that he would need to *get clean* and remain so if he were to continue to stay there. It was a wake-up call for him and he agreed.

Over the next few days, the relationship eased albeit he suffered withdrawal symptoms. They walked and talked early in the mornings and she set him some specific tasks to undertake to occupy his mind.

She would be away again for a week to complete her latest project. Upon her return, she would start on his story in earnest.

Dan had put on a brave face during their time together. He was experiencing withdrawal symptoms worse than he had ever known but concealed them as best he could. He was desperate for a fix but knew she had taken his stash when she left. He could have turned to vodka as a substitute but thought better of it. The following few days were the worst he had experienced as the drug worked its way through his system.

He suffered panic attacks several times a day and believed that the police had surrounded the property and were about to break in. Gradually, as the week wore on, and Dom was due back, he had made sufficient progress to conceal his vulnerability.

For almost three weeks, he made no attempt leave the boundary of the property but that day, the day before she arrived back, he took the moped out to explore the local area. Foolishly, though, he forgot to check how much fuel was in the tank and six miles later, the engine petered out. It was baking hot. The sun was beating down and he had no protection. He was wearing shorts, a t-shirt, and sandals that had already caused blisters on his feet. Now, he had to find his way back to the villa while pushing the moped up several steep hills. It was an impossible task.

Fortunately, his luck was in. A local farmer driving a tractor took pity on him and stopped. He spoke in the local dialect and quickly worked out that Dan was English and offered to take him and the moped to where he was going. As they approached the driveway leading up to Dom's villa, the farmer indicated that he knew the property and its owner. He was sure he had seen Dan's face before, but he wasn't sure where. This sent a shiver down Dan's spine. It was obvious his photo, perhaps of a *wanted fugitive,* had been featured on a Cypriot news station. He thanked the farmer for his kindness, put the moped in a shed, went inside and poured himself a large vodka and turned on the TV.

The chances of him tuning into a news channel and seeing his picture alongside the words *Murderer* were highly unlikely, but that is precisely what happened.

It was reported that a British citizen – Dr. Dan Thomas – travelling under the alias of Roderic Charles, had travelled to Nicosia, and as far as the authorities were aware, he was still on the island. A British woman who had travelled out to be with him for a holiday, not knowing his real identity, had argued with him over another woman and returned home only to discover that she was dating a murderer.

He was horrified. A few days earlier, he had thought he was blending into everyday life in Nicosia and that the prospect of starting a new life with all the money he would ever need was on the cards, but now everything was closing in on him, so much so that even the local farmer thought he knew his face. It surely wouldn't be long before the farmer put two and two together and made four. It was highly likely that he would then report his sighting to the local police and in no time at all, he would be detained. Dom had thought the villa would be a refuge for him but that was no longer the case. Not only could he not stay there much longer he had to leave the island if he had any chance of freedom. Dom had told him not to call her, but he felt compelled to. She was aware of the media activity around him but still thought he was safe at the villa until he told her about the farmer. She agreed he would have to leave there before the end of the day, or they would both be in the firing line.

There was no way she would trade her own freedom for the sake of making a documentary about his life story, no matter how many awards she might win.

CHAPTER 14 – IN HIDING

She left her office in Nicosia immediately and arrived at the villa in just over an hour. During her journey, she had thought long and hard about what to do with him. She was too embroiled to abandon him like a stray dog; after all, the farmer knew her and thought he had seen Dan's face somewhere, so he would twig sooner or later, and the police would be alerted. She considered the options open to her. The idea of making a documentary film about him excited her, so the last thing she wanted to do was to give up on the project at this stage. That meant she had to help him find another refuge.

Dom was well connected and knew a man who held a private pilot's license and fortunately, owned a twin-engine four-seater plane. He had transported her and her crew on several occasions to middle eastern locations. He liked Dom, and from her encounters with him, she knew he was not risk averse. Without consulting Dan, she called him and asked if he would be prepared to fly the two of them to an airfield in Beirut, Lebanon. She had people she knew there who could hide him for the foreseeable future and with her connections, it would be a great place to plan and make the documentary. She offered the pilot $50,000, believing she would make enough money from the production to justify the cost. In any case, she was wealthy enough to afford to part with the cash even if she were wrong. The pilot – Christos Kostas – wanted to know who she was planning to get off the island so quickly.

She had been hoping to avoid the question; Dan was hot property and she thought it might put him off. Fortunately, though, the money was enough to win him over.

It was agreed that the three of them would meet the following morning at 8.00 am at a private airfield, where his plane would be waiting for them.

She explained her plan to Dan, who was hugely impressed that she had made the arrangements so quickly. They both concluded that it was too risky for him to spend another night in the villa. She knew a cave in the hills nearby and took him there with the few possessions he had. She would pick him up in the morning at 6.00 am.

It was nearly 9.00 pm when there was a knock on her door. Standing before her were three local policemen. They had been tipped off by the farmer that a man matching the description of the British murderer had been dropped off with a moped at her villa earlier in the day. She invited them in and gave them the opportunity to search her property. They declined, believing she was telling the truth. They encouraged her to leave the property for the night for her own safety in case he returned. They were confident they would find him. She was exhilarated after they left - it was just the excitement that she thrived on. How wise she had been in taking him to the cave. In contrast, Dan spent a cold and miserable night and enjoyed no sleep at all. When Dom arrived to pick him up, he was more than ready, they sped off to the airfield. By the time they arrived, the pilot had moved his plane to a quiet part of the airfield and carried out all the mandatory safety checks.

They were given clearance for take-off and fifteen minutes after boarding, they were in the air heading for Beirut. Dom told Dan not to speak to the pilot and provided a mask for him to wear, which concealed his face. The less the pilot knew about him the better. The flight took an hour and twenty minutes. There were few people at the airfield when they arrived. People travelling from another country ordinarily needed to go through a procedure for customs and immigration, but security was lax. They walked away unchecked.

She had arranged for a Lebanese man to pick them up and he was waiting for them as they landed. He had no idea who his passenger was and cared even less. Dom spoke to him in Lebanese as they drove off in his rusty Russian-made Moskvich car that was anything but roadworthy. As they got into the car, Dan smiled at her. Her plan had worked; he had escaped justice once more.

Dom had covered the aftermath of the initial Beirut conflict in her filmmaking some years earlier and knew the region well. They would be staying on the east side of the city, the most damaged area following the Lebanese civil war. It was a multifaceted war that had lasted from 1975-1990, killing well over 120,000 people. According to estimates over 78,000 people remained displaced in the region but over a million had made their exodus from Lebanon during this time, leaving Beirut a shell of its former self.

The architecture of Beirut had been the envy of the Middle East prior to the conflict, but almost all the buildings were now damaged beyond repair and those that still stood did so in constant danger of collapse.

It hadn't deterred the poor and destitute from occupying them, though: there was nowhere else to go.

As they drove away from the airstrip and toward Dan's new home, at least for the foreseeable future, he had no idea what lay in store for him. Dom's so-called *friends* that had agreed to house him were no more than people she had met in the street while filming one day. She offered to pay them if they would take him in until he could be moved somewhere more permanent. Of course, desperate for cash, they agreed.

His new home was on the third floor of a partially destroyed block of flats accessible by concrete stairs that were exposed to the elements. The flat itself had three bedrooms, two of which were undamaged and watertight. There was a kitchen partially exposed to the elements; after a wall had collapsed into the street, a small sitting area, and one tiny bathroom which they all shared. Dan would be living with a family of six, including four children aged between 3 and 9.

Unlike Dom, who was accustomed to war zones and living rough, he was a novice. This was all new to him. Even though he was a murderer on the run, an international pariah, a wanted man, he felt a fraud. In his mind, he didn't see himself in that way. Yes, he had throttled Tanya, but it was not a premeditated act. Rather, it was an accident that had happened in a moment of rage and one that he regretted deeply.

How he had come to be hiding in Beirut was the stuff of fiction, and that was why Dom had taken such an interest in him.

Having given the family some money to take care of him, she returned to Nicosia the same day, in the same light aircraft in which they had arrived. It was important to her that she maintained her presence there so as not to raise any further suspicion. She had been visited by the local police at the villa and had got away with it. For the next few weeks at least, she had to maintain a profile in the city and be seen at the villa to create a sense of normality. She had plenty to occupy her time including scoping out her plans for Dan's documentary.

Dan was given the bedroom where the window had been blown out by a rocket or mortar bomb. Most of the summer in Beirut was steaming hot and while thunderstorms and heavy downpours were rare, they were not unusual. A particularly bad storm would flood the room in an instant. There was certainly no need for air conditioning. He surveyed the scene, and his heart sank as he took in the inventory: a single bed with a well-used and badly stained mattress, a single, greasy pillow with no pillowcase, and a torn scarlet red blanket that had probably covered many a dubious body and was in desperate need of a wash. The floor was partially covered in a threadbare rug and dust was everywhere. This was so different from the four-star hotel he had left after his encounter with Charlotte and Savvina back in Nicosia, and more like the shack in which he had been imprisoned and held hostage by the rebels in Africa.

The children were not inquisitive of his presence at all - the room had probably been rented out on many occasions to dubious guests.

No one in the family spoke English and Dan's Lebanese was of course non-existent. He was lonely but not alone. The clothes that he had bought on his shopping expedition in Nicosia where he had met Dom that fateful day were there, ready, waiting to be worn as he opened his suitcase. As he pulled them out one by one, he knew how ridiculous he would look wearing them in this environment where the men were dressed in the same sand-dyed robes. It was still dangerous in Beirut, especially for westerners who were known to be kidnapped and held ransom.

Before leaving on her return journey to Nicosia, Dom had told him to spend as much time as he could with the family in the flat and to avoid going out.

Looking around him, he wondered how long he could maintain his sanity cooped up in this way.

Over the next few days, the family made no effort to engage with him other than providing a small amount of inedible food and water. The children spent their waking hours screaming or shouting at each other as their mother tried to pacify them. He rarely saw the man of the house. The shared bathroom was disgusting as the sewage system had failed years earlier; make do buckets were in use and left open, attracting flies. The place was filthy. He had at least managed to pack a toothbrush, toothpaste, a flannel, and a bar of soap, so for a limited period, he would be able to maintain a level of hygiene. Whenever he attempted to clean his teeth, he gagged. The smell in the room was overbearing. The family bathroom was a hell hole.

On the fourth day, he knew he had to escape the mayhem. He had spent the previous three days since arriving lying on the bed, trying to avoid breathing in the filth from the pillow, and trying even harder to block out the noise that persisted from dawn to dusk throughout the rest of the flat. He went through his unpacked suitcase and found the only items of clothing that would give him the best chance of blending in. A brand-new pair of blue Levi's and a pure white t-shirt. He got changed without attempting to wash; the thought of a visit to the bathroom made him feel nauseous.

Despite having been in the flat for four days, he had barely exchanged a glance with his hosts. He walked out of his bedroom and into the sitting room, paused, and nodded at the man and the woman. His appearance was enough of a sight for the children to stop screaming momentarily as he opened the door and walked down the three flights of stairs to the outside world.

They watched him walk away from the building and wondered where he was heading. He wondered the same thing. The sun was high in the sky and sat majestically in an uninterrupted, vivid blue sky, and it was hot. The war had not only wreaked havoc on the city's building infrastructure it had also upended the road system, so much so that the once-thick tarmac layer that had provided a flat surface for people and vehicles to travel on was almost gone. What was left served no useful purpose: roads were now sandy dust tracks incapable of accommodating any vehicles.

His presence on the street did not go unnoticed. Even though he had chosen the least controversial of all his new clothes, he attracted attention. As people sat crossed legged in their robes outside their decaying properties, drinking and talking, they looked up and fell silent as he passed. It was as though he were an alien who had just descended from a far-off planet. He desperately needed exercise and to be away from the hullabaloo and smell of the flat, but he was reminded of Dom's advice to stay off the streets. He walked cautiously, taking in the environment wondering how long it would be before she returned to take him somewhere else, anywhere but there.

As he walked on, he became accustomed to his celebrity status and the comments aimed at him in Lebanese. He didn't know what they were saying or thinking although he had a pretty-good idea. A young boy threw a stone at him that caught him on the arm. It was clear he wasn't welcome. Other children gathered and they, too, hurled stones at him. He had little option but to run away from them. As he did, they followed him, shouting and gesturing. Eventually, he gained enough distance from them and they gave up pursuit.

He had been on the streets for about twenty-minutes; he was breathing heavily and sweating profusely. It was clear he had to return to the flat using another route if he were to avoid another conflict with the children.

Taking a right turn at what had previously been a crossroads, he headed west along yet more dust tracks with decaying buildings on either side. Dogs barked and old men spat at him as he passed. Despite the temperature and exhaustion after running, he tried walking at a tidy pace, eager to get back to the relative security of the flat. Less than an hour earlier, he couldn't get away fast enough. The irony was not lost on him.

As the dust track twisted and turned, he lost all sense of direction and was disoriented. He stopped and looked around. Everywhere looked the same. Crumbling or fallen sand-stone buildings on either side of dusty tracks. Noticing that he appeared lost, a middle-aged man came out of his home and waved to him. Fortunately, he spoke English. "Where are you going...?" Ordinarily, Dan would provide an address in response to such a question and, hopefully, the directions received would take him to where he wanted to go. In this case, though, he had no idea where he was staying.

He didn't have an address and he couldn't adequately describe the flats as they all looked alike.

"Oh, you speak English! Thank you. I'm not sure where I am headed. I don't have an address..." The man smiled broadly. "There are no addresses anymore. We know places by family names. Who you stay with?" Rod could only recall a name that Dom had mentioned to the driver of the car that took them to the flats. "Khalil. I think his name is Khalil..." The man muttered to himself. "Four children and wife?" The likelihood was that there were several 'Khalil's with four young children in the vicinity, but it was enough of a description for him to nod and smile.

He started to give him directions in Lebanese before switching to English, but Dan was already confused. It was a pointless exercise. The man saw the dilemma and offered to walk him there. Dan was relieved and thanked him over and over as the man smiled politely. As they walked and talked, the man asked Dan what he was doing there. He quickly fabricated a story that he was a documentary filmmaker. The man, Ahmed, was an academic and had worked as a lecturer in biological sciences at the university until the government had stopped funding the faculty. He had no income and the prospects of working again in the discipline or indeed doing anything else were zero. Of course, this was Dan's real area of expertise, although, having declared he was a filmmaker, he thought it unwise to confuse his real background with his now-declared profession. That said, he asked Ahmed several science-based questions to which he was delighted to have the opportunity to respond. It stretched his mind and provided a respite from the everyday, tedious life he now suffered.

In no time, they had arrived at a block of flats Ahmed thought were occupied by the Khalil family, and he was right. The two men shook hands.

Dan was desperate not to lose contact with his newfound friend. They agreed to meet again in two days' time, exactly at the spot where they would now part company. Dan was elated he had an English-speaking companion and could not wait to see him again. He hugged Ahmed tightly, as though he were a long-lost friend, and the man reciprocated.

As he entered the flat once more, the foul smell hit his nostrils and the persistent shouting and screaming of the children returned to his ears. The parents sat staring vacantly at the children: they had little else to do. They looked up briefly to acknowledge his return. His clothes were now covered in dust and would stay that way. At least their appearance better reflected the world outside.

Despite his predicament, he was remarkably upbeat. Meeting Ahmed had cheered him up. His time imprisoned by the rebels in Africa had taught him the value of relationships. Ahmed was his link to humanity and the outside world, at least the world outside his bedroom in a block of flats that could literally fall to the ground at any moment.

A few days later, as planned, he met up with his new friend.

Ahmed lived on his own. His wife and children had died some years earlier, although he seemed reluctant to talk about the incident. He welcomed Dan into his home and provided a meal and a drink. Dan had been living on meagre rations that were barely edible, so an authentic Lebanese meal was a welcome reprieve. He had lied to Ahmed by telling him that he was a documentary filmmaker and, knowing little about the profession, he was keen to focus the attention on Ahmed and his work instead. It was an awkward conversation at first because Ahmed was eager to hear about Dan and he, too, wanted to steer the conversation.

Dan was used to storytelling, so to sound plausible, he told Ahmed that he concentrated in science-based filmmaking and that he had started out his career as a research scientist. Problem solved. They were on a wavelength.

After several hours of non-stop conversation, he left Ahmed's home. He wished he were staying there and dreaded having to return to the flat. He had thought of asking if he would be interested in having him as a lodger for a few days until Dom returned, but decided it was inappropriate as they hardly knew each other. He was also aware that he had no money with which to pay him.

The two men met on several occasions over the next few weeks.

Dan was becoming anxious because Dom had not contacted him, and he was unable to connect with her either as his mobile 'phone was unable to pick up a signal anywhere in the area between the flat and Ahmed's home. This new friendship was a life saver. The conversations helped maintain his sanity when he would ordinarily have gone into a downward spiral and craved cocaine. He was eating little at the flat, relying instead on the generosity of his new friend to sustain him. Ahmed never asked for money for feeding him, despite his own lack of funds.

He had been in Beirut for almost three months and had still received no word from Dom. Eventually, his host family stopped feeding him and asked him to leave.

As far as he could make out, the money that she had given the family to look after him had run out; they, too, had lost contact with her. He wasn't their friend nor a family member; they had provided a room for a stranger in return for cash, so when the cash ran out, he had to leave.

He immediately packed his suitcase and departed, knowing there was only one place he could go. He knocked on Ahmed's door and was welcomed in. He had no choice but to whip up a story, part truth part fiction, to persuade him to take on a paying lodger with the promise of reimbursement. Ahmed liked him, so it was an easy decision to make. The backstory he told him was that he had been filming in Nicosia and was abducted for a ransom and all his equipment was stolen. He managed to escape but needed to get off the island for his own safety. A female friend knew the Khalil family who had agreed to house him for a fee, but the money had run out and they had asked him to leave. Within a few weeks, he would receive funds, pay Ahmed for his generosity, and return to the UK.

Ahmed was relaxed about the arrangement as he enjoyed Dan's company and the opportunity to talk in English about a range of subjects in which they had a shared interest. He was unaware that the following week, Dom had travelled out to Beirut to see him. She had been embroiled in work stuff and had not been able to contact him by 'phone. She went to the Khalil home and was told that he had left, although they failed to mention that they had asked him to leave for lack of payment.

She had handed over $300 and they agreed to keep the room for him, should he return. They knew it was highly unlikely; it was money for old rope.

Dom was concerned. Had he been abducted? She knew enough about him to know that he would not have gone far on his own accord. The last thing she wanted was to lose out on the opportunity of covering his story; potentially the most rewarding project to date, both professionally and financially. She had already scoped out the production. She spoke Lebanese and she also knew the city of Beirut well, and as a documentary maker, research was her forte, so she set about trying to track him down. She made local door-to-door enquiries and several people confirmed sightings of a westerner in jeans and a t-shirt but had no idea where he was. After two days of door knocking without success, she decided to return to Nicosia, planning to make the journey again within a fortnight to carry on the search for him. They were both unaware that her enquiries had led her to within 300 meters of Ahmed's home, where she would have found him.

A month passed and she had no time to return to Beirut. Dan had no money to pay Ahmed for his hospitality, despite having said he would be returning to the UK within a few weeks. Ahmed remained relaxed about the arrangement.

By now, Dan had picked up a little Lebanese, enough for him to engage in stilted conversation.

He gained confidence in being out and about and walked the streets unaccompanied most days, always wearing his stained blue jeans, whiteish t-shirt, and trainers that blended in perfectly with the local terrain.

On one of his walks, he got talking to a local man who mentioned that three weeks previously, he had spoken to an American woman who was looking for him. He described Dom perfectly. She had given him her card and asked him to call if he saw him. This was the breakthrough Dan was so desperate for. The man agreed to call her number on his 'phone and she answered immediately. He handed the receiver over to Dan and they spoke for several minutes. There was tension between them. Dan tried to contain his anger at being abandoned in a filthy hell hole with screaming kids and feckless parents who had almost starved him to death. Dom, though, was used to hell holes and living rough.

She even quite liked it, thinking she would rather spend her life in squalor and filth if she were able to make great documentary films than live in a 5-star hotel. They were different, and they knew it.

It was in her interests to offer an apology rather than snap back at him, though. After all, she had gone to the trouble of rescuing him from being apprehended by the police and would have nothing to show for her efforts. She mumbled an apology and confirmed that she and her pilot would fly out in two days. She would give thought to whether he should remain in Beirut to make the documentary or travel into Syria, where she also had production contacts.

Dan mentioned that he had been told to leave the family's home and had moved in with a local he had befriended. He wanted her to bring some cash so that he could pay him for his troubles. She agreed. He returned to Ahmed's home and told him his good news that his contact from Nicosia would be arriving in Beirut in two days and would pay him what was owed before he left. Despite Ahmed's precarious financial situation, he had never seen Dan staying with him as a way of making money. He enjoyed his company and the opportunity to speak English and discuss science. They had become good friends and he would miss him. Ahmed's life as a lecturer at the university had given him pride, status and, relatively speaking, a good living, but all that had gone and would not be returning. He was now like so many other people in the region: poor with few prospects of working again, at least certainly not where his knowledge and intellect would be put to good use. He was inquisitive, he had a good mind, and given the opportunity, would prove to be an asset wherever he worked.

Ahmed was disappointed that his friend would be leaving him and asked him if he would do him a service. *Was it possible he could travel with Dan as a translator?* He spoke nine languages including several Middle Eastern dialects. He was a competent writer and would be willing to assist Dan with his documentary filmmaking. Dan could see how desperate Ahmed was to improve his life and with his command of so many languages, he could see his value.

Dan explained that Dom would be making a documentary about his life and he would insist that Ahmed travel with them as a production assistant. If Dom wanted to make the film, she would have to accept Ahmed as a part of the team.

Over the next two days and in anticipation of Dom's arrival, Ahmed arranged his affairs so he would be able him to travel with them. Both men were excited at the prospect of working and travelling together and celebrated with a special meal. Dan had been cocooned in Beirut from the outside world and, importantly, news about his fugitive status. He had no idea whether he was still front-page news or yesterday's story gone cold. He hoped it was the latter. He worried about his mother having to deal with the media and police and was desperate to speak to her again.

He took the opportunity on a walk to call in on the man who had connected him with Dom on his 'phone and asked him if he would allow him to call his mother in the UK. He, like Ahmed was a poor man and could ill afford to make international calls but agreed. Dan promised he would be brief. His mother's phone rang for some time before she answered it. "Hi Mum, it's Dan, how are you?" She was taken aback to hear from him. Her voice shook and he knew something was wrong. She tried to reassure him she was okay, but he pressed her. He quickly learned she had had a nervous breakdown, unable to cope with the media harassment she had received after his news story broke.

He was her only surviving relative and she wanted him home, she couldn't cope alone anymore, and begged him, not for the first time, to give himself up. The emotion was intense. He promised he would return but only after a documentary which was being made about him exonerating him from Tanya's murder was aired, otherwise, he feared he would not get a fair trial.

The conversation lasted longer than he had anticipated and could see the old man fretting at the likely cost of the call.

CHAPTER 15 - SYRIA

Two days passed and there was no sign of Dom and her pilot. She had already demonstrated how unreliable she could be, perhaps she had finally abandoned him? Ahmed was restless, too. This was a life changer for him, and he kept seeking reassurance from Dan that his contact was coming.

On the fifth day, when he had almost given up hope of ever seeing Dom again, she arrived at Ahmed's home on foot. Her pilot had to return to Nicosia but would return the following day to take them to Syria. He spoke to Dom about Ahmed and his insistence that he travelled and worked with them. At first, she was adamant he could not go with them, but she could see Dan was uncompromising. Either Ahmed joined them, or the project was off. After speaking with Ahmed for a while, she concluded he would indeed be extremely useful to her; his language skills would come in very handy.

They had a meal cooked by Ahmed and they talked. She gave Dan an update on his status back in the UK and in Nicosia, where the media were still featuring his story.

She had made several enquiries, and as far as she could gather, the Cypriot government believed he was still somewhere on the island and had agreed with the British government to return him once he was captured. They had no idea he was in Beirut. That at least was a relief, but he knew his freedom, if you could call it that, was predicated on him staying under the radar long-term. He also had his mother to worry about. There was no way he could return home.

In the morning, Dom explained they would travel to the airfield and meet up with the pilot.

They would fly to Harasta, Syria, where they would be transported to a large safe house she knew well. It was an ideal location for making the film and was safe from prying eyes. Harasta, in the eastern Ghouta area, had been a rebel-held city for some of the civil war despite its proximity to the government-controlled capital. Government troops had bombed the area as recently as 2017. The property they would be heading for itself was damaged at the time.

Dan was concerned. Why did they need to leave Beirut? It had to be better than Syria? But Dom no longer had trustworthy connections in Beirut and feared it would not be long before his whereabouts would be discovered, and he would need to go on the run again. She reassured him that the house they would occupy was protected by armed guards and was the perfect hideout. She had reliable contacts there and already had production equipment stored at the house from the time she had spent covering the civil war enabling her to make his film.

In comparison to the family flat he had shared with the screaming children, this was a palace. It was enough to win him over.

Dan was reminder just how undeniably attracted he was to her, not like the other women that had come and gone in his life, out-and-out beauties who he loved for their bodies rather than their minds. She possessed great intelligence and depth and had a different kind of beauty: she was special. He thought of her as a female Indiana Jones; a tough, no nonsense, fearless adventurer who strutted her stuff around the world with tentacles that penetrated deep into the heart of where the action was. Her focus was her filmmaking, close relationships were unnecessary, sex was enjoyed when she had time for it. She had no boss to report to - she simply could not work for anyone other than herself. She decided who, what, where, when, and why in her life. It was the only way for her. To her, Dan was a commodity she happened to have sex with. It was his story that she would fashion into a documentary that she hoped would gain a worldwide audience, sitting on the edge of their chairs, desperate to watch. She was wealthy in her own right, so her life wasn't geared around making money for a living. She was free of all that subservience. Her living did make her money, at least some of the time, but it mattered not at all.

Before leaving in a taxi for the airfield, Dom had given Dan enough money to pay Ahmed and the old man whose 'phone he had used to call his mother.

He went to the old man's home and gave him $100, which was far more than he had expected or wanted. He smiled broadly.

As they set off, Ahmed cried uncontrollably in the taxi. He was leaving his Beirut, a city that had changed so much over the past decade, as had his life. It was once a beautiful city with a proud history, dynamic and culturally desirable, attracting people from around the world. It had been a business hub for the Middle East and a safe city, a place to raise and educate a family at one of the world's best universities, where he had lectured. It was now a shell, a hitherto war zone that had been promised a rebuild but never got it. Buildings and basic infrastructure had crumbled along with people's lives. It would never be the same again.

They boarded the waiting plane and flew out and over Beirut, where they had a bird's eye view of the catastrophic damage that had been served on this once beautiful territory. Not one building, it seemed, stood intact; what were once major roads, arteries meandering in and out of Beirut central, were now completely collapsed and crumbled, rubble piled high against once proud and architecturally magnificent buildings. The sight of his city in such chaos brought the tears flooding down Ahmed's cheeks. The sound of the engine and the ear defenders they were wearing concealed his grief.

As they left Beirut and the Lebanese border behind them, they entered Syrian airspace.

Dom's pilot had been transporting her and her production crews around the world for some years and knew how to navigate his way in and out of countries undetected. They landed in a makeshift dust strip in Harasta. The pilot would immediately make the return journey to Nicosia as they journeyed in a waiting car to the safe house. Dom spoke several languages but not Syrian. Ahmed was fluent. He had immediately proven his worth.

It was early afternoon when they arrived in a remote spot. From the outside, the entrance to the building looked derelict. It had been shelled many times and any passer-by would assume it was uninhabited.

A crumbling stone wall surrounded the property, and what was a courtyard and magnificent fountain in the distant past was now overgrown. The car took them through the front entrance to the rear of the property, which was undetectable to onlookers, if any ever visited. Dom took Dan and Ahmed inside, where they were in for a surprise. They entered a large, octagonal marbled floor hall with its walls adorned with Islamic art. Ancient sculptures were strategically placed for the greatest visual impact. Several rooms branched off from the hall and an imposing spiral staircase led upstairs. Dom showed them around. The property had been occupied by both government troops and ISIS, who had left without warning. The original owners, a wealthy Syrian family, were shot dead at the start of the war. Locals had then unofficially taken over the property.

Dom had used the place for filming in the past and had paid well for the privilege, so she was treated with dignity and respect. Whenever she was there, locals provided armed security. It was perfect. The men were shown their bedrooms. Dan's breath was taken away. It was a huge room, elegantly and expensively decorated with a King-sized bed covered with fine linen. There was also a bathroom the size of a living room, with a gold bath that apparently worked, a gold basin, and a toilet. Dan smiled. He had his own bathroom and could clean his teeth without gagging. After soaking in the bath for some considerable time, he got dressed in a robe that was provided in the room. His now battered suitcase containing the *western style clothes* he had bought in Nicosia were even more inappropriate in his current surroundings.

Dom, Dan, and Ahmed met in the dining room for supper. Once again, Dom took charge. She suggested that they all relax for the next few days, which would give her time to get prepared for making Dan's documentary. She had already assembled footage of material that she could use to represent the various locations in the UK, Cyprus, Africa, Lebanon, and now Syria as a part of his story.

Ahmed was surprised that Dom was taking the lead and not Dan. Wasn't he the filmmaker? He said nothing, though. He, too, was on a journey of discovery, a journey that would deliver him a better life, at least that's what he hoped.

After supper, the three of them sat talking for several hours. Ahmed was eager to find out more about Dom and her work and travels.

She was a liberated and wealthy American who had the strength of character and talent to build a career she loved. Her ability to make award-winning documentaries was in part due to her courage in taking on challenging and often dangerous assignments in parts of the world to which few would want to travel. She researched and reported on what people wanted to see and hear in situations that many in her profession were reluctant to risk their lives to pursue. She had a way about her. She was engaging and looked people in the eye when speaking to them. She was also an animated storyteller.

Ahmed himself had his own story to tell, from the other side of the camera lens. His early life had been one of privilege. He was born into a professional Lebanese family and had four siblings. He was educated privately in Beirut before attending universities in Canada and Germany. Like Dan he was a scientist – biological sciences – but rather than work in industry, he chose academia, eventually becoming a lecturer and then a professor at Beirut University. During the war his father, mother, and all his siblings were murdered. If that were not enough to contend with, his wife was abducted and never to be seen again, and his children were taken from their schools and assumed murdered. The war had wrecked the Lebanese economy and infrastructure and as a result, he lost his job and had never been able to secure gainful employment again. He owned his own home but had little else.

Dan's story was a little more difficult to recount, largely because he was unable to remember what he had told Dom when they had first met and got high on cocaine.

Whatever he had told her was sufficient for her to want to make a documentary about him, but he couldn't take the risk of fabricating yet another story that may contradict his earlier tale. Certainly, he was not about to confess to Tanya's murder. He declined to spill the beans on the basis that his story would eventually be told through Dom's camera lens.

They were all extremely tired and went to bed.

Dan wondered if he should invite Dom to spend the night with him but thought the better of it. Similarly, she made no attempt to invite him to her room.

It was almost 2.00 am and Dan was in a deep sleep. He awoke suddenly to find Dom arousing him. It was just the tonic he needed.

The following morning, Dom was up first and had already had breakfast and coffee before Dan and Ahmed appeared. Dan had had the best night's sleep in a long time despite his lengthy sexual encounter with Dom. The comfort of a real mattress and freshly laundered linen and comfortable pillows was a godsend. As he woke, he was in a positive frame of mind. Why wouldn't he be?

The sun had been up for a few hours and it was already scorching hot. Unlike most of his sexual encounters, where the previous night's activity was acknowledged by affectionate exchanges in the morning, this was different. Dom didn't do emotion, or at least that's how it seemed to him.

It appeared that their intimacy in the middle of the night, to her at least, was a function of being human, to be enjoyed in the moment and then put aside. No strings attached.

The conversation Dan had had with his mother a few days earlier worried him. The stresses and strains she had endured since it was first discovered he had allegedly murdered Tanya, had resulted in her having a nervous breakdown. He was her only living relative and he had to make sure she was okay. In truth, he knew he needed to see her, to be by her side, but that was an impossibility. He asked Dom if it were viable from their location to 'phone her. As with most things, Dom was able to help. She had a mobile 'phone that miraculously picked up a signal wherever she was in the world. He dialed the number. Unlike the previous conversation, when he had felt pressured to keep the conversation short for fear of running up the old man's bill, this time he could take his time, also knowing the call from Dom's 'phone couldn't be traced to him. The 'phone rang for some time before she answered it. Her tone was hesitant, doubtlessly from fear that it was yet another call from the media or police.

"Hello, who's calling?"

"Hi Mum, it's Rod...sorry, Dan." His mother was unaware of his alias.

"Is that you, Dan? The line's not that clear..."

"Yes...yes, I'm here. How are you?" She tried to put on a brave face, but it was obvious she wasn't coping. Apparently, Rupert had contacted her asking if she knew where he was.

That suggested to him that he was keen to speak to him, perhaps about the money he had been holding after the sale of the painting, or perhaps because he had been put up to it by the police.

After ending the call, he 'phoned Rupert on his home number. It was evening in the UK. Rupert's butler answered the 'phone and having established who was ringing, passed the call over.

"It's Dan...are you there, Rupert?" Rupert hesitated to respond, which concerned him. He tried again.

"Rupert, it's Dan."

"Yes, Dan, where the hell are you? You know that the police are keen to charge you for Tanya's murder, and there's been a media frenzy about you absconding." Dan wondered just how much he should reveal; could he trust Rupert?

"Yes, I know. I've been told."

Rupert persisted. "It's a bad line, there seems to be an echo...where are you?"

"I can't say right now... I've tried to contact you but couldn't get through. Have you wired the money to me as we arranged?" He was aware the police had found out about the sale of the painting and that Rupert had been the recipient of the funds, but he wanted to hear Rupert's take on events.

"You have no idea what's been going on back here in the UK, Dan. I assume you are still out of the country?"

"I am."

"The police have been investigating my business and personal affairs and I, too, have been dragged into your story. I'm bloody annoyed if you want to know the truth..."

"What's happened to my money?" It was perhaps an indelicate and blunt question under the circumstances, but he had to ask it for the second time, hoping Rupert still had it in his account. Rupert was agitated.

"Did you hear what I just said, Dan? Your antics have put at risk my investment business and damaged my personal reputation. The money is the last thing you should be concerned about!"

"I'm sorry, Rupert, but it hasn't been easy for me, you know. I didn't murder Tanya: you do believe that don't you?" There was a hesitation before he responded.

"Dan, I don't know, and to be honest I don't bloody care whether you killed her or not, but I can tell you that the first opportunity the police get, they will charge you with her murder." Dan paused, wondering if he dared to ask about the money for a third time, but he was agitated that Rupert would make such a cavalier statement and felt he had to bite back.

"So much for compassion. So, you care little whether I murdered her or not? That's fine. I can tell you're pissed-off, Rupert, and I'm sorry, but I didn't plan all this..."

Rupert tried again. "Dan. Tell me where the hell you are?"

"It doesn't matter, it won't help if I tell you. Suffice it to say I'm not where I would like to be."

"And where would you like to be, Dan?"

"Back home. My mother is unwell, and I need to support her. She has been through an ordeal too. Look, I know under the circumstances it's a lot to ask, but can you wire my money to the Swiss account I gave you?"

Rupert laughed. "You're either crazy or deaf, perhaps both? No, I cannot *wire you the money!* The police sequestered it soon after they raided my office and home, assuming I was your accomplice. This is all a bloody mess, Dan, so you can understand why I am pissed-off as you put it. Give yourself up and face justice, that's my advice." And with that, he slammed the 'phone down.

Dan knew the state of play. It had been an outside chance that Rupert still had his £4 million, let alone the will or capacity to transfer it.

What he had not factored in was the fallout Rupert would suffer from him absconding. He wondered if they knew that his passport in the name of *Roderic Charles* had been acquired by him? It seemed not to matter now; the whole affair was a fuck-up and he had only himself to blame. He had never been content with an ordinary life. He was intelligent and had the gift of presence – people wanted to be around him. He had his pick of girlfriends and the freedom to use his God-given talents to better the world as a scientist, but he had let his ego get in the way. He envied the lifestyle and trappings of wealth that others like Rupert had, irrespective of what they had had to do to achieve their goals. He wanted it all, and now.

He wondered how he could hope to fix things in a way that would enable him to return to the UK, be with his mother, and not face a lengthy prison sentence.

If he went to jail, his life would be wrecked. If he remained outside the country, what kind of life would he have on the run, especially without money to sustain his existence?

The call to Rupert had clarified a few things in his mind. He had been swept along by Dom's idea of making a documentary about him, but what would it achieve other than to flatter his already oversized but punctured ego? It certainly wouldn't provide evidence of his innocence. The police would have all the evidence they needed by now to successfully prosecute their case and at the end of the day, he was guilty and there was no escaping that truth. This was a vanity project. He liked the idea of being a celebrity, an actor in a movie, a star performer, but it just wouldn't work in freeing him to live a *normal life*, and he knew it.

He spent the rest of the day trying to think of a way of telling Dom that he no longer wanted to be involved in the project, but at the same time, persuade her to help him to fund his return to the UK to face justice. His relationship with her was best described as sexually matter of fact; there was no conventional bond between them. Yes, he admired her enormously, and found her an attractive woman, but he wasn't in control of the relationship as he had been with all his other conquests over the years. She was formidable in so many ways. He was not her equal, her boyfriend, or her lover. He saw himself as a helpless child being given instructions on how to get through each day.

Ahmed had spent most of the day chatting to Dom. They seemed to bond intellectually, better than Dan had with her. They had a different type of chemistry. It was evening after supper when they were finally alone, and he saw an opportunity to speak to her. At first, he told her how impressed he was with her as a human being and his affection for her. He envied her dynamism and all that she had achieved in her career. She listened to him unemotionally - she had had men say similar things over the years, but their overtures always washed right over her. She was not flattered in the least, she wasn't looking for adulation, nor was she looking for a long-term lover, friend, or confidant she could turn to in a crisis. She was a disruptor of life and sought out crises, which is what drove her from one day's challenge to another, living on the edge as she went. Dan could see that he could be talking to an android more than a human being, but in a strange way, that made him admire her even more. Her life wasn't oriented around soaking up people's affection to navigate her way through life; she represented a pioneering spirit and an attitude that everything wasn't just possible, but expected, especially by her.

In the end, he just came out with it. He could no longer see the point in making the film about him - it would serve no useful purpose if his aim were to get back to a *normal life*. Of course, she had no idea what a *normal life* was. She saw things differently.

From her perspective, it was just another in a long line of projects, but she genuinely believed this one, done well, would really put her on an international stage of award-winning documentary makers; not for the prestige and adulation that she would receive, but to satisfy her inner craving for perfection in her art form. It would be justified recompense for all the hard work over the years. Their objectives, to say the least, were incompatible.

She was surprised by his decision and disappointed. She tried to change his mind and gave a compelling justification of why he was wrong, an *academy-worthy performance*. Of course, her production would vindicate him; he would be a free man and able to return, if he chose, to his everyday life but with celebrity status and all the trappings of stardom. She knew it was those ephemeral things that motivated him.

What she was unaware of, although she may have suspected, was that he was indeed guilty of Tanya's murder, so no documentary, no matter how compelling, would get him off the hook if the evidence were there to prove his guilt. She offered him a line of coke and, as she had done before, she then offered him another and another. In no time, they were both high. Ahmed, who was tired, had gone to bed some time before. In his euphoric state, Dan thought it best to confess everything to Dom about his life, the lab, the data theft, the murder, the inheritance and subsequent sale of the painting, and the Bentley. Of course, she had conducted her own research and knew almost everything he was telling her already, but he had never actually confessed to murdering Tanya before.

It was an admission that failed to shock her; in fact, she had prepared a section for him to confess on camera in her production plan.

Having both drifted off into a drug-induced state, it was after midnight when they came around sufficiently to drag their bodies to bed. Sex followed, although neither of them would remember when morning came.

It was almost 3.30 am when they were woken suddenly. Ahmed had come into Dan's room and was surprised to see Dom lying in bed next to him. But it wasn't that revelation that perplexed and agitated him. He had been sleeping lightly but had awoken when he heard two of the armed guards talking together. As a master of languages, he understood what they were saying. It was obvious to him they were ISIS informants and had alerted a local group that an American woman and a British man were staying at the house and were planning to make a film. They were accompanied by a traitor, a Lebanese man who was assisting them. The ISIS fighters had decided they would raid the house, take the American and Brit hostage, and skin the traitor alive and decapitate him in front of his friends. The assault would take place at midday.

Ahmed was shaking as he told them what he had heard. He had witnessed his entire family killed in front of him in Beirut and knew the ISIS fighters would do as they said they would do, and skin him alive. This was not just an expression - *skin him alive* - it was a method they used regularly to bring about an excruciating death.

As Dan listened to Ahmed, he was reminded of his experience in Africa at the hands of the rebels and of Susannah's dismembered body being dumped in front of him along with Chuck, Ashley, and Stefan.

Dom was unemotional and had clarity of mind. She thought for a moment and came up with a plan. She had a contact in Iraq, an American Colonel named David Dillon, who was a serving officer in special ops. It was the middle of the night, but she called him anyway; they had no time to waste. She explained the predicament they were in and asked if it were possible for him to arrange a rescue mission. It was now 3.50 am local time. ISIS was planning their assault at noon, so that gave him eight hours to assemble and helicopter his team to the property's geographical coordinates that she had given him. He agreed to help.

Colonel Dillon knew that threats of this kind made by ISIS were invariably actioned. He also knew, in theory at least, the eight hours he had were sufficient for his team to prepare and get there early enough to surprise the enemy, and with luck, avoid an ugly battle and a serious amount of bloodshed. His mission was not to confront and wipe out the ISIS fighters, it was to rescue Dom, Dan, and Ahmed unharmed with no casualties. Dom was instructed as to how they should protect themselves leading up to the crack team's arrival. The advice was precisely what she had in mind.

The American presence in Syria was an ambiguous one. Early in the Syrian war, the US government had chosen not to back President Assad, who they believed to be a dictator accused of genocide.

Instead, they backed local militia, a ragtag group of quasi militants and disgruntled ex-government soldiers who were attempting to overthrow the government but lacked the necessary armory and infrastructure. The Americans made both available, but the strategy failed miserably. The militia were not an organized, disciplined, coherent group, they lacked leadership, and spent a good deal of time fighting each other. It was a strategic mistake that allowed the Russians to step in.

The Russians under Vladimir Putin saw an opportunity to fill the vacuum left by the Americans and agreed to back the Syrian President, not with ground forces, although there were some supposedly in an advisory capacity, but with their formidable air power, bombing rebel targets at will.

This resulted in the death of tens of thousands of innocent civilians in the process. ISIS, too, saw an opportunity in a fractured country to expand their caliphate; other rebel groups eager to grab power also got involved, making it a cocktail of confusion, an impossible war for anyone to win. Having made the decision to keep at arm's length, the American government watched impotently as the country tore itself apart. Dom's contact – Colonel David Dillon - was part of a covert group that operated under the radar in Syria, and this was the perfect operation for them...if they could get there in time.

Whenever Dom used the property, she arranged armed guards for protection, knowing that ISIS had once operated in the area. What she failed to factor in was that some of the guards would also be on the ISIS payroll.

It was always difficult to know who to trust in a country ravaged by years of war, where everyone lived on the edge in fear of their lives. She always kept at least two semi-automatic rifles, two pistols, and plenty of ammunition at her disposal at the location when working just in case she needed to defend herself and anyone accompanying her.

With the knowledge that ISIS would attempt an assault at midday, she had considered escaping in advance but knew it wasn't a viable option. They had no idea how many of the guards were working for ISIS and any attempt to leave, even on the pretext of going to the next village, would be seen as suspicious.

Dan's bedroom was the most secure of all the rooms available to them, so she decided that was where they would barricade themselves in. They would take food and water from the kitchen and the weaponry into the bedroom during the morning in preparation for the assault. Dom's leadership was comforting both for Dan and Ahmed. Within the hour, she had arranged for the Americans to rescue them and assembled the weaponry, food, water, and other essentials necessary for a long siege. She reassured Dan privately that ISIS wanted them as hostages to extort a ransom and they would not be harmed. Despite her power, influence, and enviable leadership skills, he was not convinced.

Ahmed was a concern. He was of no value to ISIS. The Lebanese wouldn't pay a ransom for him, and he was likely poor anyway. No, he would be a plaything, someone they believed had turned his back on his faith and sided with the enemy.

His rightful destiny would be an early and excruciatingly painful death; they would relish the chance to skin him alive and serve up his head to Dom and Dan on a platter.

It was a waiting game. They had breakfast and remained downstairs, making themselves visible to the guards so as not to cause alarm. At 11.15 am they would, one by one, go upstairs to Dan's bedroom and barricade themselves in.

Dom took the opportunity to explain how to use the weaponry. She and Dan would each take a rifle and Ahmed would have the pistols and be responsible for supplying them with additional ammunition if it were necessary.

11.15 arrived and within a couple of minutes, the door had been barricaded using Dan's bed and a large chest of drawers. They knew it would provide little protection if their assailants wanted to get into the room, but they had to make it as difficult as possible. After his hostage experience in Africa some months earlier, Dan knew he could not endure the mental and physical pain of being held hostage again, and had pledged, albeit only to himself, that he would shoot himself rather than be taken. ISIS were renowned to be the most ruthless of the rebel groups and the most imaginative in ways of torture.

They remained silent, listening out and, in Ahmed's case, praying the Americans would arrive on the scene first. Dom knew the armed guards she paid were simply locals that happened to have rifles and were keen to earn money, but at the first sighting of ISIS, they would likely flee. They were not trained soldiers.

Midday came and went. It was just after 1.00 pm when they heard a few rounds of gunfire outside the perimeter wall and reached for their weapons. The men looked at each other, fearful of what was about to unfold. It went silent again before they heard an approaching helicopter; it was the Americans, but they weren't out of the woods yet. Gunfire could now be heard inside the building around them, including a call from ISIS to give themselves up. Ahmed provided a translation. They froze to the spot, guns held high. The helicopter had obviously landed as a wave of automatic gunfire rang out close by. It was now a matter of timing. Would ISIS capture or kill them before the Americans were able to free them?

Having searched all the rooms upstairs, the fighters were now outside the barricaded door. An aggressive voice demanded they give themselves up or they would be killed. They banged on the door with their rifle butts but there was no answer. Dom had instructed the men to move to the back of the room at an angle to avoid being directly hit by gunfire. By now, it was clear to their assailants that the American soldiers were approaching the building in force and it was only a matter of time before they would be fully committed to a skirmish they would likely lose.

They had to get their hostages now if they had a chance of bartering their way out of the situation. They fired their semi-automatic rifles at the door, which blew open in response, offering little resistance. There was a pause as two armed men with assault rifles tentatively peered into the room. Dom stepped forward and returned fire with her semi-automatic rifle, killing them instantly. With great courage, she then advanced through the remains of the door and onto the landing, where she opened fire on two other men who were trying to figure out their options. They hadn't anticipated coming up against hostages offering such resistance. One of the men dropped to the floor injured, while the other joined four or five others in racing down the stairs, only to be confronted by the American soldiers who had entered the building. A shoot out ensued and within twenty minutes, what was left of the ISIS gang had fled, leaving several dead. The American forces liberated Dom and the men and within the hour, they were being helicoptered away from the scene toward Karbala, south of Baghdad, a secret hideout the Americans had occupied for two years. After being checked out by the medical team and rested overnight, they were flown out the following day to a US military base.

CHAPTER 16 – THE DOCUMENTARY

Over the next week, the American rescue mission was beamed around the world and the international press were given the opportunity to interview the colonel, Dom, Dan, and Ahmed.

Dan knew his exposure in the media would uncover his real identity. In his first interview, he thanked the Americans and the crack team led by Colonel Dillon for rescuing them. He openly admitted who he was and took the opportunity to tell the world's media that in time, he would return to the UK to face justice for the crimes he was accused of. He was an innocent man.

Dan's story that had occupied the headlines in the British and international press some months earlier had died down, but his appearance on US TV reignited their interest in him. How on earth had he managed to flee Britain to Nicosia as a wanted man, then ended up in Lebanon and Syria at the hands of ISIS? This was a big story, and everyone wanted to hear about it.

Now he was in the USA, the British government issued an application for his extradition. Dan's original story that Dom had wanted to make a film about him had even more resonance, if only she were able to undertake the project.

She was portrayed by the media as a trailblazing hero, responsible for saving their lives. It was just the attention she wanted to promote her career as a serious filmmaker, and she was free to go about her business.

Dan's extradition proceedings would take time meanwhile, he would have to conform to restrictions on his movements. It was agreed with the authorities that he would stay at an apartment that Dom owned in New York and would report to the police weekly.

Ahmed had applied for asylum in the US, and it was likely that because he had helped an American citizen escape ISIS, he would have his application fast-tracked. He, too, would be allowed to stay at Dom's apartment in New York.

Dom's offer to accommodate the men was not merely a kind gesture; she had a motive. She wanted to make the documentary she had planned for Dan, but now, after their recent exploits in Lebanon and Syria, she wanted the story to include Ahmed. He had nothing to lose and everything to gain, so agreed to be involved. Dan changed his mind again and agreed to participate. Having told the media that he would return to the UK to face justice for Tanya's murder, he had limited time left in the US. She had no time to waste.

Before they were flown away by helicopter after their rescue from the house in Harasta, Dom had made sure she took with her all the production material she planned to use for the documentary, so all was not lost. She had also stored material on the *Cloud,* which would enable her to patch the film together. The missing parts of the jigsaw were the scripts for the interviews with Dan and Ahmed, and the interviews themselves. Once she had that *in the bag,* she would edit and finish the production. She was well-connected in the media, so negotiating licenses for broadcasters keen to air the production would be relatively easy. She knew there would be significant interest in her work, which would then give her the status she was looking for.

Being wealthy in her own right, the substantial royalties that would predictably follow, were of little importance. It was agreed that Dan and Ahmed would be the beneficiaries of the proceeds. It was a generous gesture and both men were humbled by her offer.

For Ahmed especially, if he were granted asylum, and there was little to suggest the contrary would be the case, the cash would give him a fresh start in a democratic country. He had lost everything, and no amount of money could replace his family, but to know that he would have enough to get by would be a comfort.

Dan's circumstances were different. He was a millionaire back home, at least in theory.

There was no dispute that he was the rightful owner of the Paul Gaugin painting that was sold at auction, and the £4 million proceeds were his. Trying to recover the money might prove challenging, though, so the royalties from Dom's documentary would come in handy to access lawyers if he needed to go to court over it. His likely trial for Tanya's murder would also come at a cost.

While Dom pressed on with the project, Dan and Ahmed took time to discover New York. Ahmed had spent time lecturing in Toronto some years earlier but had never been to the Big Apple, nor had Dan. While Dan and Ahmed had *science* as a common denominator in their friendship, they were different people culturally. Ahmed was eager to visit science museums and art galleries while Dan wanted to visit jazz clubs and get high.

They indulged each other over a two-day period, although Dan made no attempt to secure cocaine in Ahmed's presence, knowing he would disapprove. He would wait to see if Dom might supply him, which she duly did.

Dom worked from dawn 'til dusk on the production until it was Dan and Ahmed's turn to be interviewed. Their stories would be weaved into the final script before filming. The interview was easy but emotional for Ahmed. He was able to recount his life story, both the highs and lows, without thinking. Memories of his family and their tragic deaths were indelibly printed on his mind. He was able to tell the truth and nothing but the truth. For Dan, though, the interview was much harder. He had told so many lies in recent months and to so many people, including Dom, that it was difficult for him to remember what was real and what was fantasy. He was high when he confessed to Dom that he had murdered Tanya, but had she remembered? He speculated she hadn't.

Before starting the interview, he reminded her that he had told the press that he would return to the UK to face justice, but that he would vigorously defend his innocence. He was insistent that the portrayal of him had to be of an innocent man who had been through so much, but to her it was a lie that would dilute the impact of the story. She had in fact remembered his confession, and she reminded him. She made it clear she wanted the truth and his confession on camera. It would be the dramatic centrepiece she was looking for.

When the reality of this hit Dan, he knew had to change tack. He had agreed to be a part of the project, but was he really prepared to admit on camera that he was guilty of murder? If he were, it would contradict his earlier press statement about his innocence, and would no doubt confound a lot of people, including the police and judicial system back in the UK. He had also sworn to his mother that he was innocent; how would she take a confession of murder having already been through so much? Was he prepared to go straight to jail for murder when there was the possibility, albeit a faint one, that he would be found innocent at trial and set free?

He decided in an instant that there was no justification for him admitting the crime on camera and told her so. Yes, it suited Dom. She would have a scoop, but he would be signing up to a long custodial term. If she were to make the documentary, she would have to find another way of telling his story or leave him out. Of course, without him, there was no story, so they reached a compromise.

He would admit to having a row with Tanya in the lab on the evening prior to her being found dead the following morning. He would admit that the row became physically sexual, and that in the heat of the moment, he had put his hands around her neck, but he did not kill her. After they had had sex, he left for home and she'd stayed on to complete her work. The first thing he knew about her death was when he arrived at the lab the following day for his shift and the police interviewed him.

It was a lame, makeshift, ill-thought-through story that she was prepared to run with. It had sex and drama at the centre of the story and would create intrigue in the mind of a watching audience. Was he guilty or was he innocent?

For Dan, a scientist with a logical brain - albeit not always a rational one - it was a mistake. His latest version of the storyline was riddled with holes. Months had passed since he murdered Tanya and been interviewed by the police, not once, but on three occasions. He had forgotten what he had told them in those recorded sessions. He had lied so often, telling different versions of the story to so many people, including his mother, that even he didn't know what to believe anymore. His admission on camera to this latest fabricated story would only serve to further prejudice his case back in the UK.

It was a Thursday morning when Dan received notification from the US authorities that he would be extradited to the UK in 30 days. Dom was hoping the documentary would be aired in the USA at the very least, before he was sent back to the UK to face arrest, but she was behind with the final edit and feared she would not meet the deadline. She had secured over $3million in advance royalties for an unfinished production and believed the final total could be as high as $5 million. In contrast with Dan's news, Ahmed was joyful, having received notification from the authorities that his asylum application had been granted and he could stay in the USA.

After working tirelessly day and night, she finished the film two weeks prior to Dan's departure.

Dan and Ahmed were given a preview, and both gave their blessing to the final product. It was a dramatic and compelling documentary and despite Dan's fictional story, which would no doubt be torn to shreds back in the UK, it portrayed him in a sympathetic light. He acted his part like a true pro. CNN had scheduled the hour-long documentary to be screened at prime time, two days before Dan's extradition.

The three of them sat in Dom's apartment in New York and watched what millions of Americans were watching at the same time. After it had aired, Dom received a flurry of congratulatory phone calls and messages.

CHAPTER 17 – THE TRIAL

When the day arrived, Dan readied himself for his flight back to London. A government car would arrive at 10.30 am at Dom's address and he would be accompanied from that moment until he was handed over to the British authorities at Heathrow. He embraced Dom and Ahmed. They had shared a great deal together. Dan and Ahmed had developed a special bond. Ahmed's kindness in helping him in his time of need in Beirut had demonstrated a degree of generosity and kindness that went beyond what could ever be expected for a poor man who had lost everything in life, including his family. He was a man of faith, an honest and diligent man who had devoted his life to the betterment of humanity, and Dan was fortunate to have met him.

Dan's relationship with Dom was best described as *clinical.* As has been said, she liked Dan, and she enjoyed having sex with him and sharing a line of coke, but she was unemotional about him personally.

She was not infatuated; she was not in love with him...but she was by his story. She was wired differently from other people and that's why Dan was attracted to her. He had spent years dating women, and aside from Tanya, who was cerebrally bright, his other conquests were sexually motivated. Given the opportunity, he would likely commit the rest of his life to a relationship with Dom, but that was never going to happen.

As he left the apartment, he was mobbed by the media, eager for a quote, any quote, but he said nothing. Both Dom and Ahmed had promised him that they would visit him in the UK come what may.

Dom had got what she wanted - a potentially award-winning documentary that would propel her into the higher echelons of film makers - but would Dan get what he deserved a lengthy prison sentence?

Overnight, the US media had widely reported on the documentary's content. As Dan sat in his seat on the plane, at an altitude of 33000 feet, heading to London without knowing his fate, he watched a live interview with Dom and Ahmed on CNN. Dan's story and his performance on camera had won the critics over. The overwhelming view was that he was an innocent man that had been through hell, but the biggest challenge of his life lay ahead in proving his innocence to a British jury.

It was a bumpy landing at Heathrow. Dan looked out of the window. The sky was almost black. There was a strong wind, and it was raining hard, the perfect metaphor for the storm that awaited him.

He was ceremoniously handed over to the British authorities and was immediately arrested and taken into custody. His time in Nicosia had aged him, the stints in Lebanon and Syria even more so. His youthful good-looks sparkling eyes, and bravado had gone. He looked older than his years and there was a pained expression permanently etched into his brow. He had lost weight and his clothes were too big for him. The new wardrobe he had bought in Nicosia for his new life of freedom were probably still lying in the Syrian bedroom amongst the spent automatic rifle shells.

He was taken to a detention center the following day for a medical check-up and a few days of rest and recuperation before his first formal interview got underway. The British media had now had an opportunity to review and comment on the documentaries airing in the US, and the overwhelming reaction was now entirely different. Far from hailing him as an innocent hero, he was seen as a murderer, a pariah who should face the full force of the law. Fortunately for Dan, he had not seen the media outpouring. His mood had already changed since touching down at Heathrow. He was exhausted. The months of stress and drama in his life had finally caught up with him and he became depressed and unable to sleep or think positive thoughts. In fact, he couldn't think about anything other than his impeding fate. He had no energy at a time when he needed all he could muster to defend his case.

If he had been innocent, the mammoth uphill challenge he now faced would have been easier to cope with. Telling the truth is never difficult, telling lies is full of unknowns.

In his mind, Dan knew all this. He was alone in a cell and had plenty of time to plan his strategy and get the story straight in his head, but which of the stories he had told would he rely on to get him through? He tried to think back to when the police had interviewed him on three separate occasions shortly after Tanya's death, and what he had said, but it was all a blur. It was too much to comprehend.

With so much incoherently rattling around in his head, he feared he would have a panic attack, as he had done when he was being held hostage. His mind wandered back, and he felt the pain and anguish of being tortured and seeing Susannah and the others dragged before him and dumped on the ground as though they were sacks of dead meat ready for animal feed. He could not recall a time in his life when he had felt so low and confused. His freedom was at stake, but his mind lacked the capacity to think straight.

Several days passed and he was advised that he would be interviewed under caution by the police the following day. He had a choice of hiring his own solicitor or being provided one by the state. A 'phone was made available to him and he used it to call his mother. She had seen the UK media reports vilifying him for Tanya's murder.

They had already made up their collective minds that he was guilty, aside from one newspaper, known for its liberal views, which argued that everyone was entitled to a fair trial. If he were guilty, he should serve his time of course, but they were concerned that his case was being decided by the media and could be prejudicial to him getting a fair trial, a point his lawyer would argue later.

Dan's mother had been harassed by the media ever since he absconded and she, too, was on the verge of another breakdown. He did all he could to mask his own fragility and reaffirmed his innocence. She wasn't prepared to ask him again if he had anything to confess, fearing he might tell her what everyone else appeared to know, that he was indeed guilty.

He was her only family member, and she desperately wanted all this to come to an end so they could both get on with their lives. In her heart, though, she knew she would never achieve the inner peace she desired.

After the call, Dan's mood changed for the better. He had lied over and over to his mother that he was innocent, knowing the reverse was true. He owed it to her to defend himself to the best of his ability. If he failed and was found guilty, it would tell her that her innocent son was being imprisoned unjustly. If he were successful in being acquitted, it would reaffirm his claim of innocence. It was all a charade, but in his mind, he could not bring himself to admit to a mother that loved him dearly that he was a murderer. Everything he would do and say from there on in would be predicated on that commitment.

Dan 'phoned Rupert. There was only a slim chance that he would have anything to do with him, but he was the first person he could think of that could help him with legal representation, or at least advice on who he should engage to defend him. After several attempts, he got to speak with him.

Rupert's position had not changed. Through Dan's actions, he had been embroiled in his back story and he and his business had suffered as a result. He took the call only to reassert that he wanted nothing to do with him or his upcoming case. He would not defend Dan in any way; instead, he would be acting as a prosecution witness if called. The passing of time had not healed any wounds. Rupert would be quite happy to see Dan incarcerated for a long time and for the media frenzy to die down enough for him to rebuild his tarnished image and get on with his life. The call lasted no more than 5 minutes, but it was sufficient time for Dan to get the message, loud and clear, that Rupert wanted nothing more to do with him. Of course, he had known he was on a hiding to nothing making the call in the first place, but he had thought it worth a try at least. As he sat with the 'phone in his hand after the call ended, he suddenly remembered he had a friend, Charlie Hagen: It was some years since he'd last seen him, but knew he was a practicing solicitor and a partner in a London firm. Of course, Dan's story had not passed Charlie by, but he was surprised to receive the call. They spoke for almost half an hour. Charlie's specialty was not criminal law, but he suggested one of his practice colleagues, Adam Spires, might be interested in his case.

He called Dan back later in the day and confirmed that Adam would represent him and recommended a barrister, Sir Conrad Spellman, who could defend him in court. Dan would meet Adam two days later.

Having established legal representation, his spirits were raised. Now, he needed to exercise his mind by trying to patch together the story he had told and compare it to the interview he had given to Dom for the documentary that had now been aired around the world.

If he had any chance of convincing a jury he was innocent, the story he fabricated had to be believable. It had to flow like silk, and he knew he could ill-afford to make contradictory statements that would give fodder to the prosecution and dash his chances of an acquittal. It was a mammoth task.

Adam Spires was about 45 years old and a senior partner in the law firm representing Dan. He had risen quickly through the ranks by taking on several high-profile clients, but none as high-profile as Dan. He was an astute lawyer with a forensic mind for detail. When he arrived, he wasted no time indulging in pleasantries, instead demanded an exhaustive account of Dan's story. He wasn't there to judge him or ask whether he was guilty or innocent of murdering Tanya. That was for jury to decide. What he did want was to assess was the credibility his story and whether it would stand up against cross examination.

Prior to the meeting, Adam had researched all there was to know about the case, especially Dan being held hostage and tortured at the hands of the rebels in Africa. His mental state would be a crucial factor in deciding if he was fit to take the witness stand in the first place.

Having established Dan's story, Adam believed they were ready for the police interview that had been scheduled for the following day. Dan was briefed on the protocol of the meeting and guided on what he should and should not say. Adam left and agreed they would meet in the morning.

Dan had a restless night. He kept reminding himself of the story he had created for himself based on his recollection of everything he had said previously to the police. It had been almost 5 months since he had first been interviewed by DI Ian Graham and he wondered if he would be interviewing him on this occasion, too. He hoped not.

He thought he would have more latitude in his story if it were someone fresh to the case.

It was morning, two hours before the interview, and Dan was nervous. Adam arrived early and they chatted for a while. He confirmed that he had spoken to Sir Conrad Spellman QC, who had agreed to act on Dan's behalf as his barrister. A preliminary meeting with Sir Conrad had been planned for the following week.

Dan had been arrested and detained upon arrival at Heathrow airport but so far, he hadn't been formally charged with Tanya's murder.

Of course, it was a foregone conclusion that the police would do so at the start of the interview, so it came as no surprise to Dan when they did just that.

Dan was not surprised to see the familiar faces of DI Ian Graham and DC David Finch when he entered the room. After they had charged him, they read him his rights. He would be interviewed under caution and the proceedings would be recorded. In contrast with Dan's demeanor, the inspector took great pleasure in welcoming him back. He had cursed his poor judgement allowing Dan to abscond before he could be formally charged. He fired a serious of questions at Dan straight off the bat, seeking to undermine his earlier statements about the events leading up to Tanya's murder, but Dan acquitted himself well. He stuck to the script. He had denied throttling Tanya, although in his interview for the documentary, he had admitted to the camera that he had put his hands around her throat during a row that led to a sexual encounter in the lab. Still, he had also emphatically denied killing her. He argued that he left the lab soon after and Tanya stayed on to finished up her work. Of course, the police had worked hard to gather additional evidence to charge him.

Having murdered Tanya and cleaned up after himself, he had left the lab, sure that the CCTV cameras were not in operation. He had been right. Unfortunately, the police had discovered that management had instructed a security guard to install several stealth cameras in the lab the day prior to the murder, as a prelude to rolling out wider CCTV.

CCTV had been delayed for several months until the announcement that a formula for the vaccine was in the advanced stages of development when it had been promptly fast-tracked. Coincidentally, the security guard and the manager had been relocated in the business soon after, and whilst the installations had been logged, no one else knew about the cameras until a forensic search by the police discovered their whereabouts.

After successfully answering the inspectors' questions, Dan was shown video footage taken from one of the stealth cameras. He was surprised that it existed. The police hoped this was enough evidence of guilt to successfully prosecute the case, despite the footage not actually showing the actual murder taking place. The lab was laid out in three sections. The camera in question covered the middle section where the lab technician's computers were situated - the computers from which Dan had copied the data. There was no sound, no date, and no time stamp on the recording and the footage was grainy, but it was evident that the two people in the recording were Dan and Tanya.

As Dan watched, DI Graham narrated the events on camera. "At this point, you can be seen sitting at one of the technician's computers." Dan knew he was downloading data onto his external hard drive, although it was not visible.

"Now, we see Dr. Waters entering the area after you have moved into her office, and it is clear from your reaction that you were surprised to see her. Now, you stand up, and point a finger at her and there is surprise that turns to anger in your facial expression. Next, you both leave Dr. Waters' office and we see you move toward her and put your hands on her shoulders as if to plead with her. Your anger clearly intensifies when she clearly refuses to agree to what you are saying. Now, you shake her by the shoulders, and she pulls away and walks off camera. You follow and this is the last image the camera caught of Dr. Waters. We believe that it is at this point, out of view, that you murder her, Dr. Thomas. Then, you appear back on camera a few minutes later in an anxious state and go over to one of the other computers. On three other occasions over the next 27 minutes of running time, you appear and disappear from the camera's view, then you collect your rucksack and are seen leaving the premises."

The inspector turned off the tape and turned to face Dan. The revelation of the footage had clearly left him spooked. Adam asked the inspector for some private time to discuss the video footage with his client and the inspector was happy to oblige, hoping Dan would change his mind and plead guilty.

DI Graham and Inspector Finch then left the room.

Adam was a smart and experienced criminal lawyer, and it was not his job to make judgements about a client's guilt or innocence, but he knew after his initial meeting with Dan that his story lacked conviction and authenticity.

Dan didn't need convincing that he had killed Tanya. He hadn't forgotten what he had done; quite the contrary, he had to live every day knowing he was a murderer, but as the days passed, the guilt had diminished. He became more able to live with his crime, manufacturing stories for his own and others' consumption. Ultimately, this strategy, deliberate or otherwise had the effect of removing him from reality.

Now, faced with that reality in black and white, he looked at Adam sheepishly. He knew the footage damaged his case and was expecting Adam to advise him to change his plea to guilty. Instead, he pointed out to Dan what the police already knew. The footage did not show him committing a murder. Yes, it showed that they had had a row and he had put his hands on her and shaken her at one point, but it was not enough evidence to convict him of murder. A jury may find him guilty at trial, but that was a battle his barrister would fight another day. Adam advised him to stick to his story that he had rowed with Tanya. Yes, he shook her, but after that, he packed his rucksack and left. This also tallied with his confession in the documentary that Dom had made.

DI Graham and Inspector Finch rejoined the meeting shortly afterwards, fully expecting him to change his plea, but they were disappointed. After the interview concluded, Dan was returned to detention. Having been charged with murder and having absconded once before, he was refused bail. The case would continue.

That evening, the inspector held a press conference announcing that he had charged a man with Tanya's murder. He named Dan in the process.

Dan was detained for four months before the case was brought before a jury at The Old Bailey in London. During that time, he instructed his solicitor to recover the £4 million pounds that the police had sequestered from Rupert after the Paul Gauguin painting had been sold at auction. There was no question that he was the legal owner of the painting when it was sold. 3 weeks before the trial £4.3 million was transferred into his bank account.

The media frenzy around the case did not die down in the interim. On the first day of the trial, all major broadcasters and media outlets were in central London, eager to catch a glimpse of the accused. Indeed, they were to remain there for the duration of the trial, which lasted seven weeks. During the hearing, Dan was portrayed as a highly intelligent but manipulative research scientist who was not content to use his skills to better mankind, as many had testified that Tanya did. He wanted wealth and power and at any cost. He had stolen data from his employer and planned to set up his own lab funded by a venture capitalist. At the point he sensed the police were about to charge him he absconded to Cyprus.

Tanya had got in his way and refused to go along with his plans, so he cold-bloodedly murdered her, leaving her body to be discovered by colleagues the following day. The video was shown to the jury by the prosecution as evidence of his intent to murder her, but this was shot down by Dan's barrister as circumstantial footage that proved nothing.

During the trial, Dan sat unemotional. Not once was he seen casting his eyes across to the jury, nor did he attempt to look at Tanya's family and his own mother in the gallery. Halfway through the trial, he was shocked to be told that his mother had died of a heart attack. He was bereft. He was permitted time, albeit shackled to an officer, to attend her private funeral. Details of her death were not reported to the media until after the funeral had taken place to avoid a media skirmish.

His mother's death hit him like a ton of bricks. She had been unwell for some months due in large part to worrying about her only son and the relentless media attention she had had to cope with. She had been unable to leave the house for fear of being mobbed. Dan had lied to her genuinely attempting to shield her from the truth that he was indeed a murderer. To her dying day, she had remained steadfast, believing wholeheartedly in her son's innocence.

After all the evidence had been presented by the prosecution and Dan's barrister had made the case for Dan's defence, the jury were sent out to consider their verdict. As Dan waited in his cell for them to return, he reflected on his life. His mother had died, and her demise had come too soon. He had never really known his father, who had served as an officer in the military but died in action when he was four years of age. His mother never remarried instead doted on her only son, doing all she could to ensure he had every opportunity in life, including a good education.

It was evident early on that Dan was academically bright, and she was proud when he went on to gain a PhD in Biological Sciences. Dan had everything any young man could wish for: intelligence, good looks, a socially amenable temperament, a good job, and enough money to enjoy a comfortable lifestyle. Of course, it was never enough for him. Something was missing in his psyche. Perhaps it was the father he never knew? A chink in his armor? His lack of contentment drove him to use people because he knew he had the presence and power of personality to do so. He used women to achieve sexual gratification, but rarely saw them as potential partners or equals. Relationships were difficult to sustain because he sought perfection in women - an illusory quality in human beings.

Commitment was always difficult for him. His desire for wealth and riches motivated him - in this instance to kill - believing these two commodities would make him happy. Another illusory concept. His fate now lay in the hands of twelve good people, democratically selected, who would determine his future life.

He consumed time in his cell thinking through the trial proceedings and all the evidence that had been presented. His barrister had done a magnificent job in defending him. He had used Dan's trauma from being held hostage and subsequently tortured to portray him as a victim not a criminal. Yes, he had a temper, and yes, he could be a bully on occasions, but he was not a murderer. There was no conclusive evidence that suggested otherwise.

The jury returned.

As Dan was brought back to the dock, he glanced at the jury for the first time and looked across to the gallery, where Tanya's family had faithfully sat throughout the trial.

Of course, his mother was not there, and he was thankful that she wouldn't bear witness to her beloved son being found guilty of murder and sent down.

The clerk of the court called for the foreman of the jury.

"On the count of murder in the first degree, do you find the defendant Guilty or Not Guilty?" There was a profound silence in the court. Dan looked once more at the jury and back to Tanya's family, then bowed his head. He knew it was all over. He had murdered her in cold blood in a fit of rage and he knew he deserved to suffer the consequences of his actions, cutting short the life of a beautiful young woman who had had so much to live for and had, at least once upon a time - loved him dearly. She could have been his long-term partner or wife and bore him children if he were not so burdened with the psychological imperfection that had led him to kill.

The verdict came in. "Not Guilty."

Dan raised his head in shock.

"On the second count of Manslaughter?"

"Not Guilty". If there had been silence prior to the foreman's utterance of the words *Not Guilty* on both counts, there was now an audible outcry of disbelief in the gallery at the jury's findings.

Dan stood motionless, scarcely able to believe that he had correctly heard the verdict.

The waiting was over; a jury of twelve had unanimously found him Not Guilty and he could walk free. The judge struggled to bring the court to order.

Dan was unaware that both Dom and Ahmed had been in the gallery for two days and had been there to hear the judge set him free. As he left the court with his solicitor, they both went up to him and hugged him. He was overwhelmed to see them. The media were out in force, eager to hear a statement from his solicitor.

"My client had protested his innocence from the start of this trial and a jury has found him innocent on all counts. My client is deeply saddened that his girlfriend, Dr. Waters, was brutally murdered and shares in the grief of her parents. He would now like the opportunity to put this sad affair behind him and move on with his life."

Dom had arranged for a private car to transport him away from court to a luxury hotel she had arranged for him in central London. She and Ahmed would join him there. That evening, he had dinner with the two of them. He was in a fragile state, torn between emotions of elation at being acquitted for a murder *he did commit* and feelings of anxiety that he could never put recent events behind him. Dom knew the truth. Ahmed did not. The jury had got it wrong on this occasion, as they sometimes do, and he had walked free, but what would freedom mean for him? Could he get on with his life as a responsible member of the community or would his experience haunt him for the rest of his days?

Dan and Dom drank heavily over dinner. Ahmed chose to leave them to it and went to bed. They slept together that night after several lines of coke and awoke somewhat worse for wear. Dan was a free man, but he had no life to go back to. What he did have, though, was £4.3 million pounds in the bank and a brand-new Bentley Continental in his mother's garage.

As the sole beneficiary of his mother's estate, he also inherited her home and other minor assets that were valued for probate at £1.2 million pounds. He immediately put the house on the market. Dom invited him to join her and Ahmed in the USA.

CHAPTER 18 - BRAZIL

The British media had been shocked by the *Not Guilty* verdict; the front pages of the red top and broadsheet newspapers covered the story in detail, and none of the editorials had anything other than condemnation for him.

As his mother had died, he could see no reason to remain in the UK, where it was clear that neither the media nor the public would ever accept him. He was seen as a pariah. For the short term, he stayed with one of his few remaining friends in Surrey that believed the falsehood of his claim of innocence and kept a low profile. During this time, he obtained a US visa and six weeks later, he flew to New York to join Dom. The US media were more sympathetic toward him. His performance in Dom's documentary - now short-listed for an award- had given him quasi celebrity status. A British court had found him innocent, so he was free to live his life.

Deciding to make the move permanent, he shipped the Bentley Continental to NY. Having been granted asylum in the US a few months earlier, Ahmed had settled into a flat that Dom had rented for him, and with her help, he had been offered a university lecturer's post in Biological Sciences. His life had been transformed, and he could once again use his talents and expertise to do what he loved.

Dan moved into Dom's apartment. Mindful that his visa would expire in no time at all, and he would then be expected to leave the country, she suggested they married so he could apply for residency. During his time in detention awaiting trial, Dom had missed him and decided they would be good together long-term.

There was no romance, no dewy eyes: this was an arrangement that suited her needs and provided Dan with the security of residency he desperately wanted. He was thrilled and of course, he agreed. Three weeks later, they married in the US Virgin Islands, a low-key affair with few attendees. The marriage was somehow leaked to the international media and it was covered extensively.

Dan had fallen in love with Dom in a way he had not experienced in the past. Physically, he wasn't overwhelmed by her beauty, although she was an attractive woman. He was captivated by her mind, her courage, and her ability to get things done. She was a powerful woman and someone he could respect and from whom he could learn a great deal.

For her, she saw an attractive, intelligent man who was vulnerable and had lost his way in life, and who was certainly unworldly compared to her. She knew he had murdered Tanya, but somehow, that knowledge had not clouded her views or her feelings for him.

Dom was inundated with offers to make documentaries about an eclectic mix of topics around the world. She had planned three lucrative projects over the following two years. The first would take her to South America to document poverty and a failing political system in Brazil. The second was a documentary about the socio-economic opportunities for Yemen post-civil war, and the third would document the rise in India's economic power and its influence on the world stage.

Now they were married, it made no sense for Dom to be travelling and working alone, leaving Dan in New York. They agreed he would join her team and would learn the art of production management. Dan was excited at the prospect of a new and exciting career travelling the world with his new wife.

For a month, they worked solidly, researching the background to the first project in Brazil. Dan was used to detailed work and proved his worth in uncovering stories Dom believed were worth pursuing.

After a long cold winter in New York, they both looked forward to their four-month trip to Brazil to make the documentary.

Dom had painstakingly made all the arrangements for the two of them and her film crew to travel out the following Monday to Rio de Janeiro, where they would base themselves in a downtown hotel.

Rio was the home of many universities and institutes, boasting the second-largest centre for research and development in Brazil, accounting for 17 percent of national scientific output, which impressed Dan enormously. Of course, it was also one of the most dangerous cities in the world, where drug-related murders were commonplace, and gangs ruled the streets. Westerners were regularly kidnapped by gangs demanding substantial ransom for their release. A high proportion of known kidnaps ended badly, with bodies dumped in refuge sites or on the streets, irrespective of whether a ransom was paid or not. Dom was not in the least fearful for her safety. She had worked in more dangerous places in the world and knew how to stay safe. Dan, however, was more than apprehensive after his experience as a hostage in Africa but he kept his thoughts to himself. He trusted Dom to keep them safe, as did her film crew. She was the matriarch.

The flight to Rio was uneventful. Dom, Dan, and the crew all travelled business class, their budget now being able to afford them a few luxuries. After arriving at their hotel, they had dinner and planned their first reconnaissance trip of the city the following morning.

Before travelling out, Dom had arranged several meetings with government officials in Rio also their detractors in the week following. After the success of Dan's documentary, which had been aired in Brazil, her status as a serious filmmaker had been established, and the mention of her name was enough to gain her access to high-profile people to interview.

Dan would accompany her wherever she went. They would in turn be accompanied by two armed bodyguards she had hired, whose job it was to protect them during their time in the country.

Her first scheduled meeting was with Paulo Silva, Head of Government Economics and one of a few centrist politicians in the current right-wing government that was prepared to speak out about corruption in High Office and the deterioration in social infrastructure.

He was also outspoken about the rampant drug culture and wanted a change in policy that would round up the drug barons. Despite his views, though, he was loyal to the junta and the President in particular. It was well-known in political circles that he had a price on his head. Given an opportunity, the drug barons would assassinate him without a second thought. What was not common knowledge, was that Paulo de Silva and the President were themselves involved in a large-scale property fraud that Dom's research had uncovered, and this, not De Silva's policy on the drug culture, would be the focus of her interrogation. It was a risky strategy.

In a volatile country, to accuse a government minister of fraud could result in the entire production team being arrested and possibly never seen again. She knew the risks and had discussed them with her team before embarking on her mission.

The interview would be held in a secret location, 20km outside Rio. As the team assembled in the hotel waiting for a government car to pick them up and take them to the location, a lone gunman burst into the hotel lobby brandishing a pistol. Within a minute, he had shot a man dead on his stool in the bar and raced out to a waiting motorbike, which promptly sped away. The man's body remained precariously balanced on the stool in a semi-upright position, his head slumped back onto the bar. Blood pumped from his chest; his white t-shirt absorbed as much fluid as it could in the following few seconds, then the bright red pool flowed freely down to his waist, soaking his belt and trousers. It was a bizarre scene one that would have prompted those observing to flee almost anywhere else in the world, but few did. People were surprised rather than shocked by what had taken place. This type of assassination was not uncommon. Dom's instinct was to find out who the dead man was after all there was a story to investigate, but there was no time to make enquiries as the government car had arrived. As they left the hotel lobby, bar staff could be seen removing the body from the bar as patrons continued to sup their drinks.

This was Dan's first mission as Dom's assistant.

Dom and her film crew were well-versed in setting up and recording interviews, albeit not quite at this senior ministerial level in such a volatile country where corruption was endemic, and certainly not with a plan to expose the interviewee's corruption.

Two hours later, they were set up ready for the interview. The team, other than Dom, were a little apprehensive not knowing how this would all turn out. All they needed now was Paulo de Silva, the minister was running late. Dom's armed security guards were banned from entering the building, which concerned her a little, but she expected as much. She thought they might come in handy if things became tense. It was certainly the case that the Minister would have his own team on hand. As he arrived, she greeted him in Portuguese, just one of many languages she spoke almost fluently.

"Bom dia, Ministro. Obrigada por concordar com nossa entrevista, eu sei que você tem uma agenda lotada..." The Minister was impressed but insisted they spoke English, which is what Dom expected and hoped for.

"No, no, no. Please. I am good with English if you not speak too quickly, thank you. I see on TV your film recently you made and we all impressed with your work. I see Dr. Thomas...is it Thomas, here?" Dom had no idea he would have seen the documentary, let alone recognise Dan.

"Thank you, Minister. Yes, Dan, Dr. Thomas and I are married and we work together now." Dan looked lovingly at his new wife and boss.

"Well, that is good, yes?" Dan nodded. The minister was accompanied by two of his aides and three armed body guards, who stood menacingly at attention, automatic weapons poised for action.

"Minister. As you know, we are here in your country to bring to the world's attention through our documentary the challenges that you and your government face with the drug culture, and I know this is a subject that you are personally working hard on bringing under control. May I start by asking you if you know what percentage of the population are addicted to hard drugs?" The Minister looked to one of his assistants who shook his head, suggesting he had no idea.

"I not sure the percentage of people but it too high, we all know that..."

"Our research, Minister, suggests that over 38% of the population are either addicted or in some way linked to the supply or distribution of narcotics. Would you say that was a fair assessment?" The drug culture in the country had reached epidemic proportions and the minister was one of only a few in government who had openly admitted to a domestic audience that something needed to be done.

Dom suspected that his words were hollow. He had taken on a stance, albeit a risky one, to gain popularity with voters in the hope one day of being President. She suspected the truth, though, was that like most of the corrupt government, he couldn't really give a damn. It was clear the minister was already feeling uncomfortable.

"I said I not know but your figure seem high. No. I say not that high, but we do have problems and I am doing what I can to make my country a better place..."

Dom spent 35 minutes interrogating the Minister on the drug culture and its impact on society, covering off a wide range of domestic and international economic issues which lay under his responsibility.

In response to almost all the questions, he either had no idea what to say or gave muted responses. He was unaccustomed to being interviewed in such a professional manner by a woman who had clearly done her research. The minister's tone and facial expression from first meeting her had changed to one of mild irritation.

Dom now approached the topic of corruption - not just any corruption, but the large-scale property fraud to which both he and the President were inextricably linked. According to her research, they stood to make millions of US dollars from the deal. Dom glanced at her crew, including Dan, as if to give them warning of what was about to come.

"Minister, thank you for your candid response to my questions so far..."

"No. Thank you. It has been a pleasure and I hope you have all you need..." Before he could finish his sentence, though, Dom stopped him in his tracks.

"Minister, if I may, there is just one other subject I would like to ask you about..."

"Of course, please, please go ahead..." He looked at his watch, Dom looked him in the eye and kept her focus on him, keen to see his reaction to what she was about to say.

"Minister, you have already said that you and the government are fighting the drug wars and the corruption in your country and are getting good results, but I would like to ask you about your personal involvement along with the President in agreeing to sanction the building of a large-scale industrial plant in Curitba, outside of Rio, without going through normal government channels."

The Minister was visibly shocked by her question and became agitated. "I do not know all you talk about...I think if you have all..." Again, she stopped him.

"Minister, Is it true that you and the President sanctioned the building of this industrial plant without agreed permissions and both of you will be rewarded with millions of dollars? Minister, is that not corruption?"

He had heard enough. He stood up to face her, and barked at his aides to leave the room. His guards would stay. He glared at her. "You insult me a government minister and accuse me and the President of corruption. I want you to stop and destroy your video recording now and you will leave our country today!" He stared at Dom.

She responded, "Minister, as a back up, we always have a live feed of interviews streamed to our office in New York. We have the recording, whether we wipe it now or not. May I suggest that we continue the interview so you have an opportunity to defend yourself on camera?" This was a risky strategy, he grunted and sat back down.

"Minister, I have alledged that you and the President are in some way involved with the building project in Curitba. Do you deny any involvement?" The minster looked nervous and paused for a moment.

"I know of this project, but yes, I deny that I am in any way involved in corruption..."

"Minister, I have evidence that both you and the President are involved and expect to receive a substantial amount of money. Do you still deny your involvement?" He got extremely angry and barked at her.

"What proof you have...show me, show me..." Dom reached into her bag and pulled out several sheets of paper, detailing email exchanges between the minister and the contractor.

The papers showed that a deal was agreed to pay eight million US dollars into the Minister and President's Swiss bank accounts. She passed the documents to him. He read them slowly, clearly trying to think how he was going to respond. The crew kept filming.

In the end, he decided to ramp up his anger thinking it was the best form of defence. He ripped up the papers he had been given, then barked at her again.

"This is false, fake documents...your governemnt sent you to cause further unrest in my country! You will go now!" Dom tried again, the camera still rolling.

"Minister, what I have shown you is evidence that you and the President..."

He cut her short this time. "Get out, get out of my country!" He signalled to his guards to round them up and frog march them out of the building.

As they did, Dom tried again, "Minister, I apologise if I have got all this wrong and you are innocent of my claim...would you like to make a final statement to camera disputing my assertions?" She knew if he agreed, and it was unlikely, that he would go on a rant that would add drama to the interview. To her surprise, that was exactly what happened. He stood facing the camera, eyes popping, cheeks red with anger as he spat out his words.

"Trump says, "fake news, fake news", and this is what America wants to do! You accuse innocent goverment ministers and the President of corruption when your country is most corrupt in the world. I have seen the US of America and it not our ally, it dying dictatorship with more drug problems and killings than we have but talk down to us..! You tell your people to look at their own government before accusing us!"

Dom's cameraman had the sense at the end of his rant to disconnect his camera and bag it. The minister ordered his guards to clear the room and remove them from the building. Dom had lied. There was no *live feed* of the interview being beamed to her NY office; it was a ploy to avoid having the recording destroyed. As it was, everything the minister had said was recorded and residing precariously in the cameraman's bag.

The four government cars that had been provided to escort Dom, Dan, and the film crew to the meeting location returned them to their hotel.

The threat they would be removed from the country that day was not carried out. Back at the hotel, the crew applauded Dom for her expertise and courage in pressing the minister as she did. She had not elicited an admission of guilt, nor had she been expecting to receive one, but she had got enough footage of a minister squirming, unable to put up a believable defence. It was almost as good.

They all kept a low profile in the hotel during the following 24 hours prior to their next secret interview with a leading drug baron – Carlos de Souza.

He had been a police target for three years but they had failed to capture him, perhaps through incompetence but more likely because he had 'unofficial immunity'.

Dom was convinced he had paid bribes to the Chief of Police and other senior officers and she wanted to expose the corruption and corroborate her research about the drug trade and the impact it was having in the country and internationally.

The interview had been granted under strict rules of engagement. Only Dom and one other person would be allowed to meet him. They would be picked up at the hotel by one of his drivers and a secruity guard. There would be no cameras - only a sound recording. Dom had chosen Dan to go with her to record the interview. The car arrived, a 1960's American Chevrolet with darkened windows. It was the perfect wheels for a mobster.

As they left the hotel and jumped into the back of the car, Dan looked out of the back window and thought they were being followed. Then, the security guard gave them blindfolds to put on. He had also twigged they were being followed. They drove around the streets aimlessly to see if his suspicion was right. Dom assumed that the minister had probably placed a tag on them. After a few blocks, they lost sight of the vehicle and headed speedily toward the secret location. Twenty minutes later, and outside of the Rio city boundary, they arrived in a village and pulled up on the driveway of palatial home surrounded by high and inpenetrable walls. Once inside, their blindfolds were removed.

Carlos de Souza looked every bit the gangster. He was short and stocky with thick black crickly hair and wore an enormous moustache.

His face had been re-arranged at some point in the past and several scars to his right cheek bore witness. It was likely that he had crossed someone or they had crossed him, and a new face was the price he had paid. Dom was facinated by his appearance and wanted to know how he received his injuries but thought the better of it.

They were invited into a large, sumptuous sitting room full of brighyly coloured ornaments, paintings, and sculptures. The whole place was full to bursting as if the occupant had too much money to spend and was given little time to spend it. None of it made any aesthetic sense.

She had always consulted with her team when they embarked on a new project, keen that whatever she did or said never came as a surprise. On this occasion, though, it was different. She only had Dan accompanying her so the crew were not at risk, and as he was a novice at all this, she feared if she told him that she was wearing a secret camera hidden in a brooch, he would freak out. She had decided to keep quiet. An audio recording of the interview would not be enough for her, no matter how provocative or enlightening the commentary was. No, she needed video footage to bring it alive. Of course, this went against one of her interviewees main conditions.

Dom asked to visit the bathroom and while there, she switched on the camera. If they were going to be searched, it would have happened by now.

She was prepared to take the risk of being caught. As she returned to the sitting room, she discovered Dan sitting opposite Don Carlos, where she needed to be if her camera was to pick up his image. She asked Dan to move to another chair, which seemed odd to both men, but he obliged nonetheless.

Once again, she spoke in Portugeuse to ask him if the interview could be conducted in English.

"Yes beautiful lady. I speak English good..." He was unaware that Dan was her husband and chose to flirt with her. He clapped his hands and a manservant appeared from nowhere. Apart from one armed guard, the man who had accompanied them to the house, no one else was present.

"Can I get you drinks?" Dan fancied an Earl Grey tea but knew that was unlikley to be on offer, so he asked for a whisky instead. Dom chose the same.

"Welcome to my home. So, you very famous lady now. I watched your documentary on TV, it was very good. The man who killed his girlfriend got off in court trial, eh?" He hadn't realised that Dan was the man in question, so they made no effort to enlighten him.

"Thank you, Don Carlos. Are you happy for me to start the interview?"

"Yes, yes, please you start if you like..."

Dom's initial objective was to get him to admit on camera that he was the wealthiest and most influential drug baron in Brazil, if not the whole of the Americas. "May I ask how wealthy you are, Don Carlos?" He laughed out loud.

"How wealthy? I am a poor man, why? You think I'm rich?" He was toying with her.

"I understand that your wealth is estimated to be over $1 billion dollars - is that true?" Don Carlos laughed again. "One billion dollars is a lot of money..."

"But is it true?" He wouldn't be drawn. "I am a humble businessman, that's all. Nothing of what you say..."

"What sort of business are you in, Don Carlos?"

"My business is import and export."

"What products do you deal in?"

"Many things, many things that are sold everywhere. We are very popular..."

"Don Carlos, it is well-known that you are a very rich man from selling drugs and you have networks that span the world. Is that true?"

"Drugs, no. I don't sell drugs. Drugs are bad for people, why would I sell drugs?" It was obvious he was not about to admit to anything.

"When I arranged this interview with you, Don Carlos, I told you that I was making a documentary about the drug cartels in Brazil, who they were, how they operated, and the amount of money they were making and you agreed to meet me. Are you denying being a drug baron?"

Don Carlos laughed heartily. "Drug baron, no! I am trying to fight drugs in my country. I work with the government to stop the selling of drugs and the people who die from overdoses. I am a respected businessman, a citizen who cares for my people..."

"If you are not a drug baron, do you know those who are?"

"Everyone knows who they are. You know who they are, don't you? Look, beautiful lady, there are many bad people in the world and many people are poor. Buying and selling drugs is a way of life for people in countries like mine, and they can only exist if they do. The government doesn't know what to do. They are involved themselves, everyone makes money from drugs."

"But you don't, Don Carlos?"

"Why would I want to make money from drugs? I am a rich man, you say $1 billion dollars? That's a lot of money, so why would I sell drugs?"

He continued to toy with her, but she hadn't yet played her trump card. "Don Carlos, I know you sell drugs. I know you're a drug baron; in fact, I know you're the richest of them all, and I know this because I have evidence to prove it."

Don Carlos enjoyed laughing. He did so again. "You have evidence to prove it...where is your evidence?" Just like earlier interview with the minister he wanted to see proof. Dom took from her bag another email exchange between a government minister close to the President and Don Carlos, then proceeded to read it to him in Portuguese.

Don Carlos. Thank you for your kind gift. I am confident the President will agree with me that the proposed reforms you say will harm your business will no longer take place. We all know how important your work is in harvesting crops and exporting them around the world....

"And you think that is proof, what you say...I am a drug baron?" He laughed for the third time.

"Don Carlos. I also have, but not here, signed statements from other people in government who are willing to testify that you have made a considerable amount of money from drugs and regularly bribe people to keep them quiet.

I also have other people who claim they used to work for you and know the business well and the number of people who have been murdered upon your instruction. I have names, addresses, phone numbers, locations where you grow and process the harvest, and where you store the drugs before shipping them to the US and Europe. I also have details of a border tunnel you use for drug runs from Mexico to the US...Are you still denying you have anything to do with the drugs trade?"

Don Carlos had sat still staring at her withour emotion but he had heard enough. His attitude had changed from convivial to aggressive. She had touched a raw nerve. He didn't believe she had any of the proof she claimed she had, but he had tired of her tirade of accusations. Few people would challenge him face to face and if they did they would suffer the inevitable consequences – a beating or worse still an agonising demise. "I heard enough from you..." He gestured to Dan who was recording the interview and demanded he hand over the audio file. Dan looked at Dom and she nodded in the affirmative.

"Don Carlos, I am sorry you didn't like what I have told you, but it's all true and you know it is. If I am wrong, I apologise, but I know I don't need to offer an apology, do I?"

There was a silence before he clapped his hands and gestured to his guard to see them off the premises. They were blindfolded and roughly bundled into the car and returned to their hotel.

As soon as they were in their room, she was desperate to check the video recording, praying it worked. She told Dan what she had done and downloaded the file onto her laptop before calling the crew together to share the spoils. Once again she hadn't managed to obtain a confession that he was a drug baron, but she had his face on camera and his reactions to her claim that she had irrefutable evidence of his illegal activities. Of course, she had lied as she had the previous day. It was all a fabrication to get him to talk, but it was enough to warrant including the interview in the final documentary.

CHAPTER 19 – GETTING AWAY FROM IT ALL

They had been in Brazil for almost two months and had conducted a wide range of interviews with people in power and those who sought to exploit them. She had a rich seam of evidence and testimony to show just how corrupt politics, the police, and the judiciary were - as well as the power and influence of drug barons.

The economy had performed well in recent years but was now on the verge of collapse as government officials who had been sucked into a culture of bribery and corruption openly granted government contracts to their friends, who were then paid billons of US dollars for doing little or nothing.

The coffers were low, but the need for rebuilding the infrastructure to provide suitable housing, hospitals, and communications was high. This paralysis of power and corruption on such a vast scale was making it impossible to offer a future for the people who were now destined for decades of poverty.

As they left the country, Dom was confident she had all the material she needed to make another *award-winning* film. Meanwhile, Dan had learnt a lot about the business of making documentaries. His admiration for Dom had grown and he was totally in awe of her. She was fearless, focused on her work, and fully deserving of the accolades that came her way.

For the next four weeks, she edited the programme and when she had finished, she called the crew together to show them what they had achieved. Everyone was delighted with the results.

Dom was visibly tired and not sleeping well. Dan suggested they took a vacation after the wrap. She agreed they needed time out. The next production could wait. They decided to go away for a month and take time out in the Caribbean and the Virgin Islands before flying to Cuba. For her, vacations were an opportunity to seek out new projects. She had made a documentary about Cuba in the past and was proud of her accomplishment, but as an unknown filmmaker at the time, the production had failed to gain the attention of major media companies.

She wondered whether an edit and new material might gain the traction she needed, helped on by her newly acquired cult status as a lauded filmmaker. She would wait until they arrived in Cuba to decide.

Her tentacles spread widely around the globe. She seemed to know everyone worth knowing and had connections in the highest places - heads of state, politicians, drug barons, businesspeople, and those in the dramatic and musical arts to name but a few.

Dan enjoyed riding on her coat tails and was adjusting well to his new dramatic lifestyle, one that he could not have anticipated. He had a beautiful and talented wife who herself was independently wealthy, he had his own new-found affluence after the sale of the *Paul Gauguin painting,* and despite the risks of the work they were undertaking together, he was able to fully relax and enjoy life. Murdering Tanya still haunted him, as did the experience being held hostage in Africa and, of course, his more recent experiences on the run in Cyprus, Lebanon, and Syria. The death of his mother had also affected him and he suffered the guilt of knowing that she had died prematurely from worrying whether he would go to prison.

They flew out to Aruba, a Caribbean island Dom loved. With its alabaster white coastline, picture-perfect weather, and crystal clear waters teeming with aquatic life, the island was as diverse as its people - a beautiful, sustainable spectrum of dry desert, limestone coves, and picturesque pastel architecture that Dom enjoyed exploring.

Wealthy friends of Dom's, had several beautiful properties on the island and would always let her stay in one of them when she visited. They were away in Europe but all the arrangements had seamlessly been put in place for her.

The villa they would occupy led onto a private beach and had every amenity. The garage housed three classic British cars - a Rolls Royce Phantom, an Aston Martin DB6 Volante, and a Lotus Turbo Esprit that were all at Dom's disposal should she wish to use them.

They were both tired upon arrival, so they had supper and went to bed. The following morning, Dom was keen to show Dan the island, so they took the Aston Martin and spent the day sightseeing. They stopped for lunch in a restaurant she had visited many times. The owner was a Dutchman named Kip Jansen, a renowed yachtsman who had sailed in the Americas Cup challenge some years earlier. Dom had been introduced to him by her friends whose house they were staying in, believing that she, a single woman at the time, and Kip, a batchelor, would hit it off. Kip had taken her sailing and for a week they had enjoyed an intimate relationship but the demands of her work had cut short their relationship. They hadn't seen each other for three years.

Her choice of restaurant was not predicated on its good food and impeccable service but on her desire to see Kip again. She had enjoyed sex with him in the past and found him interesting and amusing, although romance was not a part of the equation. Despite being married to Dan, she wanted to reconnect and reminisce .

She also loved sailing and hoped he would take them out on his yacht after lunch.

As they pulled up outside the restauarant in the open-topped Aston Martin, Kip came out to greet them, believing Dom's friends had arrived as he recognised their car. He beamed with delighted when he saw it was Dom in the driving seat and rushed to open her door; they tightly embraced and he kissed her on the lips like a long lost lover, which of course he was. "My darling Dominique, I still can't get over you leaving me, what was it three years ago?..."

As Dan got out of the car slightly taken aback by the familiarity, Dom introduced Dan. "Kip. This is my husband, Dan." Dan nodded uncomfortably and saw Kip's apparent disapproval of him etched into his expression.

"Your husband! You mean you are married? Well, what can I say... come in, come in." Kip and Dom led the way holding hands. Kip looked at her disbelievingly, she smiled back at him, all witnessed by Dan who followed like sycophant; albeit an angry one.

They were shown to a table and Kip joined them. Dan had already decided Kip was not someone he warmed to. He was too brash and it was obvious he disapproved of Dom being married to him. Kip snapped his fingers and a member of staff brought over a bottle of champagne.

"So, Dan, you were lucky enough to marry the beautiful Dominique. What did you have to do to persuade her to be with you?" Dom was about to save Dan the trouble of responding, but Kip was insistent he heard from her new man. "No, no, my lovely Dominique, I want to hear from him." Dan had gone from not warming to Kip to despising him in one short leap.

"Have I deprived you of Dom?" Kip looked at him and looked at Dom.

"Dom? What is Dom? Surely you don't allow him to call you that; it's so very unattractive." Dan needed to hear no more. There would be no camaraderie between the two men, irrespective of what Kip said from here.

"May I ask, is Kip an abbreviation for Kipper?"

Dom and Kip laughed. "At least your husband has a sense of humour, a typically British one."

It was her turn to talk. "We met in Beirut and worked together on a documentary..." Before she had time to complete the sentence, though, Kip broke in.

" I saw it, I saw it...of course! You are the doctor who murdered his girlfriend and went on the run! Well well."

"For your information, I was found not guilty..."

"Yes you were, but that doesn't mean you didn't kill her, does it? Juries get things wrong from time to time, don't they?" Dan looked at Dom and Kip looked at him. Dom insisted the conversation changed. "What are we eating?" Kip immediately rushed off to get the menus. Dan was fuming.

"Who is this fucking idiot?" Dom could see he was less than impressed with Kip but tried to smooth things over.

"He's okay, really. Just teasing you. Lighten up, go along with him, relax." Dan didn't like her response. She wasn't his boss or his mother.

"I'd rather we ate somewhere else. This will spoil what has been a lovely morning, can we go?" But Dom wasn't about to leave.

"No. You have my permission to tease Kip, say whatever you like, just don't be boring." Kip returned with the menus.

He had decided he would eat with them. "There are so many things I could recommend for you, my lovely Dominique, but you know what I'm famed for so I will leave you to choose."

"So what are you famed for, Kipper?" He looked Dan squarely in the eye and winked.

"Dominique knows what I'm famed for."

For Dan, it was an excruciating hour and a half. He stayed almost silent and scouled at Dom, eating little of the food that Kip recommended. Kip and Dom caught up on their news as if he wasn't there. "Now you've enjoyed my good food, I hope I shall take you sailing."

"No, that's fine, thanks Kipper. We have plans..."

Dan was keen to make clear he did not want to spend another minute with this loathsome man but Dom interjected,

"...Dan. I'd love to go sailing! Come on, you'll enjoy it!"

"No, thanks."

"Well, Dominique, it looks as though it's just the two of us. Let's go. We'll take my car - we're only five minutes from my yacht."

She didn't want Dan to stay and sulk. "Oh, come on Dan, it'll be fun. Please come" Dan didn't respond. Having tried twice, which was once more than her usual, she got up and left the restaurant with Kip, heading for his Porsche. They laughed together. She looked back at Dan and shook her head disapprovingly. Dan was furious, enraged.

He pushed his chair back and shoved the table out of his way, grabbed Dom's bag that she had forgotten to take, barged his way out of the restaurant, and headed for the Aston Martin. At boiling point, he searched her bag for the car keys and started the engine before roaring down the street in the opposite direction to them. He stopped shortly after and opened the glove compartment, where Dom had put some cocaine. He had already snorted one skinny, short line, but this time he chose to go longer and wider to calm his nerves. It did the trick instantly. Again, he revved the engine and tore away at speed, not knowing where he was headed. He drove for over an hour. He pictured the smugness of Kip's smile as he and Dom had left the restaurant and fumed some more. His head pounded with anger. Why had she agreed to go with him? What on earth did she see in him?

Aruba was a small island, about 19 miles long. Dan knew they would be away for at least a couple of hours and possibly more, so after more than an hour, he attempted to find his way back to the villa but got lost. Frustrated, he took a bend too quickly and collided with a stationary farm vehicle at the side of the road. He was shaken but not injured. He got out to inspect the damage to the Aston and it was considerable. It was still driveable, but the front end had been stoved in and would cost a considerable amount to repair. This was all he needed, and he knew it would likely be seen by Dom as a deliberate act of willfullness. He didn't care.

What he didn't know was that the Aston Martin DB6 Volante he was driving was a classic 1965 model in concourse condition with only 21000 miles on the odometer and had only recently been bought at auction in London by their hosts and shipped over to Aruba. It was a rare and much sought after vehicle, costing £450,000. The damage he had caused could only be repaired on the mainland and would cost a considerable amount.

He got back into the car and drove off. As he glanced at the fuel gauge, he saw the tank was low. He decided to turn round and head back in a direction he believed would take him to the restaurant and, fortunately for him, it did. He parked the battered vehicle outside on the pavement, immediately attracting attention from passers-by and a few locals, who knew the owner. Of course, on seeing its condition, one of them immediately called the police.

The sun was beating down and Dan was sweating profusely partly due to the amount of cocaine he had taken. He leant back in the driver's seat, closed his eyes, and fell asleep.

Forty minutes later, the police arrived. He was still high and confused. His face was sunburnt and raw. He was questioined about the car's ownership and the damage to the vehicle. He admitted he wasn't the owner but had been given permission to drive it, although he couldn't remember the name of the owner or the location of the villa he was staying in.

The last thing he wanted to do was call Dom's mobile tail between his legs for her to reassure the police that he hadn't stolen the vehicle, but he had no option. The 'phone rang but of course, it was in her bag in the back of the Aston Martin. She had forgotten to take it with her.

Under the circumstances, the police were remarkably tolerant. Dan suggested they call Kip's mobile - the restaurant manager had his number. They got through and it was confirmed that Dan was staying with her in the villa and had permission to drive the car. They were only minutes away from the restaurant, so the police waited for them. Kip was a local celebrity and restaurateur and known to the police, so they were satisfied when he reassured them that the car was being driven with permission.

Dom and Kip inspected the damage to the Aston. Dan was embarrassed but still in a rage that she had gone off sailing, leaving him behind. He had begun to shake awkwardly, a side effect of taking too much cocaine. Dom knew the symptoms and was immediately angry with him.

"What the hell have you done?"

"It's all your bloody fault - you've wrecked our day together!"

"Grow up, Dan. You're acting like a child and it's not attractive." Kip came across to them and wagged his finger at Dan. "Naughty Boy."

Dan could barely control his emotions. He wanted to punch Kip in the face but held off. Then, in front of him, Kip handed Dom her earrings. "You left them on the bedside table, darling. I picked them up when we left the yacht. So, you've had an accident, Dan? Were you driving too fast?" The earrings had not gone unnoticed.

"Your earrings? Why did you take your earrings off?" Kip smiled at Dan and walked away. Dom didn't respond.

"Let's go."

She walked back to the Aston and got into the driving seat. Dan followed soon after. They returned to the villa. During the journey, they didn't speak at all. When they got out of the car and went inside, Dan was ready for confrontation. He would not allow her to treat him like a child as she had done in the reastaurant. It was his turn to be heard and importantly, listened to. He raised his voice.

"I'll ask again, why did you take your earrings off?" Dom was wired differently from most people. She was not a cold woman in the least, but she was unemotional, logical, focused and never weighed down by the morals of right and wrong. She did what she did. She was honest; in fact, too honest, but she lived life according to her terms and no one else's, including her husbands.

"I took them off on the yacht."

"That much is obvious, but the question is why?"

"Dan, are you serious? Have you no idea why I took them off?" Dan thought for a second. Perhaps there was a legitimate reason why women took off their earrings when sailing and it had passed him by. "No. I don't."

Dom shrugged. "Dan...We had sex and I didn't want them to tear my ears or scratch Kip's face. That's why."

Dan's head was already pounding. What he really wanted to do was sleep for the rest of the day, but this revelation had to be a joke, so he attempted to laugh. She was cool and unflustered. She had told him the truth, what more was there to say? It only took Dan a moment to realise that she wasn't laughing with him.

"Are you serious? You had sex with that bastard?" "Dan, it was just sex. We've had sex before. We're friends. Why is it such a crime? I'm not about to run off with him; I'm married to you." With that, she turned and headed to the bedroom. Dan could not be more enraged, he grabbed her hard by the arm turning her toward him and yelled at her.

"Tell me you're fucking joking! Tell me you bitch!"

She stood perfectly still and confidently looked him in the eyes wrestling herself from him. "I'm going to have a shower. I suggest you calm down" Dan was incandescent.

"A shower? To fucking wash him off you, is that it?"

"Yes, Dan. After sex and sailing, I always think it hygienic to take a shower, don't you?" She turned and went into the bedroom and stripped off. Dan followed soon after and forced her onto the bed. He was aroused at the thought of sex with her, he couldn't help it. Now, he wanted her too, to remind her who she should be spending her time with. He quickly ripped his clothes off pinning her down until they were both naked together. Dom said nothing but used her strength and determination to push him off the bed. She stood there looking at him with distain before walking to the bathroom. Dan lay uncomfortably on the floor, humiliated, and went into a frenzy.

He heard the shower go on, he got up and went straight for the kitchen. Once there, he opened a drawer and pulled out the largest, sharpest carving knife he could find. There were plenty to choose from. Shaking, and not thinking rationally, he headed for the bathroom, burst in, and with his left hand grabbed her by the hair and violently pulled her out of the cubicle onto the floor. Then, he dragged her backward into the bedroom. He forced her onto the bed as she screamed, his right hand brandishing the carving knife in front of her. He was fully out of control by now, shrieking at her incoherently. In contrast, her wide-open eyes were full of terror but she could say nothing. In an instant he had grabbed her by the throat with his left hand and squeezed as hard as he could. She knew what was coming. In vain, she attempted to wrestle him off but he easily over-powered her and plunged the 12-inch blade deep into her body as if she were a pin cushion. It penetrated deep into her vital organs. In a manic frenzy, he repeated the assault over and over as blood spurted from every part of her torso until she could bleed no more. Spent, he lay down next to her, exhausted.

The woman he had truly fallen in love with and married, the woman he admired so deeply, the intelligent, passionate woman who was so hugely talented, was dead. He had savagely killed her in a fit of jealousy, fuelled by the effects of cocaine. Covered in her blood, he attempted to get up, but the experience had been too much for him. He collapsed back down on top of her, his face buried in her blood soaked chest.

It was six hours later when he woke. He had no idea where he was or what he had done. As he peeled his bloodied face from her chest as though he were removing duck tape from cardboard, he found them naked, the congealed blood of the attack stuck to both of them. As he raised his body and opened his eyes fully, the horror of what he had done was plain to see. He leapt off the bed, heart racing. Her bloodshot eyes were still open, her face was ashen, and her torso was mutilated with over twenty stab wounds. Fragments of her inner body parts were stuck to his own body. The blood-stained blade he had used to kill her was lying on the bed next to her. He reached over for it and was tempted to plunge it into his own heart, but didn't have the courage to do it. He had committed a heinous crime by any standards, but he had no recollection of his actions. Less fortunately, the evidence was there before him in all its gruesome glory. The chink in Dan's psyche had once more taken him into a dark space where his rage could not be controlled. Again, murder was the consequence.

He sat on the edge of the bed staring at her and wept. The room was eerily quiet except for the bathroom shower, which was still running. He got up and looked at himself in a full-length mirror, what he saw was a killer holding a blade, covered from head to foot in someone else's congealed blood. Hysterically, he rushed to the bathroom to wash away his crime.

The shower had run cold but that was of no conseqeunce to him, he stood shivvering as he manically scrubbed his body until it was raw. He watched as her blood and fragments of her organs disappeared down the plug hole. The room began to spin uncontrollably and he passed out once more.

Several minutes later, wringing wet, he dragged himself back to the bedroom, hoping desperately that he would find her asleep. Could it have been a nightmare, a figment of his imagination? He was to be disappointed.

He had been here before. He had murdered Tanya, albeit in a less dramatic way and he knew he had to make some fundamental decisions quickly, no matter how difficult they were. He could call the police and an ambulance and hand himself in, or he could do what he had done previously and find a way of escaping justice. The latter seemed the better option. He spent the next few hours trying not to think about what he had done, but how best to deal with the situation.

It made no sense to try and clean up and dispose of her body. There was far too much blood and evidence of his crime. He decided for some odd reason to dispose of the carving knife, though.

He systematically went through the possessions Dom had brought with her to the villa and put anything that might be useful to him to one side. He had to escape the island. He was travelling on his British passport as his US Green Card had not yet come through after marrying her, so he decided it would be best if he made his getaway to Cuba, where they had planned to spend the last leg of their holiday.

But how would he get there? It was about a thousand miles, over two hours on a commercial flight, but he couldn't risk that exposure. Local private jets operated on Aruba and tourists often flew across to Cuba, so he made some enquiries. For a man who had just butchered his wife, he was remarkably calm and focused. Time was of the essence.

He'd just finished a 'phone call and arranged his private flight for the following morning when the doorbell rang. Tentatively, he looked out of the window. It was Kip. He rang again and again and called out for Dominique. He knew they had to be in as the Aston Martin was in the driveway and they wouldn't have gone out without transport. He looked into the window, hoping to see them and called her name again. Dan hid behind a curtain.

Kip, like Dom, was a confident person and had already demonstrated his assertiveness and cunning in dealing with Dan earlier. He was not phased by anyone or anything and was certainly not about to drive off without seeing her. He knew the owners of the villa well, as they often frequented his restaurant when they were on the island, so he decided that gave him licence to check the back door to see if it was open. It was. He walked into the kitchen, calling her name. Dan had to do something, but what? He knew if he chose to hide, Kip would certainly wander the house looking for them, and in doing so, would find Dom's body. He had no choice but to confront him.

He went into the kitchen. He was not about to be friendly with the man who had, only hours earlier, had had sex with his now-deceased wife.

"Yes, why are you here? What do you want?"

"Not a very friendly way to greet someone who paid for your lunch, Dan, or is that the way you Brits treat friends these days?" Dan had already reached boiling point. He raised his voice.

"Friends? What makes you think we're fucking friends? You fucked my wife a few hours ago. Is that what men do in your country, fuck their friends wives without them knowing?"

"You're too sensitive, my friend. Anyway, is the lovely Dominique here? I've come to see her, not you."

"Fuck off. You're not welcome and I'm not your fucking friend. I thought I'd made that clear."

"Oh dear, a bit childish, Dan..."

Kip decided he would go and look for Dominique anyway. "Don't worry, I'll find her myself." He brushed past Dan and as he did, Dan grabbed the same knife he had used earlier and stabbed Kip several times in the back. His expression barely changed. As Kip dropped to the kitchen floor, he kicked him several times in the gut and watched him writhe in front of him. Dan laughed excitedly as Kip's eyes rolled back and his life came to an abrupt end. Dan's own eyes were full of hate. He kicked him again and again and laughed manically as he did.

He stepped back from the carcass as blood gushed from his body across the kitchen floor, then he calmly washed the carving knife in the sink for a second time before placing it into a plastic bag. As if nothing had happened, he wandered out onto the private beach that backed onto the property. He walked for ten minutes watching the sea wash up onto the beach before digging a deep hole in the sand, where he placed the bag containing the knife and covered it up. He returned to the villa. Unemotionally he dragged Kip's bloodied body out of the kitchen and bundled him into the passenger seat of his Porsche in the driveway. Then, he drove a short distance and abandoned the car in a wooded area. He walked back to the villa, snorted more cocaine, and fell asleep.

Dan woke at 3.00 am in a cold sweat from a nightmare. He had dreamt that Dom and Kip had come back to life to haunt him.

The morning arrived. He packed his bags took the keys for the Aston, then drove to the private airfield where he would be met by his pilot. What he didn't know was that the owner of the villa used the same pilot for transportation, so the car was recognised immediately. The moment Dan parked up, he went across to him.

"Mr. Thomas? So are you a friend of Señor Snelgrove?" Dan was puzzled. "Snelgrove?"

"Yes, the owner of this beatiful but damaged Aston Martin."

"Oh, yes. Snelgrove..." Dan immediately knew that once Dom's body was discovered at the villa, it would be broadcast widely.

It was a small island and later the pilot would remember that he was driving the Aston. The police would put two and two together very quickly but there was little he could do about it now. "Did you crash it, or was it Señor Snelgrove?"

"Snelgrove...shall we go?" He could see no point in continuing the conversation. The pilot was given permission to take off and within no time, they were airborne.

CHAPTER 20 - PENANCE

Throughout the journey, Dan spoke little to the pilot. Rather than land in Havana, Cuba's capital, Dan had asked to land at a small airfield in Trinidad, on the south coast. Fortunately for him, the customs and immigration point was unmanned. A familiar scenario. No one would know he was there. He paid the pilot and walked away from the airfield, suitcase in hand, to start a new life.

Within no time, he had hitched a lift to Havana and taken a hotel room for the night. There, he took stock. He recalled Dom telling him when they first arrived that the owners of the villa were not returning for at least a month, which meant that Dom's body would not be discovered for quite some time, unless of course they paid cleaners to call in. He hoped the former was the case, but it mattered little anyway - it was out of his control. Kip's body would almost certainly be discovered in his car within a few days and he wondered if the two murders would be linked in some way. Again, though, it mattered little.

Dan's cash from the sale of the painting had been transferred from the UK to a US bank and he feared at some point, when Dom's body was discovered and the finger was pointed at him as her murderer, his assets would be frozen. It was essential that he transferred the money again, this time to a bank in Cuba, but it wasn't that simple.

The following morning, he visited the first bank he came across after leaving his hotel and spoke to the manager. He told him that he was a businessman and was planning to invest a substantial amount of money in Cuba's regeneration programme, so he needed to open a personal account for the time he spent in Havana.

The bank had protocols they had to adhere to by law and one was not allowing random accounts to be opened without proof of residency. Of course, he failed at the first hurdle. But when he mentioned that he wanted to transfer several million pounds, the manager's eyes lit up. He knew a man who knew a man that could make all the necessary arrangements for him to be given 'documents' that would allow him to open an account. But, of course, it would come at a cost. He smiled and said "$20,000".

Dan agreed to pay the fee once the money had been deposited. It didn't take long. Within a few days, the account was open, the money had been transferred, and the fee was paid. Not so surprisingly, he was also offered a fake Cuban passport and residency documentation that would allow him to live on the island, no questions asked. Again, he agreed, and paid another $10,000 for the privelege.

Within a month, he had bought a discreet but sizeable property with land 20 miles outside of Havana and a 1960s Cadillac, a popular choice on the island. He was beginning to settle in when he saw a news programme on CNN reporting the discovery of Dom's murder in the Aruba villa. Kip's body had also been found and linked, with the common denominator a certain Dr. Dan Thomas. It was a major story that featured clips of the award-winning documentary Dom had made about him, their marriage, and their subsequent vacation on the island. As Dan predicted, Kip's body had been found a few days after he had been ceremoniously abandoned in the woodland, but it was a full month before the villa owners had returned and found Dom's body decomposing in the bedroom. The one element that he dreaded hearing was that the pilot had come forward confirming that he had flown him to Cuba, and an international arrest warrant had been issued.

The Cuban government had been at loggerheads with the Americans for decades and extradition requests for criminals on the island were automatically rejected. However, in more recent times, as a degree of cordiality had been established between the two countries, largely driven by an easing of sanctions, extraditions had taken place on occasion. Dan had applied for a *Green Card* to stay in the US after marrying Dom, but thus far, he was not a US passport holder and had travelled under a British passport.

There was a reasonably healthy relationship between Cuba and Britain, and an extradition agreement was in place. That meant that if he were apprehended, he would be returned to the UK and potentially face new questions over Tanya's murder, or extradition to the US, where he would stand trial for three murders. Of course, if he was found guilty in the States, he would likely face the death penalty.

After murdering Tanya in the lab, Dan's life had been turned upside down. Prior to that momentus event, he had been enjoying life. It was a modest existence but sufficient for him to have a circle of good friends, a relatively well-paid and secure job, a succession of girlfriends, and the freedom to do as he pleased. What led him to murder Tanya was a desire for wealth, the kind of wealth he saw Rupert enjoying. He believed that by stealing his employer's intellectual property rights, he could set up his own lab and make millions. If only it had been that simple.

In less than two years, he had murdered Tanya, been kidnapped in Africa, and seen his girlfriend brutally raped and killed alongside two others. He had absconded from Britain to Cyprus, then to Beirut and onto Syria, where he had been subjected to a gun battle with ISIS before being rescued by American special forces and taken to Iraq for an onward journey to the US. He had met and married Dominique and been the subject of an award-winning documentary that had given him the kind of social status he craved. He had also won a Bentley Continental in a competition and inherited a painting that proved to be worth more than £5 million.

But as if all that wasn't enough, he had then murdered his wife and her friend. It was the stuff of fiction, but it was his reality. After seeing the news programme, he became seriously depressed. How much more could he take? For how long could he continue to live a clandestine life? He was tired of ducking and diving, trying to avoid what he believed to be the inevitable – life in prison or a death sentence. He had murdered three people but in his mind, he was still trying to justify his actions. Of course, his soul would tell a different story.

None of the facts brought tears to his eyes, but when he reflected on his mother's early demise, he broke down. She had been a good mother and had given him a start in life and an opportunity to prosper as a human being. He had let her down.

Since buying the Cuban house, he had worked hard to put the recent past to one side. He had kept himself to himself and spent most of his time gardening, something he had never thought of doing before. It was a kind of therapy. Every night, he would go to bed, fully expecting to be arrested by the police and extradited, but a knock on the door never came.

It was a modest life for a man who had millions in the bank. He had built a small but intimate circle of friends, locals who lived nearby, and managed to eke out a living selling local crafts to tourists.

Eventually, he met and married Beneta Perez, a nurse at a local hospital. She was a beautiful young woman from a desperately poor family. They had two children together.

Dan's past remainded just that, his past. He never spoke about it to anyone, including Beneta, but he had constant nightmares, reliving the murders he had perpetrated.

Time had changed him. He no longer had aspirations for wealth and social status, albeit he was a wealthy man, and he no longer had a desire to exploit women or be the centre of attention. He no longer took drugs or drank alcohol, instead living one day at a time and making sure that he did everything he could to make Beneta, the children, and his friends happy.

At the age of 46, Dan was diagnosed with cancer and against his better judgement, was admitted to hospital for treatment. It was there that he was recognised by one of the hospital administrators and reported to the police. After his release following a week as an in-patient, he was arrested and held in custody awaiting extradition. The family were not allowed to visit him. The British authories had no interest in him; after all, he had been aquitted of Tanya's murder at the Old Bailey, but the US authorities were quick to seize on the opportunity to have him back in the States to stand trial for Dom's murder. Six weeks later, with deteriorating health, he was extradited, and upon arrival on US soil, was arrested and held on detention in a prison hospital.

After years of believing he had escaped his past and adjusted to a sedate family existence in which the pace of life had allowed him to regain his mental and physical health, he had got cancer, and the episode and his hospitalisation had plunged him back into the limelight.

He was a changed man in so my ways from his murderous days, but that meant little. Justice was justice, it was not time dated. Dan was weak both physically and mentally. He knew his cancel was terminal but had no idea how long he had to live.

The murder of Tanya was no longer the issue. He had lied to save his mother the pain, but she was dead now. The issue at hand was the murder of Dom and Kip, and how he was going to protect his wife and children from the realisation that he was guilty of barbarism, and the burden that would befall them from media intrusion. Their lives would be turned upside down.

Dan recovered sufficiently in hospital, allowing him to be transferred to a maximum security prison to await trial. It was then that he received an organised visit from Ahmed. Dan was accepting of his fate. He knew he was rightly being brought to justice for the heinous crimes he had perpetrated and he had developed a shielding mechanism that at least allowed him to sleep without having nightmares. He was reconciled with meeting his maker.

Ahmed was a wise old man and had suffered tragedies in his life with which few people could contend. But despite his experiences in losing all of his family, his career, and his livelihood, he had maintained his faith. He believed in his god and he believed in humanity. With Dom's financial support and encouragement, he had managed to rebuild his career and a good life in a democratic country. He wanted for nothing.

Dan's alleged murder of Dom and Kip had been reported widely by the media and the press, and Ahmed had read everything avidly. Despite all the evidence and claims of his guilt, Ahmed did not believe his English friend could be guilty of such crimes, and in his desperation to find the truth, he had made a request to meet Dan face to face.

At first, Dan was resistent to the idea. He was tired, a dying man, and just as he had tried desperately to protect his mother from the truth that her son was indeed a murderer, so he also wanted to protect his friend Ahmed from discovering who he really was and what he had done to Dom.

After reflecting, though, he decided to see him. He believed it would be a cathartic experience.

He would not massage the truth, he would not lie anymore: this would be an opportunity to come clean, to lay bear who he was and what he had done and seek forgiveness from a man he respected as a good human being; a human being that lived life honourably, and selflessly.

The day arrived when the two men would meet. They were both looking forward to seeing each other again but were also fearful of what the other may reveal. Dan was shackled and wore the customary 'inmates' bib as he sat waiting for the arrival of his friend. Accompanied by a guard, who remained at the back of the room out of earshot, Ahmed entered the room and both men's eyes filled with tears. They were not allowed to embrace. Both were eager to talk but Dan let Ahmed go first.

He had been devastated to discover that Dom and a friend had been murdered during the vacation on the island of Aruba and without hesitation, he asked Dan outright if he had had anything to do with the crime. Dan had promised to himself that he would not lie, but wasn't expecting Ahmed to be so forthright with his question. He paused and kept his eyes firmly fixed on Ahmed's face, looking for a reaction to what he was about to say.

"We have both been though a lot in life, and especially you, my friend. In Beirut, you were my lifeline. You befriended me in a way that I was not expecting, nor was used to. You barely had enough to eat, yet you shared all you had with me. You listened to me and we shared good conversation about our common love of science, and throughout my time with you in your home, I sensed you found a friend too. You are a good man. A selfless man, a man of faith...all the things I am not. But there is a side to my personality that I have found hard to control. Your humbleness and generosity of spirit are not traits that I possess. I have always wanted more from life. I craved attention and the trappings of wealth I saw others enjoying, but was unprepared to do what was necessary to achieve my aims without employing deceit and deception, lies and more lies. The truth is that I have always had every opportunity, in fact more opportunity than most, to carve out a worthy life for myself but I always looked for the short cuts, ways in which I could circumvent the hard work and investment in relationships. It has always been about me and only me. Now I am a dying man, I see the futility of my life. It has been a wasted life, one that could have been devoted to others.

I see this in you, my friend. You are enriched by your faith and your desire to use your knowledge and talents to better the lives of others..."

Ahmed's eyes were swollen with tears. He knew that Dan had murdered Dom - he did not need to hear a confession, but he knew for Dan's sake he had to wait for it.

"You asked me a direct question and I have, so far, chosen not to answer you because it pains me to tell you that the friendship and trust you invested in me was misguided. I am not the human being you thought I was. I am a cold-blooded murderer. I have killed three people." He broke down, then composed himself once more and looked back at Ahmed. "I am hoping you will forgive me..." Again, he broke down. Ahmed spoke.

"Dan, I cannot offer you forgiveness, only your maker can do that. Why you did to those innocent people I do not understand, but I do not hate you. You are my friend and will remain so to the day you die. It is important for your soul and for the souls of those you killed, and their loved ones, that you confess your crimes so they can come to terms with their grief and experience inner peace."

Dan sobbed uncontrollably. Ahmed sat patiently waiting for him to regain his composure. He knew Dan was a damaged human being and despite his transgressions, he could see he had come to terms with his failings.

Dan wiped his eyes and looked at Ahmed.

He had sought a cathartic moment with him and now he had unburdened his mind, he indeed felt a weight lifted from his shoulders. He would do as Ahmed advised. He would confess all and hoped he lived long enough to bring closure to the families of those he had murdered.

In a change of tone, Ahmed told Dan that he had learnt that soon after Dan had married Dom, she had made a will. Dan was sufficiently interested to hear whether he was her beneficiary, not that increasing his existing inherited wealth would do him any good, nor would her assets come to him after he confessed to her murder. Ahmed had been invited to the will reading. It transpired that her entire estate, valued at well-over $12m, had been left to him, not Dan. A codicil in her will made it clear that her decision was based on three factors.

Firstly, that Dan had already inherited sufficient money to sustain him. Secondly, that she feared increasing his wealth would likely cause him to live life a little too richly and his consumption of cocaine would badly influence his decsion making, if not kill him. Thirdly, she had left it to Ahmed because he was a 'good' man and knew he would use his new found wealth wisely.

Ahmed told Dan he planned to return to Beirut and invest his fortune in rebuilding the university and reinstating his faculty, something which his governemt had been unable to do. He would devote the remainder of his life to serving his country.

Again, Dan was overwhelmed as tears ran down his cheeks. Oh, how he wished he had been blessed with Ahmed's humility and generosity!

Dan would plead guilty at his trial to murdering Dom, Kip, and indeed Tanya. He asked Ahmed if he would do him the service of being at his trial to provide moral support and he agreed without hesitation.

It was the last time the men would spent time together. Despite the regulations, they embraced each other with great affection before Ahmed left the room. Dan was taken back to his cell.

The effect of telling the unmitigated truth to Ahmed had not been easy for Dan, but the payback for unburdening his mind was immense. Over the next four months leading up to his trial, he changed profoundly as a human being. He was resigned to his fate. He would be executed by lethal injection but that life-ending procedure didn't occupy his mind. He asked for writing paper, a fountain pen, and ink and set about writing to the families whose lives he had shattered. He wrote to his freinds and business colleagues, personal letters both admitting his guilt and apologising for the hurt he had caused them. He wrote to Rupert and thanked him for his friendship at the time and his help and again, he admitted his guilt and apologised for the impact his plan had had on his personal and business reputation. Of course, he also wrote a note to Ahmed and promised that he would leave him inheritance in his will.

Finally, he wrote to Kip's family. He found this the most difficult letter to write, but write it he did.

Despite his outpouring of guilt and acceptance of his crimes, he still held a deep seated resentment for the man he could only think of as 'Kipper'. Kip and Dom had betrayed him, and whilst most people betrayed in this way may seek some kind of revenge, few would consider cold-blooded murder as retribution.

Dan was a complicated character. He was highly intelligent and talented in so many ways. He was good-looking and a great communicator but deep within his psyche, he was fundamentally flawed. He was unable to take a balanced view on life. He craved what others had but was unprepared by instinct to go through the usual or accepted channels to get what he wanted. He was unable to think clearly and distinguish between right and wrong, and had an oversized ego that needed to be constantly fed. Furthermore, his thinking had become exaggerated as he increasingly relied upon cocaine and, to a lesser extent, alcohol to soothe his troubled mind.

Four months had passed since seeing Ahmed. Dan's cancer had spread still further and he was growing weaker by the day. He had several medical interventions to ease the pain but his discomfort got worse. Despite his medical condition and being barely able to walk, he was brought to trial and pleaded guilty. He was sentenced to death and placed on death row. On the announcement of his sentence, Dan looked across to Ahmed, who was in the public gallery and saw him praying for him. It was a poignant moment.

Many prisoners on death row desperately challenged their sentences in the hope that they would be pardoned or receive a stay of execution. In some instances, the process took decades to either acquit the offender or decide that they will die.

Dan had pleaded guilty for his crimes. He had offers to challenge his death sentence in the courts, too, but he refused. He was dying and wanted society to punish him for his crimes, rather than dying a guilty man from his illness.

The documentary that Dom had made about him was televised once more on the majority of US and UK media channels prior to his death, and his cult status was brought back into being.

Whilst the cancer had spread throughout his body, the prognosis suggested he had some months still to live.

Through various channels, he begged the state governor to give the order for his execution by lethal injection. He was now ready to pay the ultimate price for the crimes he had committed. He wanted closure. He wanted to close his eyes for the last time, knowing that his maker would determine his ultimate fate. The governor agreed, and a date was fixed three weeks hence.

It was a Tuesday afternoon at 3.00 pm that Dan Thomas's came to an end. It was beautiful day. The sun shone and the media were out in force.

He had lived an infamous life, one he had tried desperately hard to forget.

His Cuban family and friends had truly loved what they believed to be their *British gentleman*, a man generous of heart, a loyal family man who doted on his children and his beloved wife. To them, he appeared a contented soul that wanted for little and demanded even less. But their image and portrayal of Dan prior to his arrest could not have been further from the truth; he hoped they would never find out but of course, they did.

After Dan's life was taken away from him, they held a mock funeral in their village in Cuba and his will was read out. Beneta discovered that she and the children had been left over £3 million pounds. He had also left almost half a million pounds to his friends in the community and a further millions pounds to Ahmed. His family and friends were shocked that the man they loved, a man who had lived so modestly, had accumulated so much wealth.

A film of Dan's life story was made on the back of Dom's documentary, entitled, 'Three times a murderer'. On release, it broke several box office records. The film was dedicated to Dom and her life as an award-winning film maker and the royalties were donated to a charity Ahmed had established in Beirut.

As Dan was reviled the world over, so Dominique was adored. His story became legend for all the wrong reasons. The world saw him an intelligent and gifted man who had had every opportunity in life. He could have lived comfortably and used his talents as a scientist to better the world and save people's lives, but he chose the pursuit of greed and personal gratification.

His only consolation on the day his life came to an end was that his beloved mother had gone to her grave without knowing the truth that her son was three times a murderer.

THE END

Printed in Great Britain
by Amazon